DEAD
SECRET

AVA McCARTHY

HARPER

Harper
An imprint of HarperCollins*Publishers*
1 London Bridge Street
London SE1 9GF

www.harpercollins.co.uk

A paperback original 2016
1

ISBN: 978-0-00-736391-9

Set in Sabon LT Std by Palimpsest Book Production Limited,
Falkirk, Stirlingshire

Printed and bound in Great Britain by
Clays Ltd, St Ives plc

MIX
Paper from
responsible sources
FSC C007454

For the family unit; more important than anything:
Tom, Mark, Megan, Duffy and Goldy.

NW 11 - 3 - 20   01/16 CL

ees
ork
yst
nty
wo

By the same author

The Insider
The Courier
Hide Me

Acknowledgements

Big thanks as always to my agent, Laura Longrigg, for her continued support and patience. And heartfelt gratitude to my editor, Sarah Hodgson, for her tireless enthusiasm and wonderful suggestions. Thank you also to Rhian McKay for her eagle-eyed copy edits, and to Lucy Dauman and all the team at HarperCollins. A special thanks to Gerry Gleeson, for sharing an insight into his hometown in New Hampshire, and to Cliff Cunningham who first told me on a plane about fisher cats.

PART ONE

1

Jodie loaded the gun the way she'd seen Ethan do it: finger-checking the rounds so they were lined up flush, then smacking the magazine up into the grip.

Her jittery hands almost fumbled the manoeuvre. She clenched them steady, then racked the slider back to chamber the first round.

Clack-snap.

Nine bullets loaded, but she'd only need two.

One for Ethan.

The other one for herself.

She flashed on her husband's face; on his fixed stare, and the twisted mind-games shape-shifting behind it. Sweat prickled down her spine. Maybe she was wrong. Maybe it would take more than one bullet to kill Ethan.

Fireworks hissed and crackled outside the car, and the sky exploded into a weeping willow of light. Jodie peered through the windscreen, scanning the strobe-lit crowds that lined the lake perimeter. Ethan was out there somewhere, masquerading tonight as Mister Nice Guy, a back-slapper and hand-shaker for the Fourth of July celebrations.

She slid the gun into her bag, then reached out to the drawing pad that lay on the seat beside her, lifting it onto her lap to leaf through it one last time.

The paintings were childlike but imaginative, showing uncomplicated feelings rather than copies of objects: the tangle of scribbly black for the cranky family cat; the sunshine-yellow splodge for the spring picnic; bursts of colour splattered from a height, paint squeezed straight from the tubes to the page.

'*Look what I can do, Mommy!*'

Jodie brushed her fingertips across the rounded letters marking the bottom of every page: *Abby McCall Age 3*.

Her throat constricted. She swallowed against it, but the ache intensified, crushing her chest, choking her, smothering her, sending her spinning.

Breathe!

She bowed her head, took deep, shuddery breaths. Found a dead, flat place somewhere inside her and invited the numbness back in.

Slowly, Jodie straightened up. Touched a hand to the drawing pad. Turned a page.

Blob-figures. The family unit. Abby holding Badger, the black snarl of a cat, flanked by Jodie and Ethan.

Wide curves for mouths, vibrant red and yellow clothes. Finger-daubed by Abby.

The next few pages were the same. But by the last set of drawings, the colours had muted: faded blues, dull browns. With each painting, Ethan's blob-figure stood further apart from the others, the mouth growing straighter, the features fainter, until finally he had no face at all.

Jodie shivered. Even little Abby had seen it.

She closed the pad, cradling it in her lap before setting it back on the seat. Then she lifted her chin, shouldered her bag and clambered out of the car.

The night air was cool against her skin. Volleys of rockets sizzled skywards, erupting into starbursts over the lake. Her eyes raked the spectators by the water's edge, hunting for her husband's lean, elegant frame.

She threaded through the crowds, the air dry and flinty with the smell of burned-out fireworks. She pushed closer to the shoreline, where the water, normally tea-coloured, looked black and oily in the dark.

Up ahead, her gaze snagged on a familiar figure: the plump silhouette of Nancy Adams. Jodie went still. For an instant, she caught the other woman's eye, then Nancy glanced away.

Something small tugged at Jodie's chest. Even Nancy was avoiding her now. But she wasn't surprised. People had been talking, saying Jodie had gone over the edge. For 'people', read Ethan.

She and Nancy had settled in Hillsborough County

around the same time, Jodie as Ethan's Irish bride, Nancy as the new proprietor of Attic Corner, a quirky little café tucked into an art gallery in Peterborough. It was Nancy who'd pitched Jodie's paintings to the gallery and made them see her potential.

'Us blow-ins got to stick together in this godforsaken place,' Nancy had said once, hefting a pan of cinnamon rolls from her oven. 'Especially in the winter. All these blizzards and power outages, snowdrifts barricading your front door. Talk about isolated. Drive you five kinds of crazy.' She'd given Jodie a probing look, the scent of brown spices billowing from her in waves. 'Especially way out in the wilderness where you are.'

Jodie had smiled, shrugging off the concern, her mind skittering away from her own growing misgivings. It was only later she'd admit that the backwoods had turned oppressive.

The whirr of crickets pulsed from the lakefront.

Slowly, she pulled away from Nancy, angling wide along the embankment, still scouring the crowds for Ethan.

'Didn't expect to see you here, Jodie.'

She whipped around. A blocky, compact figure was stalking towards her, dark eyes pinned to hers. Her heartbeat tripped.

Zach Caruso, Sheriff of Hillsborough County.

She slipped a hand inside her bag. Touched the gun like a talisman.

Caruso halted in front of her, his solid bulk blocking her path. 'You sure being here is such a good idea?'

'I'm just looking at the fireworks, Zach. Like everybody else.'

His eyes were watchful. 'Ethan didn't mention you'd be along.'

'Ethan doesn't know.'

Fireworks exploded overhead, spotlighting Caruso in the dark. His expression was hard and flat with suspicion. He had to be in his fifties, over twenty years Jodie's senior, but his hair was still thick and dark. That and the high-bridged nose spoke of Italian lineage, but the accent was pure, abrasive Boston.

His eyes narrowed. 'Maybe I should let him know. You don't look too good.'

'I'm okay.'

Jodie knew how she looked: rail-thin in jeans and T-shirt; skin stretched taut, bare of makeup; up-slanted eyes dull and vacant; straight dark hair unkempt and shoved back behind her ears. Her world had been annihilated. Made desolate. Her appearance was nothing.

Caruso stepped closer. 'You had a chance to reconsider things since this morning?'

Jodie felt her jaw clench as she recalled their earlier encounter, when she'd made the mistake of thinking that the law might be on her side.

Caruso went on. 'You were overwrought, I can understand that. After all you've been through.' The sympathy was a mismatch for the guarded look on his face. 'Ethan says you're trying to work through it together. I told him, if I can help, he just has to ask.'

7

'I'm sure he's glad to know you've got his back.'

'You got to understand, making groundless accusations is rash. People can get hurt.'

His closeness was suffocating. Jodie touched her bag.

'I'm not here to make trouble, Zach. There's just something I need to give to Ethan.'

Caruso shot her a wary look. Jodie made her face bland, breezed on.

'He's catching a ten-thirty flight after the fireworks.'

'I know. He told me.'

'Did he tell you he forgot his passport?'

His gaze dug into hers, looking for the lie. The explosions paused overhead, and a mosquito whined next to Jodie's ear. Caruso's stare was unblinking.

'Not like Ethan to screw up on details,' he said. 'Usually has everything under control.'

'I guess everyone slips up once in a while.'

Caruso dropped his eyes to her bag. She groped for a distraction, gestured at the lake.

'You're a little way off your turf, aren't you, Zach?'

He darted a look out across the water that geographically resided in Cheshire County, close neighbour to his own jurisdiction. He shrugged.

'Doesn't hurt to broaden your horizons, does it?'

Jodie eyed the crowd, a new batch of voters for Caruso to get his hooks into. Whatever scheme he was cooking, Ethan was probably involved. She used to wonder what kind of backscratching they had in place to make Ethan align with such a crook. But none of that mattered any more.

Caruso held out a hand. 'Why don't I take him his passport? You get on home, get some rest.'

She gripped her bag, her heart rate climbing. 'Thanks, but I want to do it myself.'

She edged away, sidestepping his bulk.

'I want a chance to say goodbye.'

Jodie hiked along the lakefront. By now, she'd combed most of the northern shore, and she still hadn't found Ethan.

She checked her watch. He was scheduled to leave for the airport any time now. Maybe he'd already gone.

A rush of dizziness flooded her head. Her encounter with Caruso had left her shaky, but worse was the thought that she'd missed her chance. That Ethan had slipped away. She blundered onwards along the embankment.

The weight of the gun dragged at her bag. She'd only used it once before, six months earlier. Her first time ever handling a firearm.

She'd been alone in the house, finishing up another painting for the gallery. She could still recall the graveyard silence of the rooms, deadened further by the waist-high snowdrifts outside. Jodie shivered.

When she'd first come to New Hampshire five years earlier, Ethan's house had charmed her. The Irish place names had charmed her too, lulling her with a false sense of the familiar: Kilkenny, Antrim, Dublin Lake.

She'd never had a home of her own. She'd grown up on the move in Irish foster care, twelve moves in all over eighteen years, to places where nothing was ever really hers. And each time, she was told she'd be safe with the next family. She wasn't.

But Ethan had seemed safe. He'd wooed her with an old-fashioned attentiveness, and his secluded Colonial home had reinforced the gallant image. Maybe she'd finally found a home.

But the truth was, it was all a fake.

Fireworks burst into bloom overhead, brilliant red chrysanthemums of light. Jodie stumbled through the cheering crowds, out of whack with normal life.

She flashed again on Ethan's house in the backwoods: six miles from the nearest town; no neighbours, no boundaries; the garden blending without warning into dark, dense forest. Not forest like she knew it, but vast, primeval hinterland that besieged three sides of the house.

Incarceration.

She could still hear Ethan's voice echoing in the banquet-sized rooms.

'If Mommy wants to work, it means she doesn't love you, Abby.'

'It's Mommy's fault you don't have any brothers or sisters.'

'If Mommy leaves, we can't be a happy family any more.'

Jodie's throat closed over. She clenched her fingers around the gun in her bag, re-living the day she'd last fired it, six months earlier.

She'd been painting for three hours straight, her spine crunching with the backache she always got from standing for too long. She stepped back from the easel to eye her work, a vigorous landscape of the local Contoocook River. Like all the paintings she sold, it offered plenty of wild, improbable colour but almost nothing of herself.

She wiped her hands on a turps-soaked rag, stirring up a pungent, piney scent. Then she selected a fine rigger brush and signed the canvas: *Jodie Garrett.*

She eyed her signature with misgiving. Another battleground with Ethan. She still used her maiden name, signing her work with it the way she'd done ever since she was a child. Ethan railed at her to switch to his, as though the other was some kind of veiled threat; some act of defiance.

Maybe it was.

She tossed the brush aside, got ready to clean up. Then an eerie screech tore through the silence.

Raucous, inhuman.

Jodie raced to the window. Stopped dead when she saw the malevolent forest animal skulking in her back yard.

Black as the devil against the snow. Dense, glossy pelt, humpbacked like a rodent, haunches high and round. Maybe four feet long from nose to bushy tail, about the size of a family dog.

A giant fisher cat.

That was the local name, though there was nothing

11

feline about it. A gigantic member of the weasel family, to Jodie it was furtive and diabolical-looking.

The fisher froze, its eyes trained high on the birch tree by the back door. Jodie's stomach lurched. Abby's cat, Badger, was clinging to one of the branches.

Jodie yelled, and pounded on the glass. The fisher ignored her, twitched its tail. Then it streaked up the tree and wrestled Badger to the ground.

The fisher's high-pitched shrieks were blood-curdling. Badger yowled, staggered free. Jodie cried out, bolted to the study. Couldn't bear to think of Abby's face if her beloved cat was killed.

She wrenched open drawers, scrabbled for keys, unlocked the cabinet where Ethan kept his gun. Loading it with shaking fingers, praying she was doing it right, she sprinted to the back porch.

The fisher had a jaw-lock on Badger's neck, and was thrashing him against the snow. The cat emitted a keening sound. Jodie fired into the air, but the fisher ignored her. By now Badger was silent, his throat ripped open. She took aim this time, fired at the fisher, knowing it was too late. Kept on firing, round after round in a frenzy of bullets, until the fisher lay still over Badger's limp body.

That night, Abby was inconsolable. The cat had been her ally in the silent house, his robust crankiness a match for her own wilful, tomboy spirit. Jodie sat on the bed, rocking her on her lap. Ethan glared at Jodie, his eyes full of dark reproach. Eyes that looked so much like Abby's.

'You let the cat outside? What the hell were you thinking? You know those goddamn fishers attack pets around here.'

Jodie stared in disbelief. From the start, she'd wanted to safeguard Badger in the house. It was Ethan who'd insisted the cat be allowed to roam; who'd scoffed at her caution, dismissing the threat of fishers as old wives' tales. After all, he'd argued, it was his home country, he should damn well know.

His eyes challenged her to contradict him, the faint sneer betraying his certainty that no one would believe her if she did. Her gut turned cold as she realized something else: Ethan had *wanted* something bad to happen to Badger.

Dazed, she watched him lift Abby into his arms, watched his head bend to hers, the two so alike. Same dark hair, same strong brows; same stubborn set to the mouth. Ethan kissed Abby's plump, damp cheek.

'It's Mommy's fault poor old Badger is dead.'

A fireball of colour exploded over the lake.

The flash defined a knot of spectators on the shore, and Jodie's heart double-thudded. Backlit in their midst was Ethan's sculpted profile.

She edged forward. He was less than two hundred yards away. Close enough to make out the faint Van Dyke beard, its thin vertical line carefully etched from lower lip to chin. As a beard, it was barely there; just a whispered suggestion of maleness, pirate-style.

A pulse hammered high in her throat. Behind Ethan, Dublin Lake seemed on fire, the blazing sky twinned in the water like paint pressed from a centrefold. A dramatic backdrop to Ethan's buccaneer looks, as though he'd staged it with that in mind. Then again, maybe he had.

She inched closer, eyeing his group of companions. They were mostly men, their body language proclaiming Ethan as the dominant figure. She saw it all the time; that potent sway he had over people.

She watched as one of the men leaned in to make a comment, saw the other low-rankers all peek at Ethan, gauging his reaction before committing to theirs. Jodie noticed Ethan appeared a head taller than the rest, and guessed it was no accident he'd ended up on higher ground than they had.

Power and control: his motivation for everything.

Jodie clutched her bag, felt the hard outline of the weapon inside. She tried to picture the moment when it was done. When Ethan was dead, and the time finally came to turn the gun on herself.

Would she hesitate?

Would it hurt?

She probed her psyche, plumbed deep. Took an honest pulse-check of her soul.

Found no fear.

Pain would be cathartic. A final scream of release.

She took a deep breath, scanned her surroundings. Felt a twist of unease. The lakefront should have emptied out by now, but the shore was still lined with people. She couldn't risk a shot from here. What if she hit someone else?

She had to get up close. *But all those people.* One of them might try to stop her. Putting Ethan back in control.

Her spine hummed. In less than two hours, Ethan would be on a flight to New York, gone for three weeks. She couldn't last that long. Couldn't survive it. It had to be tonight.

Her gaze rolled down the shoreline, out to the road, her brain scrambling for a way to get him alone. Then her eyes came to rest on the cars by the kerb, settling on the stately black sedan that dwarfed its neighbours.

Ethan's Bentley.

Jodie's skin tingled.

With a last look at Ethan, she struck out towards the highway, willing the car to be open. He'd never given her a key. No point, he'd said, since he wasn't going to let her drive it. She climbed the slope up to the road, pinning her hopes on his complacent habit of leaving the vehicle unlocked. She could see his point. Who'd steal from the local hotshot lawyer, especially when his ally was an ambitious thug like Caruso?

She clambered over the guardrail onto the road. Stole up to the Bentley. Tried the handle.

The door eased open.

She let out a breath, unaware she'd been holding it. Then she slid into the roomy back seat, closing the door with a *thunk* that blocked out all sound. She lowered herself to the floor, crouching in the space between front and back. A travel rug lay folded in the foot well beside her, and she shook it out, covering herself head to toe. Then she slipped the gun out of her bag and hugged it to her chest.

She lay there, cramped, her nostrils filled with the scent of leather upholstery. From outside, the rug and tinted windows would hide her. By the time Ethan knew she was there, it would be too late.

Fatigue pressed down on her like a dead weight. Maybe it was the horizontal position, but suddenly the world seemed to tilt, as though she was losing her grip on it. Her mind scrabbled for a foothold. Fastened on Abby: all rough-and-tumble in her dungarees, frowning as she brushed a squirming Badger; never crying when he scratched and ran away, just wrestling him back.

A faint hum started up in Jodie's throat, and she clenched her teeth to shut it off.

Her head buzzed with tiredness. She'd been fighting Ethan for so long now. Fighting for freedom. Freedom to work and be independent; freedom for Abby to make friends outside the house; freedom for herself to do the same; freedom to sell her paintings; to paint at all.

And more recently, the freedom to leave.

Jodie closed her eyes. Felt herself drift.

None of that mattered any more. Tonight would be the last battle. After this, there was nothing left to fight for.

Not now that Abby was dead.

*   *   *

The door *clunked*, cracking open the vacuum in the car.

Jodie's eyes flared wide.

Cool air seeped around her, washing in with it the thrum of night insects.

She tried not to breathe.

Leather stretched and creaked. The door slammed shut. Jodie's heart pounded, too loud in her own ears. Something light flopped onto the back seat. Ethan's jacket. Jodie took shallow breaths, the rug trapping her respiration, turning it hot against her face.

She strained for sounds. Heard the friction of running fabric. Pictured him whipping off his tie, loosening his collar; his preferred style, since it played better to his daredevil looks.

Jodie listened for more.

Heard nothing.

Just a hold-your-breath stillness.

Ethan wasn't moving.

She stiffened, every skin cell on high alert, waiting for a hand to snatch the rug away. Then his keys jingled, the engine fired, and she felt herself being dragged backwards against the seat as the car pulled out onto the road.

A tremor started up in her limbs. She fought against it, tried to keep track of their route. She'd wait a few minutes, just long enough to get further down the unlit road where no one else was around.

He switched on the radio, scratching through the stations till he hit on a cheesy talk show. The chit-chat was banal, but he chuckled along, turning up the volume.

The grieving father.

Jodie's grip tightened around the gun.

He hadn't mourned Abby; he'd just cleaned house. The week after she'd died, he'd boxed up all her stuff and got rid of it without asking Jodie. He wouldn't tell her where he'd sent it. Just said they'd no more need of it and her railing at him wouldn't change a thing. All Jodie had left of Abby was the drawing pad.

She twitched the rug down from her face, breathing in cool air. Dense trees whipped past the window. She pictured the dark, narrow road: tall birches lining both sides, the grassy verge rising to the left, sloping downwards to the lake on the right.

As good a place as any.

She eased out of her crouched position, slid quietly onto the back seat, keeping the gun out of sight till she was good and ready.

'Hello, Ethan.'

2

The car swerved.

'Jesus, Jodie, what the hell—'

Ethan yanked the Bentley back on course, and Jodie grabbed at his seat to steady herself. His eyes locked on hers through the rear-view mirror.

'What the fuck are you doing here? You scared the shit out of me.'

Her fingers dug into the soft leather. 'We've unfinished business.'

'It can't wait till I get back from New York?'

'You're not going to New York. Not any more.'

'What the hell are you talking about?'

Jodie's mouth felt parched.

Lift up the gun.

The weapon was suddenly heavy. Her arm wouldn't move.

Ethan jerked up his chin to survey her in the mirror. 'Look at you, you're a mess.'

She closed her eyes.

Lift up the damn gun!

'You're not well, Jodie, I've been telling you that for weeks. You need help.'

Her muscles were rigid. She opened her eyes, squinted against a blaze of oncoming headlights. Then she stared at the back of Ethan's head, at the longish hair waving in S-bends down to his collar. She gripped the gun. Tried to picture herself touching the barrel to his skull.

She failed.

Do it! What are you waiting for?

She knew she was stalling. Told herself she was waiting for the road to clear, so no one else got hurt. Was she losing her nerve? Maybe she just needed to hear him say it one last time.

She swallowed hard. 'I talked to Zach.'

Ethan's gaze shot to hers in the mirror. 'I told you not to do that.'

'I don't do everything you say, Ethan, you should know that by now.'

'You're crazy. Zach's not going to believe your far-fetched story, I told you that.'

'You were right. He didn't.'

The Bentley glided around a bend, its headlights sweeping across the trees and over water lacquered black by the dark. She clasped both hands around the gun, keeping it low.

'So I wrote it all down in a letter,' she went on. 'Everything you did, everything you told me. I wrote down what I was going to do now, so there'd be no confusion later. So no one else could get blamed by mistake.'

He half-turned towards her, the shadows catching the angles of his jaw and the trademark, barely there beard.

'You're not making any sense, Jodie.'

'I couldn't trust Zach not to bury it. The letter, I mean. So I posted it to the District Attorney's office.'

There was a hitch in the Bentley's cruising motion.

'Jesus Christ.'

'By the time they get it, it'll all be over.'

'What the hell have you done?'

'They need to know why I'm doing this. They need to know what you are.'

'My God, listen to yourself. Do you hear what you're saying?'

His knuckles were taut against the wheel. He shook his head, dragged a hand over his shadowy stubble. In the mirror, his eyes looked tired and strained. He was only thirty-nine, ten years older than Jodie, but now and then his face seemed haggard.

'You've brought this all on yourself, Jodie. I hope you're happy.'

Her insides turned stony. Ethan's eyes flicked to the mirror.

'Don't give me that look, you know I'm right. If it wasn't for you, Abby would still be alive.'

Something tore at her breath. 'You were the one who took her out in the boat, Ethan.'

She flashed on that day six weeks earlier: Ethan holding Abby's hand, demanding time alone with his daughter; their voices drifting off as he closed the door behind them.

'*I want Mommy to come.*'

'*Mommy prefers her silly old paints to spending time with us.*'

Then the call from Zach saying Abby had fallen overboard; Jodie's world crashing, hurtling down; helicopters thudding over the Contoocook River; the frantic wait; and finally, darkness calling off the search, and Zach kneeling down beside her to say her precious Abby was gone.

After that, nothing.

A black hole.

Then a heart-slamming grief that snatched her up, day after day, flung her around and ripped her apart like a fisher cat.

'I had to get Abby away,' Ethan was saying. 'I explained all this.'

Headlights bore down on them, burning holes in the dark. Ethan's eyes drilled into hers.

'You were the one who wanted to leave, to take her away from me. Imagine how that would've hurt Abby. We had a close bond, everyone noticed it.'

Jodie's chest constricted. It was true. Abby had loved Ethan, and he had loved her back. It was why Jodie had

22

stayed so long in the marriage, trying to make it work. It was why everything else that had happened was so diabolical.

'I warned you over and over,' Ethan went on. 'I said, if you try to keep her from me, I'll take her away. I'll take her some place where you'll never see her again.'

Nausea stirred in Jodie's gut, her body rejecting the truth all over again. Ethan was still talking.

'I picked a pretty spot. That fishing place she likes, down by the covered railroad bridge.'

Jodie stared at the insects whirling in the headlights, resisting the urge to block her ears. She needed to hear him say it again.

'I made sure she was asleep,' he said. 'The water wasn't cold, she didn't wake up once.'

The queasiness spurted into Jodie's bowels, churning pinpricks of sweat out through her pores. Ethan kept talking.

'I stayed there in the boat until it was all over. She knew I'd never leave her alone out there in the water.'

Jodie swallowed, aware of tears streaming down her cheeks. She didn't know how long she'd been crying.

'I *had* to do it, Jodie, you were going to break the family up. I had to protect her.'

'Dear sweet Jesus.' Jodie's voice was a whisper.

His eyes darted to hers in the mirror. Watchful, assessing. As though checking to make sure she was in pain.

Her fingers clenched around the gun. She took in his fine-hewn profile, the dark hair that brushed his collar.

He looked so charming, so normal. That was what made him so terrifying.

'Why didn't you just kill *me*, Ethan? I was the one who was leaving, Abby did nothing.' She was sobbing now. 'For the love of God, why didn't you just kill *me*?'

His eyes turned shrewd, and he didn't answer. His gaze slid back to the road.

'No one can prove anything.'

But Jodie didn't need his answer. She knew why he'd done it. He'd killed his little girl because he wanted to punish Jodie.

Retribution.

A twisted revenge for a broken marriage; a last monstrous act of control, knowing she'd suffer for the rest of her life if he killed Abby and left her alive.

Her gut heaved, spasms of revulsion spreading to her chest, her bowels, her throat, her brain, in a torrent so overwhelming she felt it might bury her.

She inhaled deeply. Sought again that dead, flat place. Then she raised the gun and put it against his head.

Ethan went still. His eyes flew to the mirror, wide, dilated.

'Jodie? My God.'

She two-handed the gun, to be sure of her aim.

'Wait! Jodie!'

Pull the trigger!

Ethan slammed his foot on the accelerator. The Bentley roared, took off, and she felt herself being sucked backwards.

Her aim wavered. She corrected her sights. Ethan swerved the car, tried to knock her off balance. She worked to keep her hands steady.

Do it!

The engine screamed, Ethan flung her a look.

'I die, you die.'

'You think I want to live?'

Two quick shots. One for him. One for you.

The car lurched, zigzagged. She flashed on Abby's face.

'There's a place in hell for you, Ethan.'

She pulled the trigger.

The blast torpedoed her ears. Stickiness splattered her face, her neck. The car screeched, spun, hurled her sideways.

She angled the gun.

Then she took the second shot.

PART TWO

PART TWO

3

Deadlock bolts clanked through metal. Latches snapped back, lights stuttered on, and a hundred and twenty-two cell doors clattered open.

6 a.m.

The hollering on A-Wing burst into Cell 5, filling the ten-by-twelve space. Noise in the prison never stopped. People screamed all through the night, kicking at doors, banging on walls, yelling about everything and nothing, as though to drown out awareness of where they were and why.

The steel bunks creaked in Cell 5. A bout of coughing started up, loose and wet, probably Magda's. Someone urinated loudly in the alcove toilet, no door to screen off the sour smell.

'The fuck out of my face, Dixie.'

'Where's my towel?'

29

'You stink, you know that?'

'Anyone seen my towel?'

'I don't fucking believe it, some bitch stole my soap.'

Seven people bumping around, cramped in a space designed for four.

'Hey, Picasso! You dead up there or what?'

'Leave her be, she's got time.'

Jodie ignored them and stayed where she was, on the top bunk nearest the door. She closed her eyes, letting the racket wash over her, an unbearable weight settling into her chest. She worked hard to push against it, trying to summon up the strength to face another day.

Magda hawked into the toilet. 'I find out who stole my soap, bitch is dead.'

Jodie waited till the woman had lumbered out of the cell, then hauled herself down off the bunk. Her limbs felt heavy, as though gravity had doubled. She bird-bathed at the sink, using the soap she'd stolen from Magda, before dragging on her Department of Corrections T-shirt and loose, elasticated pants. By the time she was done, the others had gone, all except for Dixie who was waiting by the door.

'She sees you with that soap, she'll cut your face.'

'I know.'

Dixie rolled her eyes. In the light, her brown face looked as plump and shiny as a chestnut. Too fresh for a seasoned inmate serving her third prison term, this one a five-year stretch for forgery.

They joined the mob of inmates out in the corridor,

all making their way down to chow like slow-moving cattle.

Massachusetts Correctional Institution was the oldest female prison in the country and it showed. Despair seemed to seep from the bare cinderblock walls, like residue from some Victorian asylum. Jodie shivered. She'd had the same bleak feeling as a child, in the shelters where she'd lived in between foster families. Those places had had the same austere, brick walls. The same absence of hope.

She'd spent a lot of time in between families. Some of them had lasted longer than others, but mostly it only took two or three months before her case worker would arrive to ship her out. She'd stopped asking why after the third move, coping the only way she knew how: by acting tough, by yelling and fighting. Which meant the next family dumped her too.

Joining a new family was always hard. She could still recall the rush of fear: *I don't know you. What do you want from me? Will it hurt?*

'Look at this slop. Like something my dog'd puke up.'

Dixie shoved her porridge away. Jodie sipped at her watered-down juice, not bothering with food. The over-boiled stench turned her stomach, though after two years, she should have been used to it.

Two years, two months and one week, to be exact. Eight hundred days she'd been in this place. Serving ten to life for murdering her husband.

Jodie stared at her juice. Eight hundred days. For a

31

moment, her vision tunnelled, walls and ceiling closing in. Then she gripped the edge of the table, pushed herself to her feet. If things worked out, maybe this day would be her last.

Dixie looked up. 'Where you going?'

'Think I'll line up for Meds.'

'Again?'

Jodie kept her tone neutral. 'Cramps.'

Dixie's eyes probed hers for a long moment. Then she heaved her apple-round curves up from the table.

'I'm coming with you.'

The line for medications was already forming, though the infirmary wasn't yet open. Jodie joined the queue, Dixie by her side, and tried hard not to fidget. A lot would depend on which nurse had pulled duty that week.

Dixie flicked her a look. 'Hey Picasso, you okay?'

'Sure.'

Hardly anyone called her Jodie any more. At first, the inmates had called her Cleopatra because of her wide, up-tilted eyes. But when the art teacher learned she could paint and had made her teach a class, the nickname Picasso had stuck.

Dixie's tone turned casual. 'Hey, you ever write back to that guy?'

'What? No, I told you, I'm not interested.'

'Come on, why not?'

'I've got nothing to say.'

'What guy?' Another inmate had joined the queue.

32

Jodie glanced around. The newcomer was small and wiry, maybe twenty years old, with the buzz cut and swagger of a teenage boy. Her name was Nate, a crack addict from Boston serving four years for aggravated robbery.

Dixie cocked a thumb at Jodie. 'Reporter wrote to her, wants to do a story.'

'Awesome!'

'I'm not meeting him.'

'Bullshit, you should do it.' Nate's angular face lit up. 'Me, I'd take a visit from anyone on the outside. It's a distraction, right?'

Dixie nodded. 'That's what I said.'

Jodie sighed, bracing herself for another debate on the topic. 'I told you, he's just some hack journalist desperate for copy.'

'But he wants to write a story about you,' Nate said. 'How fucking awesome is that?'

'What story? I killed my husband and they sent me to prison. You think I want to re-live all that with some stranger?'

Nate shrugged. 'Me, I'd just talk to him. Beats seeing the same old faces in here every day.' Her dark eyes widened. 'Hey, maybe he'll pay you.'

Jodie shook her head. They didn't get it. Talking about Abby to some journalist was out of the question. And talking about anything else wouldn't net the guy much either, since trauma had obliterated most of it.

She remembered pulling the trigger, but not much else.

They'd told her at the hospital that the car had overturned; that she'd been thrown clear of the wreckage but that Ethan had been found dead at the wheel. They'd been kind at first. Until the police had discovered Ethan had died from a bullet to the head.

The trial had only lasted a couple of weeks. The letter she'd written to the District Attorney had proved without doubt her intent to kill and made it an easy conviction. Her lawyer had tried his best to plead extenuating circumstances, though she'd tuned much of his arguments out, absorbing only snatches.

'*Ethan McCall was a family annihilator. That's what the criminologists call them. Fathers who kill their own children . . .*'

'*. . . not the first father to decide that a dead child is better than a child he can't raise himself. That killing his little girl is a fitting way to punish his wife . . .*'

'*. . . monstrous self-obsession . . . incapable of perceiving his child as a separate human being . . .*'

'*. . . a domineering man . . . determined to have the final word . . . to prove he was still in control . . .*'

'*Grave provocation for my client . . . unimaginable grief . . .*'

But in the end, no one had believed that Ethan had murdered his daughter.

Jodie hadn't fought it. She'd killed him and was prepared to accept the consequences, not planning on being around to endure them for very long.

A lock *snicked* up ahead. Shutters rattled, and the line

34

of inmates stirred. Jodie craned her neck but couldn't see who was manning the hatch. Her nails dug into her palms.

Nate nudged her arm. 'Orianne's back.'

Jodie followed her gaze to the round-shouldered woman who'd joined the end of the line. Her recently pregnant belly looked slack and deflated. Dixie spoke out of the corner of her mouth.

'Got back yesterday. Left her baby in the hospital, kissed him goodbye and walked out in shackles. Seven more years to go.'

Jodie stared at the woman's dull eyes, made blank from the anti-depressants she was most likely on. Her flaccid midsection looked oddly barren.

Jodie looked away. Her own mother had given birth to her while in prison, triggering Jodie's life on the move in the foster care system. She'd never given much thought to how her mother might have felt at giving her up. Too busy hating her for it.

Her mother had died shortly after giving birth, so when Jodie was old enough, she'd tried to track down her father. His trail had led her from Dublin to Boston, but ended abruptly when she discovered that he was dead too. It was while she was in Boston that she'd first met Ethan McCall.

Nate shifted from foot to foot, shoulders hunched. 'This fucking line is taking forever.'

The inmates shuffled forward. Jodie glimpsed a white uniform at the dispensary hatch, the face obscured by the women at the head of the line. If Nurse Santos was on duty, she had a chance; if it was Kendrick, she was in trouble.

Dixie threw her an uneasy look. 'Hey Picasso, let's go. You don't need nothing.'

Jodie didn't answer. Dixie edged closer.

'Honey, I know you're stashing them pills.'

Jodie regarded her steadily. 'You need to stop worrying about me.'

'Bullshit. We're family, we look out for each other.'

Family. Ironic that the closest she'd come to having one was in prison. Many of the women here built family structures amongst themselves: mother-figure, father-figure, sisters, brothers. Something most of them never had at home.

Dixie had taken Jodie into her family when she arrived, relegating her to the role of younger sister, though she and Jodie were the same age. Nate was the wayward brother, and there was an uncle called Meatloaf, a two-hundred-pound female wrestler serving ten years for second degree murder. The family unit was presided over by Momma Ruth, a lifer who'd been in prison for almost thirty-two years.

Jodie inched closer to the dispensary, her heart rate picking up.

She knew Dixie searched her belongings for pills, not trusting it to the Correctional Officers who conducted daily shakedowns of the cells. None of the inmates dared to sell Jodie drugs, not since Dixie had said Meatloaf would crush the kneecaps of anyone who tried.

The hatch was closer now. Two inmates peeled away from the head of the line, giving Jodie an uninterrupted view. Steel-wool hair, rimless glasses. Shit.

It was Kendrick.

Dixie lowered her voice. 'You won't die in your sleep, like people think. That stuff'll take days to kill you. Days of pain, real slow, with you lying there waiting for your liver to fail.'

Jodie closed her eyes briefly. 'I know.'

She moved up one more place in the queue, watching the nurse's brisk dealings at the hatch. Santos would have given her the pills to take away, which meant she could have added them to her stash. But Kendrick was a stickler. Kendrick would remember Jodie's stint on suicide watch, and the rule that all her medication had to be supervised from now on.

Kendrick was going to make her swallow the damn pills in front of her.

Jodie moved forward. Almost her turn. Small hairs prickled up her arms. She'd been planning this for some time, collecting pills no more than once a month so as not to attract attention. One more dose should do it.

Her termination plan, she called it. Ceasing to live, rather than planning to die.

Sometimes she woke up and forgot that Abby was dead. In her dreams, her little girl was alive and warm.

Those mornings were the worst, full of gut-ripping pain, the agony waiting to annihilate her all over again.

She didn't believe in the hereafter. Not really. She didn't know where Abby was supposed to be now. All she knew was she wanted to be with her daughter. And if her daughter was nowhere, then nowhere was fine by her.

Jodie stepped up to the hatch. Coached herself to relax. The nurse watched her over her glasses, eyebrows furrowing up into her forehead.

'Back again, Garrett? Let me guess, more cramps?'

Jodie shrugged. 'Every month, regular as clockwork.'

The nurse eyed her for a moment. Then she tipped two tablets into the palm of her hand and passed them through the hatch, along with a plastic cup of water.

'Tylenol. Let me see you take them.'

'Can't I save them for later? It gets worse as the day goes on.'

'You know the rules, Garrett. Swallow them now, or I take 'em back.'

Jodie prised the pills up between her fingertips. Took the cup in her other hand. Physical movement was suddenly onerous. She clamped her mouth shut, biting down on the urge to cave in. She could wait till Santos was back. Another week, maybe two. She could last.

Slowly, she raised the tablets to her lips.

'Hey bitch! Picasso!'

Jodie paused. Turned round. Magda was thundering towards her, the woman's frizzy tangerine hair marking her out like a beacon. Her huge thighs swished together as she moved, pushing her legs outward, knock-kneed style. She barged up to the hatch and thrust her face close to Jodie's.

'I heard you stole my soap, bitch.'

The funk of sour sweat radiated from her like heat. Jodie made her face blank.

'You hear me, doll-face?'

Jodie shrugged. 'It was mine to begin with, you stole it from me.'

Dixie grew still beside her. Jodie sensed Nate stepping back a pace, while the other women in the queue shifted uneasily.

'You know you're gonna pay for that?' Magda's eyes looked dead; dull marbles, half-buried in pasty flesh. 'You know I'm gonna cut you, right?'

Jodie kept her mouth shut. Rumour had it, the woman was in prison for kidnapping and assault, having tied up her best friend for seventeen hours while she tortured her with knives and hot skewers.

Magda whacked the plastic cup from Jodie's hand, sending it airborne. Behind the hatch, the nurse was on her feet, craning her neck to locate a CO.

'Got something for ya, doll-face.' Magda's tongue flicked along her lips. 'You and me'll get together later. You'll enjoy it, I know you will.'

Then she held out her arm, wrist upwards, third and fourth fingers curled against something that poked out from under her sleeve: a razor blade melted into the tip of a toothbrush. A homemade slashing device.

Jodie's gut tightened. She flashed on confrontations from the past, in the shelters where older kids had bullied the newbies. And on the advice from an ally: *Make your face dead-pan, like a soldier on parade. Make them think that you just don't care.*

She stared straight ahead. Impassive. Aware that the faint tilt to her features helped to make her expression unreadable. Sphinx-like.

Beside her, Dixie snorted in disgust. 'You're wasting your breath, lunkhead. She ain't afraid of you. She ain't afraid of pain, nor death, nor nothing. Can't you see that, you dumb bitch?'

Magda's eyes became slits, still trained on Jodie's face.

Then her gaze shifted. Rapid footsteps smacked along the corridor, and the line of women parted to make way for two approaching COs. In one practised movement Magda relaxed her stance, backed away, then raised her palms, the weapon already tucked out of sight.

She wheeled away, herded on by the COs, with a final look at Jodie that said this wasn't over. One of the COs caught it, a gruff, heavyset guy by the name of Grochowski, though the inmates all called him Groucho. He threw Jodie an uneasy glance, then marched his charge away.

The line of women seemed to exhale. Movement rippled through them as the queue reformed, and behind the hatch the nurse was settling down, preparing for the next inmate.

No one noticed as Jodie slipped away, two pills buried deep inside her fist.

4

Jodie flicked another look at the clock.

Still only 3:45 p.m.

All day, time had seemed bloated, every minute feeling like five. She leaned against the wall, clamping down on an urge to pace the room.

'Jodie?'

Mrs Tate peered at her from behind an easel, white hair fluffed around her head like an ermine hat. She pointed with her brush.

'Ruth needs some help back there.'

Jodie glanced past the other inmates to where Momma Ruth was sitting, hunched in front of a large canvas. She nodded and set off across the room, picking her way around the jumble of desks and easels, avoiding the small, plastic mannequin posed for figure drawing on the centre table. Art paraphernalia cluttered every surface: jars of brushes, tubes of paint, thick blocks of drawing paper carefully meted out by Mrs Tate.

The woman's sharp eyes were like needles on her back. Normally she made Jodie participate in the class, but so far today she'd left her alone. As though she'd sensed that today was somehow different.

For a long time, Jodie had avoided the art room. When Mrs Tate had finally summoned her there, six months into her sentence, she'd hovered in the doorway, reluctant to go in. The retired schoolteacher was rinsing brushes under a tap, her skirt and high-necked blouse protected by a billowing smock.

The woman had turned and beckoned her in, clattering another sheaf of brushes into the sink. Jodie edged over the threshold. Immediately, the woody scent of turps filled her brain and slammed so many memories into her head it almost sent her reeling.

'Have a seat. I'm almost done.'

Jodie shook her head, struggling with the reminders of her lost life churned up by the heady smell. Mrs Tate turned off the water and reached for a towel, regarding her with shrewd eyes.

'I'm sorry to find you in this situation.'

Jodie didn't answer. The woman went on, still drying her hands.

'When the papers connected you with Garrett the artist, I didn't want to believe it. I have one of your paintings on my living room wall.' She paused, her hands suspended, as she waited for a response. 'Don't you want to know which one?'

Jodie managed a shrug. Mrs Tate folded the towel into a regimented square and turned to put it away.

'It's the covered bridge on the Contoocook River. All those spellbinding colours. As though it's drenched in rainbows, I always think.' She turned back to Jodie, her loose-skinned face pleated into a faint smile. 'It looks like paradise.'

Jodie recalled the painting, a snow scene caught between freeze and thaw, laced with her signature fantasy colours: chartreuse over lilac, vermilion cut with rose madder. She'd finished it less than two months before she'd killed Ethan.

Mrs Tate must have made the same connection, for she suddenly lowered her gaze. 'Things are never quite what they seem, are they?'

Jodie shifted her feet. 'Look, I don't mean to be rude, but what is it you want?'

Mrs Tate drew herself up, the brisk air restored. 'I want you to come to the art classes.'

'Sorry, I'm not interested.'

'And may I ask why?'

'Isn't it obvious? I don't paint any more.'

'I don't care if you paint or not. I want you to teach the other women.'

Jodie frowned, and cast a look around the room: at the pencils, the charcoal, the tinted pastels; at the creamy slabs of paper and cotton-textured canvas. All the materials that had fed her and that she'd shared so much with Abby.

She shook her head, stumbled backwards towards the door. 'I can't help you, I'm sorry.'

In the end, it was Dixie who'd talked her into it.

'Bullshit. Just because you've checked out don't mean you can't help the rest of us.' Dixie's eyes had strayed meaningfully to Nate on the next bunk, whose arms had been freshly scored that morning with self-inflicted welts. 'It could help some of us get through another day in here, you know?'

Doors slammed outside the art room, and Jodie stole another look at the clock.

3:48 p.m.

Twelve more minutes till the class finished up. After that, she'd be free until the cell count at six. Free to retrieve the hidden stash of pills she'd been stockpiling for the last eighteen months.

Hiding stuff in prison was always tricky. The COs spent their days on the hunt for contraband, ransacking cells, scouring common areas, conducting random body searches. Not to mention the added hindrance of Dixie watching her every move.

Jodie had been forced to switch hidey-holes a couple of times, but so far her stash had been safe. Counting today's dose, she had thirty-six pills, which by her reckoning had to be enough. Tonight she planned to use them.

'You okay?'

44

Momma Ruth's strong-boned face was turned up towards hers. Jodie nodded.

'I'm fine.'

The older woman tilted her head, the light catching the broad, olive cheeks that hinted at Cherokee ancestry. Deep lines criss-crossed her skin, like grids for tic-tac-toe. She was fifty-two years old, and had been in prison since she was twenty. She would never leave.

She held Jodie's gaze. 'If it's Magda you're worried about, she's in Seg. They frisked her and found the blade.'

'I heard.'

Seg was the Administrative Segregation Unit, where inmates were isolated in lockdown for disciplinary offences. Most women came out of there a lot meaner than when they went in.

Momma Ruth's dark eyes still probed hers, and not for the first time Jodie imagined how she might paint her. For the skin, a blend of earthy tones: yellow ochre, cadmium red. For the black hair, layers of ultramarine blue, flecked with titanium white. The challenge would be the eyes; how to capture that taciturn acceptance.

She recalled Momma Ruth's quiet words of advice the day she got here.

'Don't fight it,' she'd said. 'I fought it every day for fifteen years, and that just made it worse. Make your peace with it.' Then she'd held up a finger. 'But you got to know how to survive. You got to be careful how you walk, how you hold yourself. Always look ahead. Don't stare at anyone, but don't look down at your feet. And remember, for some of these women, the more violent it is, the more fun they're having. You're dealing with women who don't care.'

Jodie blinked. She fought the urge to check the clock, and tried to focus on Momma Ruth's easel.

'Let's see what you've got here.'

'It's not very pretty.'

'Art's not about pretty, you know that.'

As usual, Momma Ruth had ignored the plastic manne-quin the others were drawing and had painted something abstract of her own. Jodie took in the series of dark, concentric whorls, all rippling outwards across the canvas from a pale blue core.

She glanced at Momma Ruth, then back at the easel, her eyes drawn to the warm blue kernel. 'You're not happy with it?'

'Loops went all sludgy. The browns all look like muck.'

'What about the blue bit?'

'Yeah, I like the blue bit.' Momma Ruth's eyes flicked to Jodie's face. 'Sort of tugs at you, doesn't it?'

Jodie nodded, studying the pattern of elliptical swirls. 'It's important, the blue bit?'

Momma Ruth pushed some paint around her palette with a brush, stirring up the resinous smell of linseed oil. 'It's supposed to be . . . I don't know. Like, who we are before we make all these bad choices.'

'You mean innocence?'

'Sort of. More like a clean slate, you know? Before you make that first bad choice and start up all of these consequences.' Momma Ruth gestured with the brush at the murky ripples. 'But the browns aren't right.'

'You just mixed too many colours.' Jodie nodded at the muddy-looking palette. 'You could fix it when it's dry.'

'Make the best of a bad mistake? Maybe.' Momma Ruth shrugged. 'Not all bad mistakes can be undone, though, can they?'

Jodie let her gaze fall away, the question floating between them. No one knew for sure what Momma Ruth had done. If ever anyone asked, she'd say it didn't matter; she'd done a terrible thing and now she was paying for it, and that was as it should be.

She'd tried to teach Jodie the same acceptance, but Jodie already knew she could endure her prison sentence. It was the loss of Abby she couldn't live with.

She flashed another glance at the clock. Only five more minutes to go.

Nate drew up beside them, on her way to the sink with a jar of brushes. Her freshly buzzed hair made her look like an army recruit.

'Jesus, what the fuck is that?'

Momma Ruth flapped at her to go away. 'You wouldn't get it. And I don't need any of your smart-ass comments.'

'Hey, come on, try me.'

Momma Ruth rolled her eyes. 'Okay, it's us. Our choices and mistakes.'

'It's a fucking mistake alright. Looks like a giant fingerprint.'

To Jodie's surprise, Momma Ruth looked pleased.

'You can see that?' She glanced at Jodie. 'It's what I was aiming for. You know, like our mistakes are hard-wired into our DNA? Like we don't really have any choices.'

Nate made a face. 'Fuck, that's depressing. You believe that crap?'

'I believe I would have ended up here no matter what, yes. Because of who I am. Wasn't in my blood to make different choices.'

'Well, I got choices. And I choose to call that bullshit.' Nate banged her jar on a nearby desk. 'And I choose to dump these brushes with you, because I ain't fucking cleaning them.'

She stomped back across the room, and when she'd gone Jodie said, 'Is that really what you believe?'

Momma Ruth got to her feet, her eyes on a level with Jodie's. 'Think about it. About what you did. If you had the chance to do it over again, would you really do anything different?'

Jodie stared at her, and for an instant, she was back in Ethan's car: his gaze challenging hers in the rear-view mirror, watchful, twisted.

'I picked a pretty spot . . . she didn't wake up once.'

The air rushed out of Jodie's lungs. She clenched her fists, her whole body.

She'd kill him again in a heartbeat.

Mrs Tate clapped her hands. 'Time's up, ladies, start clearing away.'

Jodie's pulse picked up. The whole room seemed to move at once. Desks and chairs chirruped against the floor, easels clattered. Jodie fumbled with jars and tubes, working hard to stay calm, while the other women queued up at the sink. They straggled out to the corridor in dribs and drabs, until finally only Jodie and Mrs Tate were left.

Together they tidied away the last of the mess, clearing the counters and stacking the desks and chairs in a corner. Mrs Tate looked tired. She thanked Jodie briefly, then led the way out of the room, Jodie following her as far as the door. There she hung back, watching as Mrs Tate took a left down the corridor.

Jodie scooted a look around. Then she quick-stepped back into the art room, reached up into a cupboard and retrieved the plastic mannequin.

Her fingers were shaking. She twisted the head to detach it at the neck, at the same time moving closer to the tray of tweezers Mrs Tate kept for jewellery-making. She'd need them to prise out the cotton wad of pills from inside the hollow doll.

'Garrett!'

Jodie froze. Her gaze snapped to the door. To the scowling, heavyset officer standing on the threshold.

Groucho.

The mannequin seemed to scorch her hands.

But Groucho's eyes weren't on the plastic doll. He jerked his chin in the direction of the corridor.

'Let's go. You got a visitor.'

5

'If it's my lawyer, I don't want to see him.'

Jodie trudged down the corridor after Groucho. From behind, he looked bulky with protective gear, his heavy leather duty belt creaking with every step. He spoke over his shoulder.

'This guy's no lawyer. He's a real live human being.'

Jodie frowned. 'But I didn't sign any visitation form. I didn't ask to see anyone.'

'Got the paperwork upstairs, your signature's on it.'

'That can't be right.'

'You saying it's a fake?'

Jodie's step faltered. Visitors had to be approved by inmates in advance, with a signed form submitted to the Department of Corrections. She hadn't signed one, but the niggling in her gut told her she knew who had.

She trotted to keep up. 'This visitor, is it a guy called Novak?'

'You should know, you put his name down on the form.'

'Is it him?'

Groucho relented. 'Yeah, it's him.'

Shit. Matt Novak. The reporter who'd written to her, asking for an interview; the guy Dixie kept urging her to see. Dixie, who was locked up for falsifying cheques and counterfeiting identification documents; who could copy a signature after seeing it only once, in Jodie's case probably from the painting Mrs Tate had brought in to show the class.

Groucho swung round to face her, his belt clinking with keys and cuffs. 'Do we have a problem here? You saying the paperwork's not legit?'

Jodie took in the grumpy lines of his face, the pouches under his eyes. The guy had a tough job. The first to unlock the inmates in the mornings, he usually took the brunt of everyone's resentment. Jodie let him do his job, never gave him any lip. In exchange, he wasn't above bending the rules, often letting her stay longer in the art room than she should. But rumour had it he was close to retirement now, and Jodie guessed he wasn't about to risk his pension by breaching major rules.

She dropped her gaze, then made herself shrug, side-stepping the fuss that would only get Dixie into trouble.

'The paperwork's fine. I guess I just forgot.'

He gave her a long, penetrating look. Then, with a

quick glance around, he stepped up closer and pointed a finger at her face.

'You need to watch out for Magda. She's a psycho, and she won't be in Seg for long.'

Jodie opened her mouth to reply, but he'd already turned on his heel and was continuing on towards the visiting room. She hurried after him. The blare of loud voices echoed through the closed door, like the racket of a large, unruly class left unattended. She hung back, her stomach knotted, while Groucho stepped in to deal with the Officer in Charge.

She'd never had any visitors. No family to worry about how she was doing, no friends who hadn't already moved on. All except for Nancy, who'd written two or three times, asking if she could come. But Jodie wouldn't see her. They'd be strangers now, separated by Jodie's pain and by the magnitude of what she'd done. A visit like that would take down both of them.

Groucho gestured her forward, and Jodie hesitated, suddenly tuning in to the sound of children in the room. She swallowed hard.

She'd get in and get out. No chit-chat with Novak, just a long enough visit to allay suspicion over Dixie's handiwork. If she was quick, she might even get back to the art room before it closed and retrieve the mannequin she'd replaced inside the cupboard.

Jodie lifted her chin and stepped forward through the door. The din of voices filled the air. She took in the rows of tables and chairs, all occupied by inmates and their families. Most of the women in prison here were mothers.

She averted her eyes from the toddlers in the play area, and let her gaze travel the room. The windows in here were larger than most. Sunlight slanted through the grilles, casting trellises onto the floor. Jodie's eyes followed the grid lines to the far corner of the room, where a dishevelled-looking man sat alone, drumming his fingers on the table.

Her arrival snagged his attention. He clambered to his feet, as she started off across the room. Up close, he looked younger than she'd thought: probably about her own age, mid-thirties at most, though his raggedy, days-old stubble made it hard to tell. She stood in front of him, assessing his unkempt, curly hair, the wrinkled shirt, the crumpled jacket slung across the back of his chair. He looked like he belonged in prison more than she did.

'I'm Jodie Garrett.'

'Yeah, I know. Matt Novak.'

He made as if to shake her hand, then glanced at the Officer in Charge and seemed to think better of it. He gestured instead at the chair opposite his, and waited for her to sit down before resuming his own seat.

'Thanks for agreeing to see me.'

'Actually, I didn't.' She went on, forestalling objections. 'My cellmate forged the paperwork on my behalf, she thought the visit would do me good. I disagree.'

His expression shifted into neutral while he processed the information. He regarded her with clear, slate-grey eyes.

'And yet you're still here.'

'I'm here for five minutes. We can talk about the weather or your favourite baseball team, but I'm not interested in discussing my past with you, Mr Novak.'

'I think you'll want to hear what I've got to say.'

He gave her a long, assessing look, and eventually, he added,

'I was in court for your trial. You haven't changed much. Thinner maybe.'

'You were doing a story about me back then, too?'

'No offence, but my story's not about you.'

'I see. Who, then?'

'Your husband.'

'Ah, I get it.' Jodie closed her eyes briefly. 'Successful lawyer, popular family man, tragically slain by evil wife.'

She felt her lips compress. The media had run that angle for months after the trial and she wasn't about to submit to it again, not even for Dixie. She shifted in her seat, made a move to get up. Novak put out a hand.

'Would it surprise you to know he was involved in fraud?'

Jodie cut him a sharp look. She thought of Ethan's secretive nature; of the quick-thinking lies he'd routinely told, always doctoring reality to suit his own needs. Swapping one lie for another when he had to, adapting without notice to changes in circumstance.

She scraped back her chair. 'It wouldn't surprise me in the least.'

'Don't you want to hear about it?'

'Not really.'

Novak's flinty-grey eyes regarded her with speculation. 'You don't seem the type to fall for such a take-charge kinda guy.'

Jodie paused, and flung him a wry look. 'Most people found him charming.'

'I've been digging for three years, and his charm escapes me. Thought you'd be too smart for all that baloney.'

Jodie gave a rueful shrug, recalling how Ethan had been when they'd first met: clever, affectionate, impossible to dislike. He'd always worked so hard, always looked so tired from trying to do his best by his clients. But six months into the marriage, he'd already been devising small tyrannies: objecting to the time she spent with Nancy; belittling her painting; challenging her need to escape the suffocating house. Over the years, he'd flung many allegations at her, accusing her of affairs, often claiming that Abby wasn't his daughter. Jodie had railed at him.

'*You want me to arrange a paternity test, Ethan? Is that what you want? I'll do it, I'll prove it to you!*'

He'd smiled, looked smug. He'd always known his accusations weren't true. He and Abby were so alike, all he had to do was look at her to see that she was his.

But Novak was right. Looking back, her radar should've flagged it at the start, should've warned that something was out of whack. In truth, her defences had been down. She'd been searching for her father at the time, desperate to find him and to finally know that maybe she looked like someone. Then suddenly she'd found out he'd been dead for twenty-three years.

He'd died in an accident at the age of nineteen. She'd talked to a few of the people who'd known him, come away with an impression of a quiet young man, kind-hearted, well-liked. The discovery had left an aching emptiness, and Ethan had been there to fill it.

Jodie gave the journalist a level look.

'People make mistakes, Mr Novak.' She eyed his wrinkled clothes and uncombed hair, willing to bet he'd spent the night in his car. 'I'm sure you've made your share.'

He dropped his gaze, seeming to take in his own appearance for the first time. He shifted uncomfortably, then flung her a challenging look.

'So how come you stayed with him so long?'

Jodie debated whether to answer, then relented to make up for her pointed glance at his clothes. 'Not that it's any of your business, but I'd never had a home, and I badly wanted to give my daughter a stable one. Is that so hard to understand?'

He looked at his hands, clenched them together. 'No. No, it isn't.'

He went silent for a moment. Briefly, she wondered if she'd hit a nerve. He didn't exactly look like a guy with a stable home life. She dismissed the thought and got to her feet.

'Look, I'm sorry you were misled about the visit, but I really have nothing more to say to you.'

He gave a humourless laugh and shook his head. 'I should've known.'

'Known what?'

'You were just the same in court, all polite and aloof. Like a brick wall.'

Jodie raised her eyebrows. He charged on.

'You don't make it easy for people to help you, do you? God knows, your lawyer did his best for you, but what could he do with all that remote, ice-queen bullshit?'

Jodie blinked. It wasn't the first time her self-protective shell had been mistaken for coldness. But she'd learned things the hard way: better by far to appear distant than afraid.

Novak was glaring at her, and she wondered just what he had at stake that had got him so riled up. He leaned forward, and when he spoke again his voice was low.

'You said in court that Ethan was a monster.'

Jodie felt her posture stiffen. Novak went on.

'You said he was evil, twisted.'

'I won't talk about this, I told you.'

'A family annihilator, isn't that what your defence attorney called him? A father who kills his own child?'

Jodie flinched. Her hearing seemed to tune in and out, Ethan's voice washed in on the ebb and flow.

'*The water wasn't cold, she didn't wake up.*'

Her gut churned.

'Your attorney brought up other family annihilator cases,' Novak said. 'Other fathers, cold-bloodedly murdering their own children. Devoted family men, losing control.'

'Stop it—'

'Happens more often than people think, right? Several cases a month, your attorney said. All those monsters. Just like Ethan.'

Jodie managed a whisper. 'I can't do this, I told you—'

'Only no one believed you, did they? No one believed he was a monster.' Novak's eyes were latched on to hers. 'Well, I may be the only person who does.'

Jodie turned to go. Novak jerked to his feet.

'Wait!'

She shook her head, moved away.

'Listen to me Jodie, you need to hear this.' Novak's voice grew urgent, louder. 'Ethan is still alive.'

6

Jodie froze. Then slowly, she turned around.

Novak was on his feet, his chair kicked back. Beneath the rumpled shirt, his frame was stocky, the bedraggled hair and stubble giving him a wild, mountain-man look. She shook her head.

'You're crazy.'

'Didn't you ever wonder about the bullets?'

She shook her head again and turned away. His voice rose over the racket in the room.

'They said four shots had been fired from the gun, but you only took two. Didn't you ever wonder about that?'

Jodie halted, keeping her back to him. 'So maybe I fired more, I don't remember. Does it matter?'

'You swore in court you only fired two. Should've been seven rounds left in the gun, so why were there only five?'

'Maybe I only started with seven bullets.'

'You said you loaded a full magazine. Nine rounds.'

Clack-snap. Nine bullets loaded.

Jodie squeezed her eyes shut, driving the memory away. Then she spun round to face him. 'What the hell does it matter how many shots I fired? However many it took, Ethan is dead.'

'The prosecution claimed you fired a round into the gas tank of the car.'

'I don't remember doing that. Why the hell would I do that?'

'To finish him off in the explosion, is what they said.'

'I know what they said, but Ethan was already dead. I shot him, for God's sake. Point blank range. There was blood, it hit my face—' She clamped her mouth shut, inhaled deeply through her nose.

'You may have shot him,' Novak said. 'But you didn't kill him.'

She opened her mouth to object, but his gaze had moved past her, his expression guarded. She flicked a look over her shoulder. The Officer in Charge was scowling in their direction, motioning at them to sit down. Jodie glanced back at Novak, intending to wrap things up, but he cut across her.

'Ethan was in Belize less than two weeks ago and I can prove it.'

The skin on Jodie's arms puckered. Novak's eyes burned into hers. She checked on the Officer in Charge who was now striding in their direction, and with a twinge of misgiving, she stepped back to the table, yanked out her chair and sat down. Novak took his seat opposite hers, but before he could speak, she leaned forward and said,

'This is pointless. I don't know who was in Belize, but Ethan is dead. His body was in the car.'

'That wasn't his body.'

'Oh, come on.'

'I'm serious. The body wasn't his. Did you identify it?'

'No, I didn't *identify* it, the fire in the car made that impossible. But I didn't need to, the dental records confirmed it was Ethan.'

'Yeah, the dental records. I've got a theory about those.'

'A theory? Jesus.' Jodie flopped back against the chair. 'This is the basis of your story? A theory?'

'Come on, humour me a second.' Novak shoved a hand through his wayward hair. The brown curls looked tough and springy; irrepressible. 'Let's back up a bit. How much do you really remember about the last moments in the car?'

'I went over all this in court, you said you were there.'

'Please, bear with me. How much do you remember?'

Jodie rolled her eyes. 'Not much. I know I took a second shot, but after that, nothing.'

'Why two shots?'

'I explained all that. The first shot was for Ethan, the second one was supposed to be for me.' She indicated herself with a sweeping flick of her hand. 'Obviously, I missed.'

'Maybe you didn't.'

She squinted at him, and he went on.

'Maybe you had to change your plan. Maybe when it came to it, you needed that second bullet for Ethan. Because you knew the first one hadn't killed him.'

'The gun was inches from his head.'

'But the car was speeding, swerving all over the road. You said in court you were flung around, thrown from side to side, so how can you be sure your shot was accurate?'

For an instant, Jodie was back in the car: lurching, pitching; her head dazed, the Bentley screeching, spinning out of control.

A cold sweat settled on her skin. It wasn't possible. She'd killed him, she knew she had.

Novak said, 'So where was Ethan going?'

'Boston. The airport.'

'On his way to New York, that's what you said, right?'

'Yes.'

'Do you know for a fact he was going to New York?'

Jodie paused. 'If you put it like that, I suppose I don't. New York is just what he told me.'

'Did you know there are no flights to New York that time of night?'

Jodie frowned. 'No. No, I didn't.'

'It was a business trip?'

'I assumed so. But he never told me much. Look, Mr Novak, Ethan had a lot of secrets. More secrets than we'll ever know about.'

'Yeah, I'm getting that.'

He broke eye contact, and scratched his stubble for a while. He seemed to have trouble forming his next question. The cacophony of families echoed around them, punctuated by the *clunkety-clunk* of cans being dispensed from the vending machine. Eventually, Novak said,

'How many other cars did you see on the road?'

'One or two. Not many.'

'What? That can't be right. On the fourth of July?'

Jodie raised a brow at the argumentative tone. 'I can see that's not the answer you wanted. But it was late. Most people had gone home.'

He drummed his fingers on the table. Jodie checked over her shoulder at the clock on the wall. Time was almost up. Some families were already getting up to leave, preparing for the long ride home. Chairs rumbled against the floor, and a low-level wailing started up. The sound of children and mothers parting.

Jodie's throat constricted. Her mind flicked back to the mannequin in the art room, to the stash of pills that would bring an end to everything. Instead of the usual release, the notion stirred up a worm of unease. She shifted in her chair.

'You said you could prove Ethan was still alive.'

Novak nodded. 'He's come up in a fraud case I've been investigating. Actually, he first came up three years ago, but then he conveniently died.'

'Came up how?'

He hesitated, his expression wary. A journalist protecting his story. Then he went on.

'We can go into the details later. Bottom line is, he's heavily implicated. Along with his buddy, Sheriff Caruso.'

She flashed on the sheriff's fleshy face, his dark, hard eyes. 'That's no surprise. Where does Belize come into it?'

'I'm getting to that. One of my contacts called me. About a bank account I'd linked to Ethan three years ago, an offshore account in Belize City. It's been dormant ever since Ethan died, but six weeks ago it suddenly became active. He's started moving money around.'

Jodie sat back. 'Activity on a bank account? That's all you've got? That could have been anyone. It doesn't prove a thing, it's absurd to think that was Ethan.'

'That's what I thought.' He clasped his hands in front of him, his knuckles tense. 'So my contact got me a photograph.'

Her stomach jolted. She stared at Novak, who wasn't quite meeting her eyes. Every muscle in her body felt rigid, and for a moment, neither of them spoke. Eventually, she managed,

'Aren't you going to show it to me?'

He scraped a hand over his cheek. She could see some kind of debate chase back and forth across his face, and from the tremor in his frame, she guessed it had sent his leg jiggling. He finally seemed to make up his mind, and reached into his jacket pocket, drawing out a single photograph. Jodie's mouth felt dry. He held the photo close to his chest, still unwilling to part with it.

'This was taken from the security camera in the bank.' He peeked at it, like a poker player unsure of his hole card. 'It's a little grainy, you may not recognize him.'

Jodie swallowed hard, waiting for him to hand it over. When he didn't, it occurred to her he was as anxious as she was. She squinted at him.

'You're not sure, are you?'

'Of course I'm fucking sure.'

She studied the taut line of his jaw. 'No, you're not. But you badly need it to be him, don't you?'

He shrugged, avoiding her eyes. 'It's just a story.'

But the sheen on his forehead spoke of desperation. The guy had more riding on this than he was prepared to say. Slowly, Jodie held out her hand, aware that her pulse was hammering. He gave the photo one last look, then slid it across the table.

She picked it up. Looked at it. Her breath caught in her throat. Nausea rolled in the pit of her stomach, and she shoved her knuckles against her lips, fighting the urge to fling the photo back across the table. She made herself study it long and hard, just so she could be sure.

It was a half-body shot in gritty-looking monochrome. The man's image was over-magnified, his outline defined by small, pixelated blocks. Jodie scrutinized the longish dark hair, the jaded face, the hint of stubble on his chin. Not wild stubble like Novak's, but groomed, designer-style. And above it, the sculpted, buttoned-up mouth that looked so much like Abby's. A chill skittered through her.

'It's him, isn't it?' Novak's eyes were fastened on to hers.

She didn't answer. Couldn't. All around her, the babble of voices roared and faded.

Novak leaned forward, bending low across the table. 'I need to know. Is it him?'

She gave a brief nod, her fist still pressed against her mouth. Novak exhaled a long breath. Then he hiked his chair in closer and jabbed a finger at the photo.

'See the date? In the bottom corner? That was taken less than two weeks ago.'

Jodie shook her head. 'That's a mistake. A fake.'

'That date is genuine. Frankly, I wouldn't know how to fake it, and my contact has no reason to lie.'

She shook her head again. Managed a whisper. 'It's impossible. His body—'

'There was another car. There had to be.'

Jodie frowned, dazed. 'What?'

'Ethan's car had overturned, hurtled into the ditch. Why? Because he'd swerved to avoid another vehicle.'

'He was speeding, I'd shot him—'

He waved that aside. 'The guy in the other car was dead or hurt or something, it doesn't matter which. So Ethan just switched places.'

Jodie's brain felt sluggish. Novak rushed on.

'He dragged the guy into his own car, maybe even switched clothes, then shot him in the back of the head. He pulled you clear, along with his own jacket and ID to make sure that stayed intact. Then he fired a round into the gas tank to incinerate the body, and took off in the other car.'

Novak sat back, his arms spread out in a hey-presto gesture. Jodie kneaded her forehead, trying to process the information, sifting out the feasible from the far-fetched and wondering how to tell the difference.

She stared at the photo of Ethan and clenched her teeth. Novak dragged a hand through his hair and got ready to drive the point home.

'Look, it explains the two extra shots from the gun. Ethan was the one who fired into the gas tank, and the other bullet was for the guy in the car.' He started counting things off on his fingers. 'Ethan's finances were threatening to come crashing down, you were going to leave him, Abby was gone, you'd contacted the DA and accused him of murder. What better way to solve all his problems than to disappear? He was never going to get a better opportunity.'

'But the dental records—'

'Zach Caruso.'

'The sheriff?'

'Sure. He was in charge of the investigation, he'd plenty of opportunity to falsify evidence. I bet if we dug around, we'd find his grubby prints all over this.'

'But why?'

'You're forgetting he was heavily involved in the same fraud as Ethan. Maybe Ethan contacted him later that night, strong-armed him into it. Threatened him with exposure if he didn't cooperate.'

Jodie's head felt log-jammed. Her eyes flicked back to the photo. Was Ethan really alive after all this time? While her Abby was still dead? The queasiness in her gut swirled some more. She glanced at Novak, who was watching her closely, and shook her head again.

'You said he pulled me clear of the car. Why would he do that? Why didn't he just kill me too?'

'Because you were the clincher. A witness to his death. Think about it. You'd recover from the crash believing you'd shot him. Your letter to the DA would predispose the authorities to believe it too, not to mention prove the case against you. Ethan knew you wouldn't deny it. What better way to convince people he was really dead than have you admit to the police that you killed him?' He glanced at his surroundings. 'Plus, I guess he got to punish you by sending you in here.'

A shiver twitched down Jodie's spine, sending ripples along her arms that made her hands tremble. She slapped the photo down on the table, shoved it away. It couldn't be true. *It couldn't*.

Novak narrowed his eyes.

'What, you think he wasn't capable? He wasn't devious enough to pull off a stunt like that? Or ruthless enough? You think he didn't have the cunning to spot his chance and cook up a scheme to exploit it?'

Jodie squeezed her eyes shut, the simmering nausea threatening to come to the boil. She whispered, 'He was a liar, not Houdini.'

'He was a twisted, clever, conniving man, and you know it.'

He grabbed her hand, and her eyes flew open. He jammed the photo between her fingers, clenching his hands over hers. He thrust the photo up close, his hands warm and rough.

'Look at him. *Look at him!* He's alive, you know he is. Look at him and tell me he's not capable of doing this.'

Ethan's face filled her vision: the sculptured bone structure, the dark brows, the familiar smirk nudging his tired lines into folds.

'*I stayed there in the boat until it was all over . . . you'll never see her again.*'

She shut her eyes, shook her head. Tried to drive Ethan's voice away.

'*You've brought this all on yourself, Jodie . . . If it wasn't for you, Abby would still be alive.*'

She choked back the urge to scream, every cell in her body clenched tight.

'*No one can prove anything.*'

Jodie snapped her eyes open. Something icy stole over her, and she felt her jaw lock down tight. She stared at the photo. Novak was right. If anyone could have pulled off a conjuring trick like that, it was Ethan.

He was still alive.

Impossible! She'd killed him!

But her gut felt cold.

The bastard was still alive.

She lifted her chin, gave Novak a long, steady look.

'If he's alive, then where is he now?'

He released her hand. 'I don't know. That's why I'm here. You know his friends, habits, contacts, family. I wanted you to help me track him down.'

Slowly, Jodie nodded. 'I see.'

Possibilities formed and shifted in her head. Something stony and primitive hardened inside her, crystallizing the answer to the cardinal question: what's worth living for, what's worth dying for?

Eventually, she said, 'Okay, Mr Novak. If he's really alive, I'll help you find him.'

And when she found him again, she would kill him. For good, this time.

7

'Anyone ever break out of here, Dixie?'

Jodie stared at the horizon through the chain-linked fence, and figured she already knew the answer. Beside her, Dixie was stamping her feet to keep warm.

'Are you crazy? Have you taken a look around here lately?'

Jodie shrugged and blew on her hands, her breath clouding up around her like a facial steam bath. The view through the fence resolved into a mesh of diamond shapes, a bleak jigsaw of stretching, snowy scrub land.

She glanced at the snarls of razor wire above her, the jagged barbs spiking out through crusts of snow.

'Hasn't anyone ever tried?'

'Sure, they've *tried*. Some of 'em died trying.'

'And the rest?'

'They just got caught. Got thrown in Seg, with a few more years added to their sentence.'

Jodie nodded, her gaze drifting back out to the horizon. It was mostly obscured by maple trees and phone cables, all burdened with a heavy load of snow. Behind her, she knew the guards in the tower were watching.

Dixie stomped her feet some more, and squinted up into Jodie's face. Her round amber eyes looked watery from the cold.

'Why the sudden interest?'

Jodie shrugged again. 'No reason.'

'Bullshit.' Dixie hugged her chest for warmth, her plump shape bundled into so many layers she had trouble bending her arms. 'With you, there's always a reason.'

'The ones that got out, how did they do it?'

'How in hell do I know?'

'Come on, you must have heard something. Did they dig tunnels, overpower the guards, or what?'

'Who the fuck knows? Ask Momma Ruth, if you're so interested. Thirty-two years, she's seen everything in here.'

An officer hollered at them to keep on moving. Slowly, Jodie turned away from the fence and resumed her circuit of the yard. Her feet scrunched through the cakey snow, and Dixie's footsteps padded after her.

'Hey, Picasso, what's this about?'

Jodie didn't answer. Her glance flickered over the guard tower as they passed, the air traffic control of the prison yard. Except these guys had sniper rifles. A light shiver rippled down her spine, and she quickened her pace.

Dixie caught up. 'This have anything to do with that reporter guy?'

Jodie shook her head. She'd tackled Dixie the previous day about her forgery stunt with the form. Dixie's response had been unapologetic: just a shrewd look, with a pointed remark that at least now she seemed alive instead of ready to lie down and quit.

Jodie hadn't explained what Novak had wanted.

Dixie slogged through the snow and flicked her a curious look. 'What was he like, anyway?'

Jodie pictured Novak's slept-in clothes; his intensity, the air of desperation. 'He looked like a guy who could do with a lucky break.'

He'd be back tomorrow, digging for information about Ethan. The truth was, Jodie didn't have much to tell. Ethan's secrecy was elaborate, tending to unfold in recursive layers so that the more you knew him, the more you found you didn't know him at all. She rewound through his trail of revelations so far, through his mutation over time from loving partner to controlling husband, to murderous father, to fraudulent crook. And now to a man who'd come back from the dead. Jodie shuddered. What other secrets of his would she unravel?

She shook the thought of him away, and turned back to Dixie.

'The women that broke out of here, how long did they have on the outside? Before they got picked up again, I mean.'

'Not long. A day, maybe two.'

'Two days? Is that all?'

'People always get caught, usually 'cause they do

73

something dumb. They get drunk or get high, or visit their family.' Dixie snorted. 'Like the cops ain't going to have a fugitive's family under surveillance.'

She was starting to sound out of breath and Jodie slowed up a little. They were on their second circuit of the yard, getting closer to the cellblock where Nate stood shivering in the doorway. They trudged on, their feet munching in unison through the fresh snow. Dixie got her breath back.

'Mostly they get caught 'cause they got no money. Takes cash to get far enough away and hide. So they end up stealing, get arrested all over again.'

Jodie expelled a foggy breath. Money was a problem, Ethan had seen to that. Everything they'd owned had turned out to be in his name, and since the law ensured she couldn't profit from her crime, the upshot was, she was broke.

Dixie shot her a sharp look. 'What's going on here? You're not thinking of doing something stupid, are you?'

'Stupider than swallowing a fistful of pills, you mean?'

Dixie missed a step. 'Shit. I don't like the sound of this.'

'I've got to get out of here.'

'Are you out of your mind? Look at this place. You know what you're up against?' Dixie held up a thumb and started itemizing things off. 'Electrified fences, guard towers, motion sensors, dog patrols, CCTV,' she switched to her other hand, 'remote-controlled doors, alarms, armed officers at the gate, you name it. Anyone thinking about going up against all that'd have to be a fool.'

'I know.'

'Jesus.'

Jodie hesitated, and felt her heart rate climb as she formed her next question. 'If I needed a passport, could you get me one?'

Dixie halted in her tracks. 'Are you for real?'

Her eyes raked Jodie's face, and whatever she read there made her groan softly.

'This is fuckin' crazy. You know what Momma Ruth would say, right? Don't fight it, just do the time and get out. She has a point. Play your cards right, you could be out of here in a few more years.'

Jodie looked away. A few more years while Ethan lived and breathed; while his trail grew cold; while her Abby was still dead. Her jaw clenched.

Dixie swore some more. 'I know that bull-headed look of yours. You're not listening to me, are you?'

'I need a passport. Plus, I'll need some clothes.'

Dixie huffed out a breath, and stared up at the sky for a long, cold moment. Above them, the clouds had turned lavender-grey, bloated with the threat of forecast blizzards.

'Shit.' Dixie shook her head and looked at Jodie. 'I guess I know a guy.'

'I heard you're getting out of here.'

Jodie sat bolt upright. 'What—'

'Relax.' Nate plonked herself down on the next bunk. 'I overheard Dixie and Momma Ruth talking.'

Jodie swung her legs to the floor, flicked a glance around. They were alone in the cell, waiting for the 6 p.m. count. Outside, the yelling and clatter of trays told her chow was still finishing up.

Jodie shook her head. 'I'm not going anywhere.'

'Don't worry, Dixie thinks I can't keep my mouth shut either, but I won't say nothing.'

Nate leaned forward, elbows on her knees, hands clasped together. Her thin face looked pale, the dark brows and eyes made vivid by the harsh buzz cut.

She'd told Jodie she'd first buzzed her hair when she was eight. Did it herself, she'd said. To discourage her father's attentions and stop him coming into her room at night. She'd deliberately wet the bed most nights for the same reason.

Nate lowered her voice. 'It's wicked awesome, man. A second chance, right?'

'Look, it's not—'

'All that stuff Momma Ruth said? About our mistakes being hard-wired, how we don't have choices? That's bullshit, right? We have choices, we can change our lives.' She gestured at Jodie. 'Look at you, you're doing it.'

Nate jerked to her feet without waiting for an answer, and started pacing the cramped cell. Jodie watched her boyish frame as she dodged bunks, slammed her fist into lockers, kicked at stray shoes on the floor. The place was roomier now that Magda was in Seg, but it still wasn't designed for this caged prowling.

'Come on, Nate, sit down, you're getting fired up over nothing here.'

Nate fetched up in front of her, her eyes feverish. Behind her, Momma Ruth had stepped quietly into the cell.

Nate dropped back down on the bunk. 'I can make my own choices too. You could take me with you.'

'Listen to me. I'm not going anywhere. And even if I was, I couldn't take anyone with me.'

'But I'm clean now, I detoxed in the med unit. I can stay clean when I get out, how fucking hard can it be?' She clutched at Jodie's arm. 'We can make different choices any time we like, right?'

Jodie took in the over-bright eyes, the brittle fervour. She looked at Nate's forearm, at the cuts the girl had made to help her forget, trying to obliterate one pain with another when crack was unavailable.

She patted Nate's hand. 'Sure we can. We can change our lives any time we want.'

She glanced at Momma Ruth, who sent her a bleak look, and knew it wasn't true. Not for Nate, not for herself. Their choices were locked in tight. For Nate, it was crack. For Jodie, it was Ethan. She'd chosen to kill him once before. It wasn't in her blood to choose differently second time around.

'I know what you're going to say,' Jodie said.

She glared at Momma Ruth, who'd taken a seat on Nate's bunk after the younger girl had edged over to the door.

Momma Ruth waited, her broad face passive. Jodie had never known anyone with such a capacity for stillness, and right now it bugged the hell out of her. She lifted her chin.

'Acceptance, am I right? Soldier on, wait for parole, what's another eight years. Not to mention, I suppose, that escape is just about impossible.'

Momma Ruth shrugged. 'That last part's true, at any rate.'

'But some women get out of here. At least for a couple of days.'

'Breaking out is tough, especially this time of year. Last woman who tried it died of exposure in the blizzards. Days later, they were still trying to thaw her out.'

Jodie swallowed, and tried to block the image out. 'But people still try?'

'Oh sure.'

Momma Ruth folded her arms, her posture tranquil, and seemed content to leave it at that. Jodie leaned forward.

'How does anyone even make it past the main gates?'

'I guess mostly it happens while they're being transported somewhere else. To another prison, usually. They see a chance somewhere along the way and they take it.'

Jodie frowned. Her gaze drifted back to Nate, who was still fidgeting over by the door. Momma Ruth went on.

'You can't get far on foot, especially not in the snow. Boston's only twenty miles away, but it may as well be two hundred.'

Jodie chewed her bottom lip. Outside, the clamouring backdrop surged: yelling, banging, metallic crashes of lockers and doors. Her eyes stared unseeing over at Nate while her mind riffled through an array of scenarios, discarding most. Hovering over one.

Was it possible?

Momma Ruth was eyeing her closely. 'You think you've got a way out of here, don't you?'

Jodie shook her head. 'It's not foolproof.'

'Nothing is.'

Jodie's fingers gripped the side of the bunk as she played through the details in her head. If anything went wrong, chances were she'd end up dead. And with Ethan still alive, she was no longer ready for that.

Momma Ruth was still watching her. 'Dixie reckons you've got no money.'

'I'll find some.'

She had to. Dixie was right. Without money, she'd never get anywhere. Momma Ruth shifted her weight on the bunk.

'I got money. You can have it.'

Jodie looked up, startled. 'I can't take your money.'

'Why the hell not? No use to me in here. Been sitting untouched for thirty-two years.' She lowered her voice. 'It's not in any bank, you'll have to go find it. Should be over sixteen thousand dollars. If it's still there.'

'But why would you help me? I don't get it, what happened to acceptance, and making peace with my lot?'

Momma Ruth leaned forward, her gaze penetrating Jodie's.

'Something's changed in you. Clear as day. For the last two years, you've had a look in your eyes I've only ever seen in two kinds of people: the ones on drugs, and the ones on suicide watch.' She shook her head. 'But you don't have it any more.'

Jodie looked at the floor. Momma Ruth was right, though she'd never guess why. Ironic how hate could destroy you, but at the same time could keep you alive.

Momma Ruth squeezed her hand. 'Looks to me like you've decided to live. And if getting out of this place is the only way you can do it, then I'll help you any way I can. Hell, anything's better than watching you lay down and die.'

Jodie closed her eyes briefly, and felt like a fraud. If Momma Ruth knew the reason she wanted to live, she might not be quite so supportive.

After a moment, Momma Ruth said, 'When will you do it?'

Jodie's adrenaline spiked. She swallowed, and whispered,

'Tomorrow. I'll do it tomorrow.'

8

For the next twenty hours, Jodie slogged through the prison routine: sitting tight through the cell count; lying on her bunk till lights out at ten; up at six, down to chow; on duty as porter from seven till two, cleaning the unit, her movements robotic; and all the while, her brain manic, replaying the risks over and over, rehashing all the things that could go wrong.

It was mid-afternoon before she got back to the art room, doubt still gnawing at her gut. She stared at the mannequin in her hands.

Her muscles felt rigid. Stupidly paralysed. She swore softly at herself. How hard could it be, for God's sake? It wasn't so different from her original plan. Except this time, she wanted to live.

It was Nate who'd given her the idea, with her talk

of detox in the prison's med unit. A unit that dealt mostly with cold-turkey and routine healthcare.

Jodie grasped the mannequin's head and wrenched it off, peering into the hollow torso. The white cotton wads were still snugly packed inside. Her stomach dipped. Some part of her had been hoping the doll would be empty.

She reached for a pair of tweezers from Mrs Tate's trays, using them to prise the wadding out onto the counter. A handful of Tylenol pills clattered out after it, the rest still wrapped up in cotton. Jodie unfolded the bundle, tipping the white oblongs into a pile. Thirty-six pills in total.

Her last plan had been easy: swallow the lot, the more the better. But this time, things weren't so clear-cut. This time, she needed to strike a balance: swallow enough to get seriously ill, but not so many that they'd kill her.

She'd tried to research it in the prison library, tried to find a magic number that would keep her from tipping over the edge. But the few available medical textbooks were vague on the topic.

Jodie filled a beaker of water at the sink. Set it down beside the pills. Then she gripped the edge of the counter with both hands.

Just do it.

She gathered up half a dozen tablets, cupping them in the palm of her hand, staring at the white capsule-like shapes, at the Tylenol brand stamped in orange on the surface. She recalled what Momma Ruth had said about inmates who'd escaped: *Mostly it happens while they're being transported somewhere else.*

She gripped the beaker. The prison med unit wasn't equipped for emergency cases. It could handle detox and everyday complaints, but the serious stuff got shipped out. To the local hospital in Framingham, under CO escort.

Transported somewhere else.

Jodie stared at the pills. Stage one of a half-assed plan. Stage two, she'd figure out once she got to the hospital. Escaping from there had to be easier than breaking out of here.

She rolled the pills around in her palm.

Just do it!

Jodie tossed the pills into her mouth. Crunched down, ground them up. They tasted chalky. Bitter. Dixie's words tapped at the base of her brain: *That stuff'll take days to kill you. Days of pain, real slow.*

She gulped some water, washing the gritty pieces down. Shuddering, she grabbed another fistful of tablets, counting them out.

How many more should she take?

Her plan could fail, she knew that. Take too few pills, and the prison doctor might just treat her in the med unit. Take too many, and there was still no guarantee she'd be recognized as an emergency in time.

Her eyes settled on the rest of the pills. A part of her longed to take them all. Swallow them whole, sluice them down. She needed oblivion. Craved it.

But not before Ethan was dead.

She took a deep breath, and tossed five more pills into her mouth. Chewed. Drank. Swallowed. Reached for more.

'Hello, doll-face.'

Jodie dropped the pills, jerked her head around.

Magda's two-hundred-pound frame filled the doorway.

The woman's eyes darted around the room, two black studs in bloated flesh. The tangerine dye-job had leached her face of colour, sapping it to a putty-grey. The eyes leapt back to Jodie.

'Knew I'd find you here.'

She lumbered into the room, head held high, buttressed up by a neck-brace of chins. Jodie fought the urge to back away. Magda smiled.

'Guess you thought I was still in Seg, huh?'

Jodie managed a shrug, and Magda went on.

'Gets crowded in there. They needed the cell.' She shambled closer, swapping the smile for a mock-hurt expression. 'What's the matter, doll-face? Aren't you pleased to see me?'

The woman rolled to a halt, her right arm held apart from her side. Light glinted at her wrist. Jodie stiffened. Magda smiled, opened her fingers and let the weapon slide all the way down into her palm.

'Didn't think I'd forgotten about you, did you?'

Jodie stared at the makeshift knife: a glass shard, maybe five inches long. Jagged and sharp. One end narrowing to a deadly point, the other taped up with fabric to form a handle.

Magda moved forward, her eyes raking Jodie in a head-to-toe flick. 'I been thinking about you a lot, doll-face.'

Jodie's heartbeat drummed. She whipped her gaze around the room, scrambling for an escape. Magda stood between her and the door, the only way out a wide sweep around her and a prayer she was slow on her feet.

The glass shard gleamed in Magda's hand. Jodie stumbled back against the counter. Groped for a weapon. The worktops were bare, everything tidied away. No chairs or desks for improvised shields, all of them stacked in the corner behind Magda.

The woman bore down on her and Jodie's adrenaline surged. She pitched to the right, lurched wide across the room. Magda braked, swerved, lunged after her, and Jodie bolted for the door. The woman's bulk swished close behind her, then ploughed into her as she tackled Jodie's legs and slammed her to the ground.

Jodie's forehead smacked against the floor. She scrambled to get up, but Magda heaved herself onto Jodie's back, pinning her down, crushing the breath out of her. Jodie's right arm was trapped beneath her own chest. She lashed out with her left, scrabbling for contact. Magda grabbed it, wrenched it high behind her back. Pain screeched through Jodie's shoulder.

Magda leaned in close. She was panting, her breath hot against Jodie's neck.

'I thought about you every day in Seg. Picturing what this'd be like.'

Jodie struggled for purchase against the floor, tried to roll over, blanking out the shrieking muscles in her arm. But the woman's heft was immobilizing. Grunting, Magda humped herself further along Jodie's body, flopping back down with the full force of her weight. Jodie gasped, couldn't breathe. Tried to yell. Couldn't do that either.

Mounds of flesh crammed her face sideways into the floor. Her right arm grew numb, wedged beneath her. She strained to free it, to nudge it out, elbow first. Then Magda slid the shard of glass in front of her eyes.

Jodie froze. The blade filled her vision: splintery, lethal; a greenish tint to its slicing edge. Magda ground herself into Jodie's body, rhythmically, urgently, moaning softly.

'Your crackhead girlfriend do this to you, doll-face?' Her breathing was fast. 'You do it to her?'

The shard's tip tilted towards Jodie's neck. Pierced it. Pain bit into her as the glass carved out a line along her skin. Warmth oozed down her throat. Magda's tongue licked her neck in long, lingering strokes.

Jodie's flesh crawled. She screwed her eyes shut, suppressed a shudder; worked to dislodge her elbow some more. But Magda must have read the revulsion. The woman stiffened. Went silent. Then she shoved Jodie's left wrist higher up her back. Jodie cried out, the sound muffled between Magda's crushing weight and the floor.

'You prefer that junkie with the shaved head? That what you want?'

Magda pressed the shard flat against Jodie's cheek. Jodie wriggled her right arm, inching it sideways, so numb now she could barely feel it. Magda put her mouth close to Jodie's ear.

'I was only gonna cut you. But now I think maybe I'll kill you.'

Jodie clenched her fist in a final heave, jabbed her elbow sideways, releasing her right arm. Surprise gained her a brief advantage, enough to grab Magda's wrist, shove it straight out to the side. But only for a second. Magda's jumbo arm tensed, and slowly drove back against hers.

Jodie's eyes locked onto the glass shard. Watched it, transfixed, as it crept back towards her. Tremors shook her arm, numbness making it feeble. She couldn't stop the blade, didn't waste time trying. Concentrated instead on redirecting it away from her throat.

The glass dagger arced down towards her ribs. Magda shifted her weight to get a better purchase, and the crush on Jodie's head slackened. Jodie wrenched her neck to lift her face from the floor. Opened her mouth to yell.

Then her brain quickened. She stared at the blade. Flashed on the pills scattered behind her. Pills she hadn't finished taking, that she mightn't get the chance to take again. Pills that gave no guarantee she'd be shipped outside.

But a stab wound would do it.

A serious wound, with internal organ damage. Where surgery might be required.

The glass shard hovered below her ribs. Jodie's right arm quivered.

What's worth living for, what's worth dying for?

She closed her eyes and let go of Magda's wrist.

The blade plunged deep into her side. She gasped in shock. Waited for pain. A crushing pressure built up inside her, and she opened her eyes, saw blood seeping out to the floor. A dull throbbing pulsed along her body. Then white-hot pain blazed through her like fire.

She cried out, her torso burning. Magda swivelled the glass shard in the wound, and Jodie screamed, her brain shutting down on everything except the pain.

Violent shivers wracked her body. The room tilted, and she shut her eyes. Sound receded. Dimly, she was aware of Magda's weight shifting, lifting off her.

Jodie half-opened her eyes. Saw Magda's foot draw back, then swing towards her like a wrecking ball. Pain punched into her skull. Jodie tried to yell, couldn't tell if she managed it.

She braced herself for another blow. When it didn't come, she lay there shaking.

Knowing she was alone.

Praying someone would find her.

PART THREE

9

Muffled voices thrummed far away.

They surged in closer, then rippled out. Back and forth. A tide of sound, smothered in a fleecy layer. Jodie struggled with her eyelids. They wouldn't open.

Lighter notes filtered through: tinkling, rattling, steady beeps. But her ears felt plugged, some sounds still blocked. She groped for them, lost them. Floated for a while.

The next time she woke, she knew what was missing. The racket had stopped. The yelling, the screaming; the clank of deadbolts slamming home.

All gone.

She dragged her eyelids open.

A bulky-looking monitor blipped by the bed. Beside it was a plastic bag of fluid on a pole, and beyond that a single empty chair set back against the wall.

Jodie thought about sliding her eyes to the right. Couldn't

manage it. Stared instead at the empty chair, and took stock of her vital signs.

A low-level throb squeezed her skull. With each breath, a jagged pain ripped through her, biting her abdomen like a savage jaw. Clammy sweat pooled from her pores. She fought the urge to close her eyes, flaring them wide open. She needed to stay awake, needed to be sure.

Slowly, she eased her gaze to the right. Saw a closed door; beside it, a Correctional Officer on sentry duty inside the room. He was middle-aged, heavyset, his mouth turned down into an undershot jaw. She didn't recognize him.

Jodie's eyes slid back to the empty chair. The room seemed bare. No way to tell for sure if she'd made it out to hospital. For all she knew, she was still in the prison med unit.

She clutched the pillow. The drip line tugged at the back of her right hand, pinching the skin where it snaked into a vein. Below it, a white ID band scratched at her wrist.

Jodie frowned. She squinted at the details printed on the plastic bracelet: her name, sex, date of birth; a barcode and long identification number; then a footer inscribed along the circumference of the band: *Franklin Pierce Memorial Hospital, Framingham.*

Jodie closed her eyes and felt her extremities tingle. She'd made it out. Stage one of her half-assed plan. All she had to do now was get out of this room.

She opened her eyes and snuck a glance at the CO.

He was staring straight ahead, his eyes glassy, probably from hours of standing on guard. She shifted in the bed. Ragged pain tore through her abdomen, shredding her, paralysing her.

Jesus!

She clenched her teeth. She *had* to sit up. Had to test her mobility, maybe fake a bathroom trip to scout out her surroundings. She swallowed hard.

Two hands on the mattress, just push yourself up.

She raised her head. Slipped her right hand under the pillow, palm down. Lifted her left from under the sheet to do the same.

Metal rattled and yanked her arm back.

She paused, frowning. Then her insides sank.

Her left hand was cuffed to the bed.

'You'll be handcuffed at all times, no exceptions.'

The CO was standing beside Jodie's bed, next to a nurse who was adjusting the drip. His downturned mouth had a jutting, bulldog look. He'd told her his name was Marino.

'Cuffs don't come off,' he said, 'not for eating, sleeping, bathroom visits, nothing. If I need to leave the room, you'll be cuffed to the bed. If you need to leave the hospital, you'll be cuffed to me.' He leaned in closer, his low-slung stomach nudging the side rails of the bed. 'You were cuffed to me in the ambulance all the way here, and you'll be cuffed to me all the way back. Just remember that, Garrett.'

Jodie avoided his gaze, suspecting eye contact might constitute a challenge. He looked capable of leaving her chained up out of spite.

She raised her left arm, the cuffs rattling. 'You're in the room now, so is it okay if I get unlocked from the rails?'

Before he could reply, the nurse elbowed him out of the way and positioned herself by Jodie's shoulder.

'She needs to sit up and eat. Can't do that shackled to the bed, now can she?'

The notion of trying to sit up sent Jodie's pulse racing, and she looked at the nurse in alarm. Nurse S. Regis, according to her nametag. Middle-aged, with nut-brown skin and the tough, stringy build of a lifelong jogger.

Marino jingled through the keys on his belt, taking his time about selecting the right one. Finally, he clicked the cuff free of the rail, and in one deft movement, grabbed her right wrist and snapped the bracelet around it.

Jodie lay there, manacled. Nurse Regis placed a reassuring hand on her shoulder, then slid it down under her back and with her other hand, grasped Jodie's elbow.

'Now, dear. One, two, three, up!'

Blades of pain slashed through Jodie's gut, hot and vicious. She bit down on the urge to cry out, somehow making it into a sitting position while the nurse punched the pillows into submission behind her. Then she eased back against the downy pile. The lack of movement, when it came, was a blessed relief.

The doctor had been in to see her earlier, a brisk woman in her forties with tired eyes and cropped, cherry-red hair.

'We had to open you up,' she'd said. 'Nasty weapon, glass. Serrated and dirty. Did a lot of tearing on its way in.'

She'd ignored Jodie's wince and consulted her notes.

'Long blade, got through three layers of muscle, dodged your ribs and managed to pierce your liver. Quite a mess. Internal bleeding, cuts, bruising.'

She glanced at Jodie, then went back to her notes.

'We tidied you up, sutured the liver tissue, now we're dousing you with antibiotics to ward off peritonitis. So you should be out of here in a few days.' She snapped the notes closed, and fixed Jodie with a steady look. 'Whoever found you saw the Tylenol, so we dealt with that too.'

Jodie was suddenly unable to meet the woman's eyes. The doctor went on.

'We got you in time. Administered acetylcysteine.' She added as an afterthought, 'That's an antidote to paracetamol overdose.' Then she paused, and said, 'How many did you take?'

Jodie plucked at the sheet. 'Eleven or twelve, maybe, I'm not sure.' She gestured at her midsection. 'I guess I got interrupted.'

The doctor had given her a frank look. 'Well then, whoever stabbed you did you a favour. A few more pills, and things would have ended very differently.'

Jodie closed her eyes now, recalling the doctor's words, bypassing the gory details and worrying instead at the prospect of being discharged. A few days didn't give her much time.

She opened her eyes. By now, Nurse Regis had gone, and Marino was by the door, quizzing an orderly before admitting him into the room. Sounds flowed in from the corridor: the rattle of trolleys, the swish of curtains, the easy swing of unlocked doors. The orderly came in and set a tray down on the bed table, rolling it within her reach before departing again.

Jodie surveyed the tray. Tea, toast, butter, jam. The sweet scent of it churned her stomach up, and she nudged the table away with her manacled hands. Then she ground her teeth, furious at her own weakness.

Over by the door, Marino looked smug.

'Plastic knives and forks for you, Garrett. Paper plates, paper cups. Won't be nothing here you can use as a weapon.'

Jodie lay still. Right now, she couldn't lift a plastic knife, much less go on the assault with a weapon. Marino stepped closer.

'This room's been swept clear. Nothing sharp or heavy lying around. Bathroom's en suite, so no jaunts outside for you either. That's been swept clear too, in case you're wondering.'

Jodie managed a nod to show she understood. He jerked his undershot chin in the direction of her tray.

'You eating that?'

She shook her head. He helped himself to a slice of toast, his eyes sliding over the elevated bed, the computerized drip, the nearby en suite bathroom.

'Makes me sick, all of this. Hard-working folks never broke a law in their lives don't get a tenth of the medical care you stinking jailbirds get.'

He washed the toast down with Jodie's tea, and was wiping his mouth when Nurse Regis bustled back into the room. She held out two white pills and a plastic cup of water.

'Take these.'

'What are they?'

'They'll help you sleep. First night after surgery can be rough, I'm afraid.'

Jodie hesitated. A rough night didn't appeal, but then neither did eight hours wasted in drugged-up sleep. She needed a clear head. Had to stay alert, ready to seize any chance.

She glanced at Marino, who was watching her closely. It wouldn't hurt if he believed she was sedated later. His vigilance might slip a little.

She took the pills and popped them into her mouth, then accepted the outstretched cup. The nurse tugged at a wrinkle in the sheet.

'Tomorrow we'll get you up and walking along the corridor.'

Jodie's pulse leapt. A chance to move outside. Marino's eyes snapped to the nurse's face.

'No way, ma'am. She doesn't leave this room.'

The nurse drew herself up. 'That's not going to work, Sergeant. Early walking after surgery is critical for her recovery.'

Marino thrust his chin forwards. Jodie watched them square off, using the moment to work the pills to the inside of her cheek.

'She's my prisoner,' Marino said. 'In my custody. And I say she doesn't leave this room.'

'She's my patient, Sergeant. On my ward. Are you prepared to take responsibility for the blood clots or infections she might get because you won't let her exercise?'

'This prisoner is a flight risk.'

'Oh, for heaven's sake. Does she look like she could run anywhere?'

Jodie gulped a mouthful of water, swallowing with a showy head-toss to prove she'd flushed the pills down. It wouldn't have fooled the nurses in prison, but no one here expected patients to be sneaky.

Jodie handed the cup back, the pills still tucked inside her cheek, hamster-style. Marino's jaw was set hard. She could see him weigh it up, pitting the risks of allowing her out in the corridor against the consequences to himself if he didn't. Finally, he seemed to make up his mind.

'She stays handcuffed to me, every second she's outside this room. No talking to other patients, no trips to external bathrooms. No deviations of any sort.'

Nurse Regis flapped her hand. 'More rules. Fine, whatever you want.'

She snatched up the tray and swept out of the room. Marino followed her over to the door, seeing her off the premises, as though that might put him back in charge. Jodie took the opportunity to slip the pills out of her mouth.

She rested her head back against the pillows, assessing the night in front of her and gauging her physical state. Long night, clear head. Worthless body.

What the hell use was that?

10

Jodie sat on the edge of the bed, her skin clammy.

On her right, Nurse Regis held her arm, ready to help her to her feet. On her left, Jodie was tightly cuffed to the day-shift CO.

She made her breathing shallow. She had to get up. Had to make it to the corridor to get her bearings, find the exits; get access to people who had clothes, phones, credit cards, cash.

'Ready, dear?'

Jodie nodded and bit her lip. Braced herself for the first agonizing heave. She'd already been up once for a brief bathroom visit, and the pain had almost broken her in two.

It didn't help that Marino had been right about the bathroom. It was big and empty: no windows, no weapons. Even the toilet roll holder had been unscrewed from the wall and removed.

Jodie's head felt woozy. She'd lain awake for most of the night, alternating between fever and wracking chills, watched by Marino who'd never budged from his post at the door.

She glanced at the day-shift CO beside her. He was younger than Marino; leaner, fitter, probably stronger. Marino had given him strict instructions that morning while snacking on Jodie's untouched breakfast.

'She doesn't leave this room unless she's cuffed to you, no matter what that interfering nurse says. You got that?'

The younger man had nodded, his face impassive. So far, he hadn't uttered a word the whole time he'd been here.

Jodie gritted her teeth and eased her weight onto her feet, straightening slowly, the nurse supporting her. Pain tore through her, and she swore she heard her abdomen rip. She stood still for a moment, waiting for the world to stop spinning, while the nurse adjusted the terrycloth robe around Jodie's shoulders. Then, flanked by her two attendants, Jodie baby-stepped across the room and eased out through the open door.

The corridor air was muggy, dense with chemical and stale-cafeteria smells. Jodie's gaze darted around. The hallway stretched either side of her, opening out onto other patient rooms; cut off to her left by a dead end and to her right by a set of open double doors. Beyond them somewhere, an elevator pinged. Jodie's arms prickled.

Her escorts guided her away to the left, past the

half-open doors of patient rooms and the busy nurses' station. A steady hum filled her ears: TVs murmuring on low volume, subdued visitors running out of chit-chat.

Fellow patients shuffled by in slippers and gowns, some clutching overcoats and cigarette packs, heading out for a nicotine hit. Most of them snuck curious looks at the CO. Nurse Regis had made him drape a hand towel over his cuffs to keep them out of sight. 'You'll scare my patients half to death if they see those.'

By now, they were halfway down the corridor, and the nurse patted her arm. 'You're doing real good. This'll get your oxygen flowing, stops everything from slowing down. Healing's quicker that way.'

Jodie flung her a quick, grateful look. Her abdomen still throbbed, but the pain had subsided a little. Already, she felt better than on her earlier trip to the bathroom.

She hobbled further down the corridor, peeking into patient rooms and noting other doors along the way: discreet doors, camouflaged into the walls. Some stood open, others were closed, and most had small signs: 'IV Fluids', 'Linen Store', 'Sluice Room', 'Dirty Utility'. She spied sinks, chairs, trolleys, cupboards. One room marked 'Staff Only' was lined with lockers and benches.

Jodie's pulse quickened. She recalled Dixie's words from the previous morning, just a few hours before Jodie's encounter with Magda.

'I rung my brother again. Says he's stashed a bag of clothes in the hospital like you said, along with that other thing you asked for, but he won't leave no money.' Dixie's amber eyes had been wide with concern. She hadn't known what Jodie was planning, but knew enough not to try and change her mind. 'Says he's put them in St Ann's Ward, fourth floor. It's the only one he knows, on account of his buddy got brung in there for appendicitis. Says he found a staff locker room and stashed the bag in there. Best he could do. Can't guarantee it won't be gone when you get there.'

Jodie came to a halt. The corridor had terminated in a small storage area with a sink, some cupboards and a large window to one side. Jodie glanced at the CO.

'Mind if I look out the window?'

He gave her a hard stare. Then he glanced at the towel that covered their manacled hands. He shrugged his assent, and the three of them moved like conjoined siblings towards the window.

Jodie watched their approaching reflections in the glass. She looked small between her two companions; too thin and pale; her eyes large, dark holes, like the orbital sockets in a skeleton. A thin strip of plaster was angled along her neck, another reminder of Magda's blade.

Outside, dusk had leaked over the day, though it was only about 5 p.m. The hospital campus looked tranquil, layers of snow draped across trees and ledges like bunting. Jodie scanned the other buildings, counting the floors. By her reckoning, she was six storeys up.

Her eyes travelled to the middle distance, beyond the campus to the streets outside. Headlights rinsed away the shadows, probably ordinary people heading home, maybe to shovel their driveways, or fill water containers in preparation for another freeze.

And out there among them, among ordinary people somewhere, Ethan was alive and hiding.

Jodie made the nurses walk her at intervals all evening, blasting through the pain, determined to get mobile. Finally, they talked her into sleeping for a while, and when she woke again, Marino was by her side.

He'd uncuffed her right hand and was snapping the bracelet tight around the bed rail. 'Don't you go anywhere, now, I'll be right back.'

He smirked and turned to leave the room, just as an orderly rattled in with a trolley of tea and toast. Jodie's stomach shimmied. Her appetite was still poor, most of her meals ending up in Marino's belly.

A young nurse swept in with water and two pills, which she set on Jodie's tray with instructions to take them when she'd eaten. She fluffed up Jodie's pillows, folded her robe over the end of the bed, then breezed back out and closed the door behind her.

The room fell silent. Jodie's spine tingled, and she hitched herself upright in the bed. It was the first time she'd been left alone since she got here.

She whipped her gaze around, her brain racing. The room was still bare, apart from the IV drip no longer in use, its old-style monitor and the empty seat over by the wall. Jodie yanked at the cuffs, sending them rattling and biting at her skin. *Goddamnit!*

Her eyes flashed around the room one more time, then settled on the tray in front of her. She stared at the toast. At the two white pills.

She bit her lip. The nurse hadn't told her what the pills were for. They could be painkillers or antibiotics, for all she knew. Or sleeping pills, like the ones she'd dodged the previous evening; the ones she'd snuck out of her mouth and shoved out of sight somewhere.

Where the hell had she put them?

She twisted around, ran her free right hand under the pillows, feeling across the bed, palming down the sides, until finally she detected two hard lumps, tucked in under the sheet.

She prised the pills out, being careful not to drop them, then set them alongside the others on the tray. They looked the same. Same size, same shape; similar markings carved on the chalky surface. Four sleeping pills?

With one hand, she smoothed out the paper napkin and popped the four pills into the centre. Then she folded the napkin over, parcelled the tablets up and buried the bundle in her fist.

Jodie shoved the table out of her way. Lifting the bed covers, she eased her legs out and planted her feet on the floor. The familiar pain throbbed through her midsection.

Ignore it!

With a quick glance at the door, she stood up and reached out towards the IV monitor with her right hand. Her manacled left wrist brought her up short. She lengthened her stride, giant-stepping away from the bed, stretching her torso till her abdomen felt it might rupture.

Her fingertips touched the underside of the console. She coaxed it towards her, a millimetre at a time. It felt leaden and cumbersome, its wheels stiff. When it was close enough, she grabbed the stand and lugged the whole contraption to her side.

Jodie set her parcel on the floor, unfolding it till only a single layer of napkin covered the pills. She grasped a corner of the console, tilted the heavy stand, raising one wheel a few inches off the floor, and toed the folded napkin beneath it. Then she slammed the monitor down with a crash.

She stiffened, straining for sounds from the corridor. Heard none. Bent down, opened the napkin and fingered the broken pills. She heaped them together, covered them over, then lifted the console and hammered it down hard. For good measure, she repeated the manoeuvre twice more.

She hunkered down, opened the napkin. The pills had been crushed to a gritty, white powder. Not as fine as she'd have liked, but it would have to do.

She worked the powder into the napkin crease, then straightened up and reached for the paper takeout cup of tea. With one hand, she removed the lid and funnelled the powder into the steaming liquid. She swirled it around with a plastic spoon from the tray, and noticed her hand was shaking.

Voices rumbled outside in the corridor. Jodie popped the lid on the cup, clambered into bed and was easing down on the pillows when Marino barged back into the room.

Jodie lay still, trying not to wince at the pulsing after-shocks of pain. Marino approached the bed. His eyes narrowed as he took in her rapid breathing. He jerked at the cuffs to make sure they were intact, then swept his gaze around the room.

Jodie's heartbeat tripped. *Shit*. The IV monitor. She'd forgotten to shove it back out of reach.

Marino's eyes tracked a slow, second circuit of the room, his expression dull and flat with suspicion. But his gaze skimmed past the IV monitor without snagging. He drilled her with a final glare, then unlocked the cuff from the rail and ratcheted it tight around her wrist.

'Just you and me for the night now, Garrett. I'll be watching you. Every second.'

He lumbered across the room and took up his post by the door. Jodie waited for the throb in her gut to subside, then raised her head from the pillows and shoved the bed table away: an unmistakable signal that a snack was up for grabs. She lay back and waited for Marino to help himself.

She couldn't be sure what effect the tablets would have. There was no guarantee all four were sleeping pills, and even if they were, a man his size might need twice that dose to go under. Jodie closed her eyes and waited. Just another half-assed plan.

Marino didn't move.

Jodie's limbs felt heavy. The night nurse came and

went in a squeak of soft-soled shoes, dispensing sympathy and advice to eat up. The brisk mothering squeezed at Jodie's chest and, unexpectedly, she found herself thinking of her parents.

All she knew were their names, and some sketchy background. Her mother, Sarah Garrett, had been a young drug addict who'd died in an Irish prison when Jodie was six weeks old. According to Jodie's case workers, the Garrett family wanted no part of any grandchild, and Jodie had told herself the feeling was mutual. Who needed a mob of reluctant relatives, all filling each other's lives with unwanted obligations?

So she'd blocked the Garrett family out, her mother included, and from a young age had invested all her hopes and dreams in her father.

His name was Peter Rosen. He'd arrived in Dublin from North Dakota, a place that to an Irish child sounded adventurous and wild. Growing up, she'd always imagined he'd be her protector; that he'd guard her and be on her side. She'd known it was all a fantasy, but had cherished the notion all the same.

By the time she'd found out he'd died at nineteen, she herself was twenty-four. Already older than he would ever be. After that, it was hard to think of him as a father figure. Instead, she'd felt an odd protectiveness of her own; a nameless regret for a boy who'd died young.

Would things have turned out differently if he'd lived? She floated with the notion for a while. Felt her head drifting.

Her legs jerked, jolting her awake. She dragged her

108

eyes open, checked on Marino. He was still standing by the door, hands clasped behind his back, gaze fixed straight ahead. The tea and toast lay untouched on the tray in front of her.

Her lids felt leaden and this time she let them close.

Just another half-assed plan.

When Jodie opened her eyes, the room felt different.

Darkened. Hushed.

How long had she been asleep?

Rhythmic breaths shushed back and forth. Jodie frowned, turned her head. Marino sat in the chair, arms folded, chin on his chest. Eyes shut tight.

Jodie snapped her gaze to the bed table. The tray was gone.

Jesus.

Had he drunk the tea?

She studied his face: the pugnacious jaw, slack from sleep; the drooping jowls. His breathing was steady; slow and regular. No way of knowing if he was comatose from pills, or just taking a quick nap.

Her eyes lingered on the bunch of keys clipped to his belt. She hesitated, then eased herself upright in the bed, slipped her legs out from the covers, swung her feet to the floor. Marino didn't stir.

Jodie stared at the keys, then down at her cuffs. Maybe she should leave them on. Grab her chance now, get out while he slept. Why risk waking him by fumbling with his keys?

Mentally, she shook her head. Getting out would be hard enough without brandishing a set of cuffs to mark herself out as a felon.

She edged off the bed, crept towards Marino. Held her breath. His belt had over a dozen keys. Which one was it?

She'd seen him use it. Tried to picture it: stubby, dull; the business-end projection short and plain, like a baby tooth.

She flexed her fingers. Maybe she should just unclip the lot and take them with her. She reached out a hand, tried to stop it from trembling.

Then she saw it: small and compact. Like a toy key.

She flicked a glance at Marino's face. Listened for hitches in his breathing. Nothing.

Slowly, Jodie separated the key from its neighbours, and lowered her cuffs towards it. The tremor in her fingers wouldn't stop. She angled the key, missed the lock. Tried again and felt it slip inside.

Metal snapped. Pressure slackened on her wrists. She slid her right hand free and detached the key. Silently, she reached back and set the cuffs on the bed, picked up her robe, and back-stepped over to the door.

She groped for the handle. Eased the door open.

Then she slipped out into the corridor.

11

Jodie scanned her surroundings.

The corridor was quieter than before. Nurses flitted in and out of rooms, most of the ward darkened by now. An elderly voice moaned somewhere, a hopeless note, not expecting to be answered.

Jodie shrugged into her robe. To her left, the staff at the nurses' station were bent over patient charts, probably catching up on clerical work while their charges slept. No one paid Jodie any attention.

She padded barefoot towards the double doors on her right. Scooted through them. No one stopped her.

Jodie's pulse raced.

Ignoring the elevators, she blundered through to the stairwell, noting the signs that confirmed she was on the sixth floor. The air here was cooler, the stairway dimly lit. She jogged down the steps, clutching her stomach, her bare feet making rapid, *pit-pat* sounds. For now, adrenaline was power-washing away the pain.

She reached the fourth floor, inched the door open and slipped through to a replica of the floor she'd just left. All except for the sign: *St Ann's Ward.*

Jodie made her way through the double doors, her heartbeat drumming. The urge to break into a run was overwhelming.

She made her pace casual, drilling herself to relax. This was a hospital, for God's sake, where people were free to come and go. Not a prison where every movement was challenged.

The nurses' station was only a few feet away. The staff stood huddled together behind the desk and Jodie raked their demeanour, searching for signs that Marino had already sounded the alarm. But their eyes skimmed over her, preoccupied with what looked like a handover for a change of shift.

Jodie strolled past. Checked the clock on the wall. One fifteen in the morning.

Her gaze scoured the corridor in front of her. If the layout matched the ward upstairs, then the door to the staff room was just up ahead. She lengthened her stride, and a spasm of pain twisted through her without warning, fierce and deep. Her step faltered.

Keep going. Left foot, right foot. Left. Right.

The pain bit hard. She clamped her mouth shut to keep from crying out, and suddenly, the whole notion of escape seemed so absurd. She could barely walk.

Did she really think she could hunt Ethan down like this?

One step at a time. Don't think too far ahead.

Left foot, right foot.

Clothes. Money. Passport. In that order.

Left foot, right foot. Left, right.

Gradually, the wrenching in her gut eased, movement acting as its own anaesthetic. Jodie inhaled slow, steady breaths, and made her way along the corridor, past the linen store, toilets, bathroom, sluice room, until finally she came to the staff room. The door stood ajar, the room empty. Jodie slipped inside. Lockers and benches lined the walls, and her gaze whipped around, hunting for an unclaimed bag.

Nothing.

Padlocks secured all the lockers, but she rattled a few, just to make sure. None of them budged. Her eyes strayed upwards and her heart leapt. Shoved into a corner on top of the lockers was a large blue holdall.

She sprung onto the bench, reached up to grab the bag. Her abdomen gave a sharp wrench and she sucked in air through her teeth. She fumbled for the holdall, grasped the rough canvas and hauled the bag down.

She ripped it open, rummaging through it: jacket and sweater on top, other items underneath. She sent up a quick prayer of thanks, then slung the holdall over her shoulder and tiptoed out of the room.

Jodie headed back down the corridor, her pulse rate climbing. She ambled past the clutch of nurses behind the desk, her limbs twitching with the need to run. She held herself in check till she'd reached the elevators, then she sprinted through to the stairs.

She raced down three or four flights, lost count, double-checked the signs. Car Park, Level -1. Too far. She climbed back up, her bare feet smacking against the cold steps, her abdomen throbbing. Level 1. Jodie paused to catch her breath, then pushed through the door and out into the main hospital concourse.

The place was quiet at this time of night; wide and spacious, like an airport at four in the morning. A bank of vending machines hummed on her left, and to her right, a small coffee shop was still catering to the grave-yard shift. Her gaze roamed over the straggle of customers, settling on the nearby restrooms.

Jodie ducked into the ladies', a single spacious cubicle, then clicked the lock shut and emptied the holdall on the floor.

Something hard clattered out onto the tiles: short, wooden handle; pointed, scoop-shaped blade. She picked it up, tested its weight. Sturdy and solid. Dixie hadn't known what a gardening trowel was, but thankfully her brother had.

Jodie shoved the trowel back in the bag, then stripped off her hospital gown and dragged on underwear, jeans, two T-shirts, a sweater, and a dark blue hoodie. Dixie's brother had been considerate, packing multiple layers for the climate outside, though in truth she probably had Dixie to thank for that. Jodie belted the jeans tightly at the waist. Everything was several sizes too big, except for a worn pair of snow boots which fitted snugly with two pairs of socks.

She pulled on the padded parka jacket, discovered gloves, scarf and woolly hat stuffed into the pockets. She tugged the hat down low over her forehead, and wrapped the scarf around the bottom half of her face. Then she turned to inspect herself in the mirror over the sink.

She looked hollow-eyed and undernourished, the bulky coat swamping her small frame. What little of her face that was visible looked angular and pinched, her right cheekbone heightened with a livid bruise where Magda's foot had connected.

Dismissing her image, she stuffed her robe and gown into the holdall, then eased out of the restroom, threading her way through the coffee shop tables. The main exit was a few hundred yards ahead, and Jodie steered a course towards it.

Her step faltered. A security guard was approaching the doors ahead of her, mouthing something into his radio. And trudging right behind him was Marino.

Shit!

Marino's back was towards her, but his gaze was sweeping around the concourse like a searchlight. Jodie's skin buzzed. She retraced her steps, slunk back in the direction of the stairwell. Marino's eye line was combing the area to her left, scanning over the vending machines, rotating towards her. She groped for the door, pushed backwards, slipped into the stairwell a split second before his radar could snag her.

She clattered down two flights to the basement, burst through to the car park. The place was deserted, only a few cars left at this time of night. Her heart thudded in her ears. She scoured for exit signs, wheeled to her right, half-ran, half-staggered, clutching her abdomen, zigzagging her way towards the lowered car barriers. The kiosk was unattended at this late hour, and she squeezed past, ignoring the signs forbidding pedestrians on the ramps.

Jodie clambered up the steep, curving slope, clinging to the sides, alert for any traffic that might mow her down. She kept on climbing, until finally the ramp straightened and decanted her out into the snow. Her breath fogged up the frigid air. She shot a glance around. The hospital building was now about five hundred yards away to her left. And to her right was the exit onto the street.

An icy wind whipped at her cheeks. She dragged up her hood, pulled on her gloves. Then taking short, wary steps over the ice and snow, she headed towards the exit.

Her progress was slow, the wound in her gut biting with every step. Headlights approached her, a couple of crawling vehicles, their hoods steaming from the cold. One was a cab. Jodie flagged it down, and when the driver directed her back to the official rank at the door, she offered him cash to bend the rules. He shrugged, said, what the hell, and told her to hop in.

12

'Where to?'

Jodie's gaze met the cabbie's in the rear-view mirror. Recalling Momma Ruth's bizarre instructions, she said, 'Edgell Grove Cemetery, please.'

His eyes widened. 'Jeez, at this time of night? You sure?'

Jodie nodded. The cabbie flipped on his indicator, did a slow U-turn and set the cab in a crawl towards the exit. The tyres made *slick-slack* sounds in the slush, and she flicked a quick glance over her shoulder, willing him to hurry. So far, no one was following them.

They pulled out onto the main road, and Jodie eased back against the seat. Warm air swaddled her, thick with the aroma of stale clothes and fries. The cabbie glanced in the mirror.

'Bleak places, graveyards. You know it's minus fifteen degrees out there?'

His eyes were round and gooseberry-pale, and from the back of his narrow, balding head, she put him somewhere in his fifties. The ID clipped to the dash offered a frontal view: gaunt face; raggedy, grey moustache. He half-turned his head, directing his remarks to the space between the seats.

'My cousin's in Edgell Grove. You lose someone close?'

The question was like a punch to the chest, the directness of it almost winding her. She was saved from answering by the crackle of his radio, the dispatcher's voice cutting through the static. Jodie strained to make out the scratchy transmissions, aware that the cabbies would be among the first alerted to her escape. The driver spoke into the mouthpiece.

'Hey, Joe, two-fourteen, signing out.'

The dispatcher's response was distorted and tinny. Jodie watched the driver for signs of alarm, but after a brief exchange, he flipped a switch and cut the radio out.

'Too damn cold for a late night shift. Weather report's nothing but flash freezes and arctic air masses, whatever in hell *they* are. Gets any worse, five minutes out there'll give you frostbite.'

Jodie's gaze strayed to the window. Outside, the landscape looked lit up, the night sky and snow combining to cast an eerie, luminous glow. Snowbanks hemmed the houses in, shouldering up to the windows. Christmas-card pretty or cabin-fever stifling, depending on your point of view.

Jodie hugged the holdall against her chest, feeling for

the hard edges of the trowel inside. The hand tool seemed suddenly inadequate against so much snow.

She risked another quick glance over her shoulder. The road was empty, no blaze of headlights burning holes in the dark. She guessed the police would catch up with her eventually, but till then she had to stay ahead for as long as she could; for as long as it took to bring Ethan down. What happened after that didn't matter.

They cruised along for another slow mile before the cabbie eased right and coasted to a halt by the kerb. He left the engine idling, indicator ticking into the silence, and gestured out the window.

'Rather you than me.'

Jodie followed his gaze to a pair of wrought-iron gates, set into a knee-high wall that bordered the roadside. A platoon of trees stood guard alongside, and between them, she could make out an array of snow-capped headstones.

The cabbie twisted around in his seat. 'You sure about this? You don't look too good, if you don't mind me saying. Why not come back in daylight?'

Jodie managed a half-smile. 'I'm okay. Hey, can you wait for me? I won't be long, I promise. Maybe fifteen minutes. I'll pay you double, plus tip, when I get back.'

He eyed her doubtfully for a moment, then sighed and reached for a newspaper from the passenger seat.

'I guess there's no place you can run off to.' He nodded at the gates. 'Nothing back there, only woods and wilderness.'

Thanking him, Jodie pulled her scarf up over her nose and clambered out of the car. Freezing air bit her face. She slung the holdall over her shoulder, hunching to lessen the pain in her gut, then headed through the gates and along the main path. Her feet crunched through crisp snow. The dense whiteness reflected the moonlight, illuminating the way ahead.

'Follow the path,' Momma Ruth had told her. 'Behind the church, there's a big family plot, must be a dozen or so graves. There's a statue in the middle. An angel, maybe fifteen feet tall, writing something down in a book. Right behind him. That's where I buried it.'

Jodie shivered. A money cache buried for thirty-two years. What were the chances that it was still there?

An owl hooted somewhere behind her. She trudged past the headstones, some large and ornate, others small and plain, all cloaked in snow and presided over by gloomy statues. The place felt primitive; an ancient ward where time had stopped.

She flashed on an image of Abby's headstone, anchored into the cold, hard ground miles away in Peterborough. Ethan had selected it with such care: the white-grey granite, highly polished; the gentle-looking dove carved in one corner. But nothing could soften the starkness of those chiselled dates: *Abby McCall, Jan 1 2009 – May 23 2012.*

Jodie's chest constricted, and she shoved the memory away. Tried to focus instead on Momma Ruth's instructions, noting the small, stone chapel and the cluster of

120

headstones on the raised bank up ahead. A statue towered above them, taller than the others, and as Jodie got closer, her pulse ramped up.

Momma Ruth's angel.

He was perched on top of a twelve-foot column, balancing an oversized ledger in one hand, noting down an entry inside it with the other. Like an accountant of souls. Credits and debits; payments due. It seemed a pitiless image for a family plot.

Jodie wound her way between the headstones towards the statue. The snow was thinner here, flattened and cleared away to one side, a trampling of footprints suggesting a recent gathering of mourners. She hunkered down behind the statue and dragged the trowel from her bag.

The ground was hard-packed and frozen. Jodie stabbed at it with the trowel's pointed end, chipping through the compressed layers of snow till the blade hit denser, drier earth beneath. She gouged through it, excavating a hole wide enough to get purchase to dig. Then she wedged the trowel in deep, scooping up gritty clumps of dirt. She widened the hole, drilled it, shovelled it, deepened it, till her arms felt weak, her midsection stretched and sore. She kept on digging, penetrating the earth an inch at a time, until finally the trowel clunked against something solid.

She scrabbled away the dirt, groped with her gloved fingers along a rigid, oblong shape encased in protective plastic. She plunged the trowel in deep along its sides, loosening the earth around it, wrenching the gardening tool like a crowbar beneath it, until finally she managed to prise the object out of the ground.

Jodie tore away the raggedy, plastic bag. Stared at its contents: a bulky, metal cashbox, the size of a jumbo biscuit tin. Rust crusted along its surface, and the locks showed ancient signs of brute force. She jimmied the lid open, gaped at the wads of banknotes inside: twenties, fifties, a mix of bills, all exuding a musty, dried-earth smell.

More than sixteen thousand dollars, according to Momma Ruth.

Jodie had asked her where the money came from. In truth, she hadn't expected an answer, but the older woman had lowered her voice and said,

'Botched robbery. Worst mistake I ever made.'

Then to Jodie's surprise, she'd told her the rest: how she'd burgled a nearby family home where, according to her sister, who'd cleaned there twice a week, the guy sometimes kept business cash on the premises; how she'd escaped through the graveyard, cops on her tail, and buried the cashbox to dump the evidence. It hadn't helped. She'd been caught and arrested a few days later, charged with armed robbery and first-degree murder.

Jodie's insides had chilled. Momma Ruth had shaken her head and whispered,

'He wasn't supposed to be home. The whole family were meant to be away.'

The wind in the cemetery picked up, whiplashing the

trees and slicing at Jodie's face. She shuddered, and shoved the lid down on the cashbox, burying the malignant image Momma Ruth had stirred up. She couldn't think about the man who'd died that night. Blood money or not, she needed this cash and couldn't afford to be choosy about its origins. Without it, she'd be back in prison within a few days.

She stuffed the cashbox into the holdall and lugged it onto her shoulder. With a cold look at the bean-counting angel, she made her way back to the road outside. She'd make no apology to anyone for avenging her child.

To her relief, the cabbie was still waiting by the gate, though she'd been longer than the promised fifteen minutes. He must have finished his newspaper. She could hear him scratching through radio channels, fragments of music shredding through the static. She opened the door to the back seat, as the cabbie settled on a channel.

'. . . *escaped custody from Franklin Pierce Memorial Hospital this evening, she's thirty-two years old, five foot three, a hundred and ten pounds . . .*'

Jodie froze, her hand on the door.

'. . . *dark shoulder-length hair, noticeable bruise on her right cheek, Irish accent . . .*'

The cabbie whipped around. Stared at her for an instant. Then he flung open his door, leapt out of the car. Jodie spun on her heel, raced back towards the gates.

'Hey!'

Jodie slipped, stumbled. His feet scrunched after her through the snow, gaining ground. She clawed herself upright, and from the corner of her eye, saw him reach out to grab her. She whirled around, hauled the bag off her shoulder and swung it in a wide arc towards him.

The cashbox weighted the bag like a bowling ball. It cracked against his temple, and he slumped to the ground. Didn't get up.

Shit!

Jodie hesitated, then reached over to check his pulse, felt a thready flutter in his throat. She eyed the car, its engine still idling, ready to take her wherever she needed to go. A sudden wind-gust assaulted her, numbing her face; a reminder of the plunging overnight temperatures, the brutal cold that could kill a man in a matter of hours.

Jodie grabbed the cabbie beneath his arms and pulled. He was narrow-framed, a bantam-weight, but Jodie's muscles were already spent. She lugged at his body, dragging him towards the car. The strain wrenched her arms, tore at her abdomen. She hauled him the last few feet, and wedged him up against the open car door. Then she climbed into the back and heaved him onto the seat.

She retrieved the holdall, scrambled in behind the wheel. Took a second to catch her breath.

Then she flung the car into gear and took off.

13

Jodie peered at the road.

Snowflakes swirled in the headlights, splat like insects against the windscreen. The wipers *thunk-thunked* as she flipped them up to high speed.

She darted a glance at the cabbie in the back seat, noting the rise and fall of his chest. So far, he hadn't stirred.

She'd been driving for almost twenty minutes. Dixie's directions had led her northeast, along Interstate 90 to the outskirts of Waltham, a town maybe twelve or fifteen miles from Boston. By her calculations, the place she was looking for had to be close by.

Following the signs, she nosed the cab past a disused gas station and into a dimly lit street. She eyed the buildings on either side, a jumbled mix of residential and business units. The clapboard houses looked old and buckled, slouched against small, redbrick structures that offered services ranging from insurance to electrical repairs.

Her gaze trawled the ramshackle buildings: kitchen fitters, barbers, tilers, laundromats. Tucked between BriteKleen and Frankie's Cutz, she found the sign she was looking for: 'M&R Auto Repair'.

She cruised to a halt. The small, grimy yard lay open to the road, barely large enough to contain the three rusted pickups parked haphazardly inside. The place had an abandoned, cobwebby air.

'Don't be put off,' Dixie had said. 'Looks like an old junk yard, but his real business is run from upstairs.'

Jodie's eyes travelled upwards along the rickety steps to the narrow door, and the yellow light that glowed from a window above it. Looked like someone was home.

She checked the clock on the dash. Almost three in the morning.

She drummed her fingers against the wheel. Then she swung the car in a wide U-turn and zigzagged for a couple of unlit blocks before finally pulling up outside a row of darkened houses. She doused the lights, killed the engine. Watched the snow flocking over the windscreen. The walk back would be arctic, but it couldn't be helped. Right now, the cabbie was out cold, but he could wake up any time. No sense in handing him a trail right to the door.

Swaddling herself up in scarf and hood, she grabbed the holdall and got out of the car. The ice-laden wind cut into her face. She hunched against the driving snow, slogging back to the yard. Her eyes watered, her toes grew numb. On the upside, the blizzard would obliterate her tracks, masking her whereabouts for a while.

The window was still lit. She climbed the steps to the unmarked door. Hesitated. Knocked. Wondered what the hell she'd do if no one answered.

A security chain rattled, and the door opened a crack. Shadowed eyes stared out, and Jodie lowered her scarf.

'I'm looking for Reuben. I was told I'd find him here.'

No response. She tried again.

'Dixie sent me. Dixie Johnson?'

The chain rattled, the door opened wide. Jodie raised her brows at the open-sesame effect, and stepped into a narrow hall, thankful to be out of the cold.

She peered at the guy who'd let her in. He looked to be in his thirties, with dark hair that sprung back from a widow's peak and reached down almost to his shoulders. The lower half of his face was matted with untrimmed beard.

'You're Reuben?' Jodie said.

He stared at her for a moment, dark eyes made shadowy by a heavy, ridged brow. 'I've been expecting you for the last half hour.'

Jodie frowned. 'How? Dixie couldn't have known when I'd get here, I didn't know myself.'

He motioned her into a room. The space was cramped,

and she picked her way through a mix of office and living room clutter. At the centre stood a small, kerosene stove, the air around it thick with heady fumes.

'Dixie didn't tell me.' Reuben nodded at a TV angled in the corner. 'They did.'

Jodie's eyes snapped to the screen. The sound was on mute, but she recognized with a jolt the blocky figure being pursued by the cameras: the fleshy Italian looks, the watchful eyes.

Reuben reached for the remote, flipped on the sound. '. . . you tell us any more, Sheriff?'

Zach Caruso was scowling, edging away. Someone shoved a microphone into his face.

'You were one of the investigating officers. Is she dangerous?'

Caruso paused, and stared directly at the camera, his gaze so intense Jodie felt herself shrink back. His scowl deepened.

'She's likely to be desperate, and she may be armed. The public should not approach her. Not under any circumstances.'

The screen switched to an old mug-shot of Jodie: thin oval face; razor cheekbones; the almond tilt of her eyes more pronounced than usual. She looked lifeless. Broken. The photo of a dead woman.

Jodie shuddered.

On voice-over, the anchorman was filling in the details for viewers who missed it the first time. 'Jodie Garrett was convicted of murdering her husband in 2012, after she shot him in the head during the Fourth of July celebrations in Cheshire County. Sentenced to—'

The screen turned black, crackling with static. Reuben set the remote down, and Jodie slid him an uneasy glance. He gestured at the armchair.

'Have a seat.'

His face was impassive. With the dark, pointed hairline and bulging brow, he had the look of a tall chimpanzee. She eased herself into the chair and cocked a thumb at the TV.

'That doesn't bother you?'

He shrugged. 'I want to do business with saints, I'll become a priest.' He pulled up a wooden chair. 'Dixie said you need a passport.'

'Yes.'

'She also said you got money.'

'Money's not a problem. As long as I get the passport tonight.'

'Hey, I can't promise—'

'It's now or nothing. As you can see, I don't have time to wait around.'

He paused, and gave her an assessing look. 'Dixie said you'd be bull-headed. She was right about that.' His gaze lingered on her face, his lids half-closed. 'Didn't mention you'd be easy on the eye, too.'

Jodie tensed. Kept her tone casual.

'Let's not get sidetracked here, Reuben. All I want is a passport, then I'll be on my way.'

He watched her for a moment, then shrugged in

gracious defeat. 'Worth a try.' His eyes underwent a back-to-business shift. 'Cash?'

Jodie nodded. Reuben's gaze drifted to her holdall, and belatedly she questioned the wisdom of turning up with a bag of cash in her hand. She tightened her grip on it, and Reuben smiled.

'Let me talk you through my services.' He settled back in his chair and started listing things off, like a waiter reciting the specials of the day. 'I got false passports, driving licences, birth certs, college diplomas, credit cards, social security cards, immigration cards—'

'Reuben, let me save you some time here. All I need is a passport.'

'You sure? How about a burner phone? Or a gun? I can get you a gun.'

A charge buzzed along Jodie's spine. The time might come when she'd need a gun, but not right now. Not where she was headed.

She nodded. 'Actually, you're right, I could use a phone.'

Reuben reached for a box from a stack behind him, ripped open the packaging. 'The caller ID's blocked, you get total privacy. Let's get this charged up while I take your photo.'

'These passports of yours, just how convincing are they?'

He looked offended. 'Hey, these are quality documents, cloned from the real thing. I got a batch inside, ready to go, security features all legit.' He launched into another waiter's recital. 'Special paper, watermarks, security threads, micro-printing, laser perforation, latent image—'

'Hey, Reuben?'

He halted, mid-flow. Jodie pinned her gaze to his.

'Will it get me past airport controls?'

He hesitated. Broke eye contact. When he spoke again, his tone was subdued.

'Okay, without the bullshit? Depends on where you're going. My passports'll get you out of here and into most countries. Leaving the US isn't a problem.' He gave her a quick, direct look. 'But you try and re-enter, that's when they'll take a closer look.'

Jodie nodded, trying to ignore the knot in her stomach. She'd worry about that later on.

'How much will this cost me?'

'Five thousand dollars.'

'Dixie said four.'

'Hey, it's a rush job now. But since you're a friend of Dixie's, I'll throw in the phone for free.'

Jodie made a wry face, while Reuben produced a small digital camera. He eyed her up, made her stand against a blank, magnolia wall and snapped off a series of shots. Then he told her to wait and headed for the door, scrolling through his handiwork on the way. He paused by the threshold, still studying the photos.

'I'll touch these up, get rid of that bruise.' He flicked her a glance. 'You have a distinctive face, you don't mind me saying. Those eyes, and all. If I were you, I'd find me a big pair of shades and keep 'em on. You got Asian blood, or something?'

Jodie shook her head. 'Half-American, half-Irish, as far as I know.'

But the truth was, she didn't know for sure. She'd never seen a photo of either of her parents, though eight years ago, she thought she'd come close. She'd traced her father's family home to Carrington, North Dakota, only to find out the Rosens had long since moved away. So she'd knocked on a neighbour's door, hoping to fill in the gaps, and a mild-mannered man had stepped out into the cold to talk to her. He'd peered at her through glasses so thick they distorted his eyes.

'Yes, I remember the family.' The aroma of toast and stewed coffee had seeped out through the door behind him. 'Long time ago now.'

Jodie explained who she was, and his eyes seemed to magnify. He introduced himself then as Kenneth Blane, and invited her inside, leading the way into a dark, galley-style kitchen.

'Peter Rosen.' Kenneth reached for some cups, clattered with saucers. 'Haven't thought of him in years. We were kids together on this street. 'Course, I was five or six years his junior, but he was always friendly. Protected me some-times from the bigger kids.' He smiled, indicating his Coke-bottle glasses. 'Back then, these made me a bit of a target.' The smile turned rueful. 'Still do, truth be told.'

He poured scalded, undrinkable coffee while Jodie perched on a stool, hands tightly clasped. It was the first time she'd met someone who'd actually known her father.

A shrill voice called out from somewhere down the hall. 'Kenny? Who was at the door? Is there someone in the house?'

Kenneth's face tightened. He moved as far as the kitchen door, his gait stooped.

'It's nothing, Mother. Just someone asking about the Rosen family.'

'Rosen? That old bastard from next door?'

Kenny flung Jodie an apologetic look. 'Mother, please—'

'Who wants to know? Bring 'em into my room.'

'There's no need—'

'Bring 'em in, I said. It's my house, I'll see all the visitors around here.'

Kenneth blinked at Jodie. 'Would you mind? She won't quit till she gets her way.'

Jodie hopped off her stool. 'I'd like to talk to her. Sounds like she remembers the family.'

She followed him down the hall into a half-lit bedroom. The air smelled fusty from ancient layers of floral scent and stale socks. Mrs Blane was in bed, tiny and bird-like, propped up by a marshmallow-mountain of pillows. Kenneth made introductions, fussed with some chairs. Jodie sensed the old lady sizing her up.

'Well, well. So Peter Rosen had a child.' Her face looked cadaverous, old age finally revealing the jutting cheekbones she'd probably craved in her youth. Her small, lashless eyes fixed on Jodie's. 'You look nothing like him. Or much like the rest of the family neither. Oh, don't look so disappointed. You're better off, believe me.'

'Mother, please—'

'Young Peter was nice looking, I'll give you that.' The

133

old lady curled her lip. 'But his father, old Elliot, he was an ugly brute. And his mother, Celine, well, I guess you could say she had nice eyes.' Her gaze rested thoughtfully on Jodie's. 'There's a resemblance there.' Jodie's heartbeat quickened, and the woman went on. 'But really Celine was just mousy.'

Kenny looked uncomfortable. 'Mrs Rosen was always very kind.'

The old woman rounded on him. 'What would you know, you were just a child.' She peered back at Jodie. 'Has he made you tea? Don't let him give you coffee, Kenny's coffee tastes like burnt manure.'

'I'm fine, really.' Jodie's smile felt tight. She appreciated the woman's plain speaking, but her words still grated. Could you really feel loyalty for a family you'd never met? 'Do you have any photographs?'

'Of the Rosens? Why in the world would I take any pictures of them?'

Kenneth's expression turned gloomy. 'Mother never went in much for photos. Not even of me.'

Jodie darted a glance from one to the other, not wanting to get tangled up in their grievances.

'My father,' she prompted. 'He met my mother in Ireland when he was about seventeen. Do you know why he was over there? This was back in 1982.'

Mrs Blane's eyes glazed over, tracking some internal event. 'I seem to recall he ran away from home one time. Or got sent away, I never knew which. Might have been around then. But he came back in the end.' Her face grew slack. 'Should've stayed away. He was better off far away from all of them.'

Jodie studied the woman's gaunt face, wanting to ask what she meant. She ducked the issue, and instead, she said, 'Did he have any brothers or sisters?'

'Two sisters. The younger one, I forget her name . . .'

'Anna,' Kenneth prompted.

'. . . she was maybe seven or eight years younger than Peter. She died when she was ten. Been sickly all her life, some lung disease. Then there was Lily, she was the eldest of the three. Bit of an artist, as I recall, always messing with her paints.' Jodie experienced a leap of recognition. Mrs Blane went on. 'But she was mousy, like her mother. Never stood a chance with that bully of a man. None of 'em did.'

'Mother.' Kenneth's voice held a warning note.

'Well, if she's family, she deserves to know, doesn't she?' The woman's crooked old hands plucked at the sheets. 'No sense in sugar-coating it, your grand-pappy was a cruel and violent man. He used to beat Peter as a child. Kicked him black and blue, sometimes.'

Jodie felt herself grow still. Beside her, Kenneth shifted uncomfortably in his chair.

'You don't *know* that, Mother.'

The old lady ignored him. 'And Lord knows what he did to Lily, but I can guess. When she tried to run away, he locked her up for weeks. Had the windows in her room permanently bricked over. Can you believe that? Like a dungeon. Child never was right in the head after

135

that, had to be hospitalized more than once, as I recall. House stayed that way till the new people moved in.'

Jodie closed her eyes. Felt a rush of pity for her father and his sister. How naïve to have expected her real family to be any better than the foster homes she'd known.

She opened her eyes to find the old lady watching her. Jodie kept her voice level.

'Do you know where the family is now?'

Mrs Blane gave her an odd look. Then she said,

'Your grandmother took off with Lily and disappeared about fifteen years ago. Finally got sense and left Elliot.'

'You never heard from her since?'

'She gave me a number where she could be reached, some lawyer's office. *They'll know how to find me*, is what she said, *in case of emergencies*. In case Elliot up and died, is what she meant.'

'Do you still have it?'

Mrs Blane looked doubtfully at her son. 'Might be here some place. Kenny can dig it out for you before you go. But it won't do you no good. The old bastard did die, at long last, but when I tried calling the number, it was a disconnect.'

Jodie tried to hide her disappointment. 'What about my father?'

The old woman hesitated. 'I thought you already knew what happened to him.'

Jodie stared. Shook her head.

The old lady sighed. 'Worst storms I can remember. They'd no business being out, driving so far.'

136

She paused, and Jodie leaned forward. 'Go on.'

'There were three of them in the car. Peter and two of his friends. They veered off a curve on Highway 57 and plunged into Devil's Lake. No one survived.' Mrs Blane shook her head. 'He was only nineteen.'

The kerosene fumes in Reuben's apartment were clogging up Jodie's head. She jerked to her feet, as much to drive away the memories of her father's family as to keep herself awake.

Distracting herself, she took advantage of Reuben's absence to open the cashbox and extract several wads of notes. She riffled through them, counting them out, then stuffed them into her pockets. By the time Reuben returned, the cashbox was back in the holdall.

He handed over her passport with a flourish. She flipped it open, saw her own digitized image printed on the page, with her new name of Clara Philips. She looked up at Reuben.

'Five thousand dollars?'

'That's what we agreed.'

'I'll give you five and a half if you throw in one of those trucks downstairs. Any of them roadworthy?'

Reuben grimaced. 'Dodge is a wreck. Blue Chevy's not bad, but the transmission's unreliable. Red one's older than either of them.' His face brightened. 'But it's got a full tank of gas and it's the only one with a working heater.'

'Red Chevy it is.'

Jodie handed over the cash and he counted it out,

pausing now and then to finger the bills and pass one or two under his nose.

'Where you been hiding this, in a cave?'

She didn't answer, and when he finished his count, he said, 'You got any more like this?'

'Why?'

'Well, it's old and it smells. Still legal tender, don't get me wrong. But it might attract attention if you start passing it around. And I'm guessing attention is the last thing you need right now.'

He had a point. Jodie folded her arms. 'I get the feeling you've another business proposition up your sleeve.'

Reuben's smile was broad. 'I buy your old bills. I'll give you one thousand for every two grand of yours. I can hide them in clean money, spread them around in different places.'

'So you launder money, too?'

He laughed. 'A regular one-stop shop for fugitives, that's me.'

'How do I know your clean bills aren't fake? Everything else around here is.'

He dipped his head. 'Fair question. But word gets round I'm passing duds, I'd be out of business in a week. Probably dead inside of two.'

Jodie chewed her lip, debating her next move. Reuben was right. She couldn't afford to attract attention. She made up her mind.

'I want a discount for volume. Seven thousand for ten of mine, and it's a deal.'

Reuben started to object but his heart wasn't in it, and five minutes later, they'd wrapped up the transaction and he'd handed her the keys of the truck. Shoving passport, phone and clean bills in her bag, Jodie thanked him and headed for the door.

The red Chevy started on the third attempt. Reuben saluted her from the steps as she galvanized the rusted-up truck out into the snow, steering a course back towards Interstate 90.

Jodie's breath clouded the icy windscreen. She thought of the cabbie she'd left behind. Of the merciless cold that could kill him in hours.

Shit.

She reached for her phone, dialled 911, reported the unconscious cabbie and his location. Cutting off the dispatcher's questions, she ended the call and concentrated on the road for a long while. Then she reached for the phone one more time and dialled Matt Novak's number.

14

The journalist picked up on the third ring.

'Novak.'

He sounded groggy. Jodie hesitated, then took the plunge.

'Sorry to disturb you at this hour, Mr Novak. It's Jodie Garrett.'

'What? Jesus.'

She heard a scuffling sound, presumably as he shifted in the bed. He swore some more. She pictured his dishevelled hair, the scruffy stubble.

'What time is it?' he said.

'Four thirty in the morning.'

'Fuck.'

She tried to gauge his tone. So far, he just sounded like a guy dragged from sleep, not someone who knew he was talking on the phone with a fugitive.

'How the hell are you calling me at four thirty in the morning? They have new rules in that place?'

'Someone smuggled in a cell phone. I'm borrowing it while things are quiet.'

She pressed the phone close to her head, hoping to block out the tell-tale rumble of the pickup. She peered through the windscreen, keeping her speed at a steady twenty miles an hour. Snow enveloped the truck like thick smoke, visibility so poor now she could barely see ten feet ahead.

Novak's voice cut in. 'Hey, what's going on there?'

Jodie stiffened. 'What do you mean?'

'They won't let me see you. I came in on Tuesday to visit like I said and they told me you were unavailable, whatever the hell that means. Won't tell me anything else.'

'Oh, right, I got into a fight. I've been in the hospital wing with a stab wound.'

'Shit.'

'It's not serious.' Jodie's abdomen ached in protest at the lie. 'Look, Mr Novak—'

'Jesus, call me Matt. Or Novak, at least. My old man is the only Mr Novak I know.'

'Novak, then. Look, I have a question. When you found out Ethan was in Belize, didn't you try to track him down over there?'

'Sure, I tried. But according to my contact, Ethan left Belize that same day. By the time I heard he was there, he was already gone.'

'Do you know where he'd been staying?'

'How the hell would I know that? All I know is he called into the bank and then he left.'

'What's your contact's name?'

Novak paused. 'I can't tell you that, he's a confidential source. What do you want his name for?'

'Okay, then which bank was it?'

'Why?'

'Jesus, I don't know. Ethan must have left some kind of trail, and we've got to start somewhere. I thought you wanted my help here?'

He seemed to consider this for a moment, and then he said, 'Belize International Bank. On Coney Drive, downtown Belize City.'

Bingo. Jodie stored the information away.

'So when can I come in?' Novak said. 'I've got stuff I want to show you.'

She felt the back wheels of the truck slide. She recovered traction, slowed to a crawl. 'What kind of stuff?'

'Some paperwork of Ethan's. The cops impounded it from his safe during the investigation of his so-called death.'

'How did you get your hands on it?'

'Ex-cop who worked the case,' Novak said. 'He'd always pegged the sheriff as dirty, and some of this paperwork points that way. Not enough to prove anything, but this guy kept copies just in case. Kept other stuff, too.'

'And he just handed it over?'

'He was happy to, once I told him I was digging into Caruso and a possible connection to fraud. Hold on.'

He grunted, and Jodie pictured him reaching for a drawer, heard him shuffling papers. She squinted through the windscreen. Her headlights scrubbed away the dark, meting out the road a few yards at a time. Now and then, she passed stationary cars on the shoulder: lights flashing, skid-marks tracing their trajectory into the breakdown lane. She tightened her grip on the wheel.

Novak came back on the line. 'Okay, on its own it's not conclusive, but with what I already have, there could be enough here to put Caruso away.'

'And Ethan?'

'Him for sure, if we can find the slippery bastard. He was the major player.'

'What kind of racket did they pull?'

Truth to tell, Jodie didn't much care about Ethan's fraud. Nothing he did could surprise her now, and she'd already got the information she wanted from Novak. It was time to hang up. But somehow she found herself reluctant to end the call. She made a rueful face at herself in the mirror. Fact was, she was glad of his company.

'Fraudulent loans,' Novak was saying. 'Between them, they falsified property records so that Ethan could transfer some of his clients' homes into his own name. Without the clients' knowledge, I might add. Then he used the homes as collateral for substantial bank loans. Probably borrowed over forty million dollars from half a dozen institutions.'

'Jesus. And you can prove all this?'

'Not all of it, but I've been digging into this for a few years and I know what was going on. This wasn't just a sly dip in the till, this was screwing with people's homes, their life savings.'

'But what about the banks, didn't they come looking for their money?'

'Ethan paid it all back, every cent. See, he used the borrowed money to invest in legitimate businesses: shopping malls, office blocks, residential units. And he just paid back the loans like a regular businessman. Rectified the property paperwork after the fact, covered his trail. Ended up a wealthy man.'

Jodie nodded. It sounded like Ethan's kind of plan: cunning and secretive, modifying reality to fit in with his own wishes. Novak went on.

'But it was starting to unravel. A few years back, one of the home owners accidentally discovered his house wasn't registered in his own name. I'm still trying to unwind all the shell companies behind it, but everything I have points to Ethan and Caruso.'

'So why not go to the cops with it? Get Caruso indicted for fraud?'

'Because Caruso is nickel and dime. Big deal, so we uncover another corrupt official. Happens every day, where's the story in that?'

'You don't care he's getting away with it?'

'I care about the story, and the real story's Ethan. Picture it: *smooth, charming lawyer, back from the dead;*

swindler fakes his own death, lets his wife rot in prison. That's the scoop.'

'And the scoop is important?'

Novak gave a humourless laugh. 'Yeah. Yeah, you could say that.'

The hint of desperation wasn't lost on Jodie. 'I'm guessing you're not on the payroll of some big national newspaper here.'

Same humourless laugh. 'With a steady salary and pension? You're kidding, right? Those days are long gone. Freelancing without a safety net, that's all I got left.'

'Anyone lined up to buy your story?'

There was a pause. 'Not yet.'

A pocket of silence filled the space between them. Then Novak rushed to fill it.

'But it'll sell. It has to sell, this story's hot—' He stopped short, then switched tack. 'Look, that fraud stuff isn't what I wanted to show you, anyway. There's something else.'

'Oh?'

'Did you know Ethan was keeping a dossier on you?'

'He was what?'

'Yeah, he had a file full of stuff. I haven't read it all, but it's mostly photos, newspaper articles, addresses—'

'Photos? What kind of photos?'

'Shots of you. Day-to-day stuff. Walking around, mostly. Let's see. Shopping, getting out of a car, walking down the street. Here's one of you having coffee with some plump brunette.'

Nancy. Jodie's eyes widened. Novak went on.

'One of you outside an art gallery, one carrying a little girl in dungarees—'

Novak broke off. Missed a beat. Pain rushed up through Jodie like a wind, snatching at her breath. She closed her eyes, drove blindly into the snow. Surrendered to agonizing memories: Abby's beloved dungarees; the baby-blue T-shirt she always wore beneath them; her soft warmth; her scent so sweet, like soap and vanilla.

Novak cut back in, his tone over-rough. 'If you ask me, he was having you followed.'

Jodie opened her eyes. Closed them again, cradling the pain. Unwilling to let Abby go.

'Jodie? You still there?'

She dragged her eyes open. Noticed she was drifting close to the crash barrier. She pictured herself slamming hard on the accelerator, smashing into oblivion.

Novak barged in on the image. 'You wanted a divorce, right? He was probably looking for ammunition, some-thing to use against you.'

Memories of Ethan punctured her stupor. Recurring arguments.

'You've been seeing someone else, haven't you, Jodie? How do I even know that Abby's my daughter?'

Jodie exhaled a long breath, suddenly weary. 'It wouldn't surprise me.'

She flexed her shoulders, warding off the seductive lethargy, and straightened her course on the road.

'You mentioned newspaper articles,' she said.

'Yeah, from some years back. Looks like they've been printed from online archives.'

'Articles about me?'

'Reviews of your art exhibitions in Ireland.' He started reading aloud. '*Jodie Garrett, a graduate of Dublin's National College of Art and Design with a Masters of Fine Art Degree, has a powerful feel for themes of abandonment* . . . Sound like you?' He read on. '*Garrett's images evoke long-forgotten landscapes, lost time at the edge of the sea* . . .' Novak paused. 'Jesus, who writes this stuff?'

Jodie frowned, recalling the review. It had been written ten years earlier, during her first exhibition, two years before she'd ever met Ethan. He'd never mentioned having a copy, and he certainly hadn't got it from her.

She never kept reviews, often didn't even read them, afraid her next work would be tainted by a need to first filter it through the critic's eye. Her paintings were hers, and hers alone. Reviews could contaminate: tempt her to repeat previous successes for approval; cripple her into mediocrity from a fear of rejection. Whose paintings would they be then, hers or the critic's?

'Here's another one,' Novak went on. '*Garrett experiments with shadows, and often the work is about the shadow cast rather than the object itself* . . . *Her sombre and alienating colours portray a world of abandoned and forgotten panoramas* . . . Wow, that sounds bleak. Not like any paintings of yours that I ever saw.'

'You've seen my paintings?'

'Yeah, some.' His tone became offhand. 'I was curious

147

after the trial. All I remember are the crazy colours. Blue trees, orange rivers. Like something from *The Wizard of Oz*. These other ones sound grim.'

'The Oz colours only started after I married Ethan.'

'Really? Funny, you'd think it'd be the other way around.'

Jodie made a wry face. He had a point. Though the fairy-tale paintings said less about the reality of her life with Ethan and more about her urge to escape it.

She'd painted the first one less than a year into their marriage. She'd been playing hooky from the house, fleeing the captivity to hike the forest trails with her easel. Crisp leaves had covered the ground like a low tide, and she'd swished through them, inhaling the sweet, earthy air, letting her subconscious drift.

She never knew beforehand what she wanted to paint; just waited on the quickening in her chest that signalled she'd found it. Around her, the rain spit-spatted on the undergrowth. The light was grey, too flat for painting, really, but the open-air walk was liberating. She clambered for an hour, rustling and crackling through the forest foliage, until finally she found herself in a secluded clearing. In the centre stood a small, derelict dwelling, half-obscured by underbrush and trees.

She moved in for a closer look. Ivy hugged the walls like thick cladding, and half the roof had fallen in. Where stone was exposed, it looked cold and damp, dappled with moss. An old rusted gate marked the entrance, knitted in place with dense, ivy stitching.

Jodie stared at the cottage for a while, then gave a mental shrug. No quickening sensation. Just a dull recognition that the drab colours were a match for her mood these days.

She was about to turn away when a watery light rinsed through the gloom. A faint rainbow arched over the trees, dispersing misty, pastel hues. Something fluttered in Jodie's chest.

The house looked different. Warmed up. Then the rainbow dissolved, and the fragile light sank back to a lifeless grey. But already another image was burning against Jodie's retina. A different rainbow. A vibrant candy-stripe, dripping with phantasmagorical colours: alizarin crimson, cadmium yellow, cerulean blue.

The fluttering quickened, and she reached for her paints. She rejected conventional, true-to-life shades. Created instead a patchwork of improbable colour: magenta trees, orange grass, stone walls of vivid pink. Whimsical combinations that transformed the house from an abandoned wreck to a heart-warming, fairy-tale cottage.

The picture framers called a few weeks later. A customer had seen the painting, wanted to know would she sell it. He turned out to be a Danish architect, hired by a local landowner to demolish the cottage in favour of a modern, glass-fronted cabin.

They'd met for coffee. His name was Lucas Olsen and he was about her own age. Tanned, slender, dressed in casual-student style. He'd gazed at the painting, seemed mesmerized by the symphony of far-fetched colours. Then he'd raised intelligent, blue eyes to hers.

'I'd like to live there, wouldn't you?' he'd said.

She'd sold him the painting and he'd commissioned two more, each one designed to capture enchantment before it got hit by the wrecking ball. Soon afterwards, the fantasy colours had become her trademark.

The wipers squeaked against the windscreen, and Novak cut in through her thoughts.

'Jodie, you still there?' Pages riffled at his end of the line. 'There's a few more art reviews, no point in reading them all out. Oh, hold on. This one's different.' He paused. 'It's not a review. And it's dated 1984. That's what, thirty-one years ago?'

He cleared his throat.

'*Storms in Ramsey County claimed more lives last night when three men drowned in Devil's Lake while driving through floodwater. Damien Hynes (18), Ken Robbins (20) and Peter Rosen (19) drowned after their car drove off Highway 57 into high waters at Devil's Lake at 10.30 p.m. last night.*'

Jodie stared at the windscreen, her brain playing catch-up. The *whunk-whunk* of the wipers sounded loud in her ears. Novak cut in.

'Those names mean anything to you?'

Whunk-whunk.

'Peter Rosen,' she said. 'He was my father.'

'But he died at nineteen.'

'Yeah, I never knew him.'

150

'Oh.'

She could almost feel her brain crease up as she tried to make sense of it. Why had Ethan dug up a newspaper report about her father's death?

She'd found the same report herself online, not long before she and Ethan had met. But she'd never mentioned it, and something had stopped her from printing it out as a keepsake. She hadn't wanted a permanent reminder of his death, maybe afraid that, like the art reviews, it would colour the rest of her life.

Novak cleared his throat again. 'Look, if you want to see any of this stuff, I can show you next time I visit.'

There was a pause while she worked out how to put him off. Then his tone underwent a sudden shift.

'Hey, wait a second.' His voice was louder, sharper, as though he'd snapped to attention. 'What the hell . . .'

A low murmur sounded in the background, gradually picking up volume.

'. . . *Garrett escaped custody from Franklin Pierce Memorial Hospital earlier this evening . . .*'

'Jesus Christ.'

'. . . *could be armed and dangerous, and the police are warning the public not to approach . . .*'

'Jodie? Jesus. What's going on? You're out?'

'. . . *last seen in the vicinity of Waltham, Middlesex County . . .*'

Jodie's skin prickled. They knew about Waltham. The cabbie must have already woken up and told his tale.

151

She shot a look in the rear-view mirror. No headlights, no sirens, no flashing beacons.

Not yet, anyway.

'Jodie? Where are you? Don't run out on me, Jodie!'

Slowly, she moved the phone away from her ear. Looked at it for a moment. Novak's voice was still audible, full of urgent panic as his story slipped away from him. With effort, she made herself hang up the call.

The truck rattled into the silence. The wipers thumped back and forth like a heartbeat, and she let out a breath, oddly sorry that Novak was gone.

For a while there, they'd almost been on the same side.

15

'Next flight to Belize leaves at 6 a.m.'

The woman behind the American Airlines ticket desk added, 'You'll just about make it.'

Jodie clutched her fake passport, reluctant to part with it. The woman's fingernails clacked across the keyboard.

'Flight's almost full.' She flashed a red-lipsticked smile. 'Good thing you're heading so far south. Snowstorm's cancelled a lot of domestic flights today.'

Jodie glanced around. Logan Airport was busy, clogged with lines of disgruntled travellers, all weighed down with luggage they couldn't check in. Inconvenient for them; good crowd cover for her.

The ticket agent handed her an itinerary.

'You'll have a ninety-minute layover in Miami, arriving in Belize City at midday, local time. That'll be seven hundred and fifty dollars.'

Jodie paid over the cash, thankful for Reuben's clean-smelling bills. She'd already spent some in the airport boutiques, taking Reuben's advice and buying oversized shades, which she now wore, as well as makeup to cover her bruise and the healing cut on her neck.

She'd bought some clothes, too, and had changed into a navy business suit and smart shoes, stuffing the rest of her belongings into a new carry-on bag, along with some lighter items for Belize. She'd ditched her old holdall in the ladies' restroom, cutting the last link to any description the cabbie might have given. It occurred to her she should try to disguise her appearance; cut her hair, dye it maybe. But there wasn't time. And besides, that wouldn't fool anyone.

Her final purchases had been Tylenol for her throbbing stab wound, and a guide book to Belize City. She'd bone up on the maps during the flight.

The ticket agent held out her hand for Jodie's passport. Her stomach tensed as she passed it over, but the agent made no comment and, two minutes later, Jodie was edging through the crowds, following the signs for Departures.

Her gaze was restless behind the shades, sweeping the area for signs of ramped-up security. The police were only one step behind her. All she could do was make her next move before they had time to make theirs.

Her insides felt knotted. In truth, she didn't really have a next move. Beyond getting to Belize, her mind was a blank, and without the name of Novak's contact, her way forward was a little murky.

She paused by a monitor showing flight information, and double-checked her departure gate. The display scrolled down through the day's flights, many now cancelled, and she found herself wondering where Ethan had been headed that night of the fireworks by the lake.

She recalled Novak's words: *Did you know there are no flights to New York that time of night?*

If not New York, then where?

She scanned the display. Today was Thursday. July 4th had fallen on a Wednesday that year, so flights had probably been running to a similar midweek schedule. She waited for the list to scroll to the end, then noted the last two destinations: Zurich and London.

She wasn't sure it meant anything.

'Wondering which flight Ethan was catching that night?'

Jodie whipped around. Novak stood facing her: same scruffy jacket, same unshaven chin; brown curly hair matted from sleep. Her body pitched into fight-or-flight mode, pumping blood into her limbs. She backed up a step.

'I wondered too,' Novak went on, 'since he went to the trouble of lying about it. So I checked the flights out.'

Jodie edged away, scouring the crowds for signs of alerted security. Novak held up his palms.

'Hey, relax, I'm not here to hand you in. You want to know why? Two reasons: one, it'd break my story into the open before I'm ready; and two, think of the inside edge this'll add. Me riding along with a fugitive while we track Ethan down? That's Pulitzer Prize stuff right there.'

Jodie gave him a hard look. 'Riding along?'

He snatched the boarding pass out of her hand, checked the details, then held up one of his own.

'Snap. I made an educated guess. From the questions you were asking, it wasn't hard to figure out where you were headed.' He handed back the boarding pass. 'Now I'm coming with you.'

'Like hell you are. This is none of your business.'

'It's more than my business, it's my fucking story.'

'Are you out of your mind? The police are on my tail. You want to be an accessory? Charged with harbouring a fugitive?' She narrowed her eyes at him. 'What's going on with you, Novak? You'd do that just for a story?'

He shifted his gaze, evading the question. 'That charge would never stick, not if we can find Ethan. Once we prove you're innocent, the rest is just a technicality. Your case'll be re-opened, all the charges dismissed. Ethan's the one who's committed the crime, not us.'

Jodie's grip tightened around her bag. 'I don't want you along, this is not your concern.'

'You don't have a choice. Besides, you need me. I know you want to talk to my contact in the bank. Just how were you planning to do that without me?'

Jodie glared at the reporter. Beneath the stubble, his face was strong-boned, his mouth now set in mulish lines. She hated to admit it, but the guy had a point.

She gestured at the screen. 'Gate's closing, I haven't got time for this.'

She turned and dodged ahead through the crowds, then gradually slowed, letting him catch up. The police were on the lookout for a single female, As part of a couple, she was less likely to catch their eye. She glanced at Novak's rumpled appearance, took in the contrast with her own smart suit. Wasn't sure if the mismatch made them even more conspicuous.

They joined the line for passport control. Gooseflesh tingled on Jodie's skin, but when her turn came, Reuben's forgery went unremarked.

Leaving the US isn't a problem. But you try and re-enter, that's when they'll take a closer look.

Shelving her unease, Jodie boarded the plane and spent the next five hours in a seat three rows behind Novak's. At Miami they switched planes, and this time the reporter nabbed an empty seat beside her, though he spent most of the flight dozing. He woke just as the captain was announcing their final approach.

Jodie flicked a glance at Novak's face. His skin looked puffy, bleached to a harsh pallor by the sun streaming through the window. He caught her eye, and dragged a hand over his sandpapery chin.

'First thing I need is a hotel room and a hot shower.' He leaned forward, checking out the view. 'Soon as we land, I'll call my contact at the bank, set up an appointment for this afternoon.'

Jodie nodded, wondering what hold he had over the

guy to make him so compliant. Her gaze strayed to the window, to the sparkling turquoise of the Caribbean Sea, almost translucent beneath them. Sunlight warmed her face through the glass, a welcome contrast to the blizzards she'd left behind.

She turned back to Novak. 'You said you checked Ethan's flight from Logan Airport. The one he was meant to catch on the fourth of July.'

'Yeah. Yeah, that's right, I did.'

'So did your ex-cop tell you where he was headed?'

Novak shook his head. 'The cops never pursued it, wasn't relevant to their investigation. As far as they were concerned, Ethan was shot while driving his car, so why would they care about some flight he never caught?'

'Then how did you find out?'

'I didn't. I've no way to confirm which flight he'd booked. But I do know which flights were scheduled to leave that night, and there were only three he could possibly have caught in time: London, Zurich and some place in Oregon. My guess is Zurich. If he had an offshore account in Belize, why not in Zurich too?'

Jodie shrugged. 'Maybe the cops were right. Maybe it doesn't matter.'

'It matters because he lied about it.'

She turned back to the window. They were heading inland over Central America, its coastal terrains punctured by swampy-looking lagoons.

'Ethan told a lot of lies,' she said, 'about a lot of ordinary things that weren't important. It was his way of staying in control.'

Her gaze lost focus as she recalled petty tyrannies: Ethan secretly rearranging domestic appointments, trying to convince her she was losing her mind; Ethan hiding her belongings for the same reason. Purses, shoes, books; even Abby's toys. A favourite stuffed rabbit had gone missing for over a week, and Ethan had blamed Jodie. *Mommy lost it, honey, or just dumped it in the trash. She says she can't remember.* Abby had cried herself to sleep every night, till Jodie had found the rabbit locked away in Ethan's gun cabinet.

Novak leaned closer. 'Did you know he wasn't a real lawyer?'

She shot him a look. 'What?'

'He had no qualifications. Never graduated, never sat the bar exam.'

Jodie frowned. 'That's insane. Who told you that? Ethan was a superb lawyer, even I could see that.'

'I talked to some guys from his graduation year at BU Law, and for what it's worth, they all agree with you. I showed them an old photo, they all remembered him well. Said he was a real smart guy, popular, ambitious, and as far as they knew, he'd graduated with honours. But there's no record of him ever graduating from Boston University. He was never even registered as a student there, or anywhere else as far as I can tell.'

Jodie shook her head, trying to make sense of it. Her gaze drifted back to the window. The lagoons had given way to marshy scrubland, cleaved in two by a muddy-looking river. She stared at the ground, watching the plane's shadow track them against the wetland, watching it all the way to Belize City, and wondering if any part of Ethan had ever been real.

16

Jodie buzzed the taxi window down.

A pillow of warm air buffed her face, the glare of sunlight making her squint, even behind her shades. Outside, the streets looked run-down. Rickety clapboards lined both sides, all daubed with graffiti, some little more than shacks.

She glanced at Novak in the back seat beside her. They'd checked into a low-rent hotel called The Plaza, and taken the time to freshen up. But he still looked rumpled, like a bundle of clothes left rolled up for winter. Jodie had showered and changed into jeans and a T-shirt. By the time she'd re-joined Novak in the lobby, he'd already arranged a meeting with his contact at the bank.

She leaned back against the seat, her gaze wandering skyward. The cornflower blue was uninterrupted, apart from the occasional tall palm with its star-shaped crown of fronds. Hard to believe that two days ago she'd been locked up in prison, and now here she was in Central America, in a country she knew very little about, except that it was bordered by Mexico, Guatemala and the Caribbean Sea. Her head felt dazed. She shifted in her seat, fighting off a sudden surge of fatigue.

'How far away is the bank?' she said.

'We're not meeting him there. He'll slip out and join us in a café around the corner.'

'How come?'

'He's paranoid, that's how come. He doesn't want us on the bank's security cameras. And with good reason, frankly. He's violating bank secrecy laws. That's a criminal offence.'

'You must be making it worth his while.'

Novak didn't answer. Jodie glanced back out at the narrow streets. Some of the houses had gaily coloured roofs: sunny yellows, vibrant reds. The effect should have been festive, but up close the buildings looked derelict.

'We're heading downtown?'

Novak nodded. 'Close to the river. Almost there.'

'Sounds like you know your way around.'

'I've been here a couple of times, back when I started digging into the bogus property transfers. When I linked the shell companies to an account in Belize, I came here to find out who owned it.'

He turned to the window, and Jodie followed his gaze, taking in the rows of shuttered-up premises, separated by wire fences and scrub grass.

'This city gets a lot of bad press,' Novak said. 'High crime rates. Murders, robberies, drive-by shootings, rapes, gang wars, you name it. The place scares people.'

'I'm not surprised.'

'Me, I like it. It's got its own charm. All the hustle and bustle. There's a sort of carnival feel, you know? Reminds me of New Orleans.'

Jodie cast a doubtful look out the window; at the unkempt lots, speckled with litter; at the mess of slack overhead power lines, dangling everywhere in sagging loops. The party atmosphere eluded her.

Up ahead, the river slid into view, dark and narrow. The taxi dropped them at a small café on the quayside where they nabbed an outside table and ordered two strong coffees.

Jodie watched the river. It was murky and sluggish, lined with sailboats that knocked against the quays. The sun blazed down on her arms, and somewhere nearby a steel drum beat a lazy, calypso rhythm. The overall effect was soporific, apart from the dense, rotting smell that seemed to ooze from the water.

According to her maps, this was Haulover Creek, the Belize River inlet that emptied into the Caribbean Sea. It was hard to reconcile this dank, muddy water with the crystalline, turquoise ocean.

Jodie felt Novak watching her and flicked him a look. His head was cocked to one side, his gaze speculative.

'Must feel pretty good to be out of prison,' he said.

She raised a brow. 'Is this the journalist gathering human interest for his Pulitzer Prize?'

'Hey, no. I'm just saying. Must feel good to be free after all this time.'

Jodie let her gaze drift away to the river. She wasn't sure what freedom felt like any more. In truth, she'd probably felt freer in prison than she ever had with Ethan. She folded her arms tight across her chest, aware her body language was turning defensive; couldn't do anything to change it.

Novak was eyeing her with curiosity. 'I guess surviving prison was rough.'

'Who says I survived it?'

'You're still alive, aren't you?'

'You think that was my choice? They had me on suicide watch most of the time. Put me in isolation for the first six months. They made me wear a paper gown because it couldn't be torn into strips to make a noose.'

'Jesus.'

'I didn't *survive* prison, Novak. I may still be here, but believe me, that's not the same thing.'

He stared at her. 'But it's got to make a difference knowing you didn't kill Ethan, right? Knowing you're not a murderer after all? You can wipe the slate clean. Start over.'

Start over. Without Abby? Jodie's head reeled, swamped by a familiar black, unbearable loss. She closed her eyes as Novak went on.

'All we have to do is find Ethan. Then we call in the authorities, and they can do the rest.'

Find Ethan. Jodie latched on to the notion, zeroing in

on it: a pinpoint focus to steady her brain. Novak was still talking.

'I get my story, your case gets dismissed and you get a second chance.'

All neat and tidy, wrapped up in a bow. Jodie dragged her eyes open.

'You really don't get it, do you, Novak? You don't understand what it's like to lose a child.'

Something flickered across his face. He broke eye contact, his expression undergoing a subtle shift. Jodie wondered what she'd missed. Repenting, she said,

'Sorry, I guess I've no right to make that assumption.' She hesitated, then added, 'You have any children?'

His eyes jumped to hers, then down to his coffee.

'I have a son,' he said, after a moment. 'He's six years old.'

Jodie noted the present tense, and experienced the pang of envy she always felt for people whose children were still alive. She stifled it and said,

'Where is he now?'

'With his mother in Florida. We're divorced.' He kept his eyes on his coffee. 'I haven't seen him in six months.'

His face took on a fixed expression, and Jodie was visited by an urge to reach out and touch his arm. The impulse alarmed her and she kept it in check, casting around for a way to retreat to safer ground. Then he lifted his gaze, his attention sharpening, snagging on a point over her shoulder. She turned as Novak stood to pull out another chair.

*   *   *

'I don't have much time, I'm expected back.'

The banker stirred in his seat, his eyes restless. His name was Barrow. He was probably in his late fifties, maybe a hundred pounds overweight, with a damp sheen on his dark skin and a snowy dusting on his beard and hair.

Novak gestured at Jodie. 'My associate here has a few questions about Ethan McCall.'

Barrow turned large, expressive eyes her way. She leaned forward, hands clasped on the table.

'I need to know where he is. Do you have an address on your records?'

Novak waved a dismissive hand. 'I already checked that, it's your old home address in Peterborough.'

Jodie stared at the banker. 'He hasn't lived there for some time. How did you communicate with him?'

'By email. He designated that as the primary mode of contact when he set up the account.'

He spoke in a deep baritone, his diction slow and precise, with a mellow, Afro-Caribbean cadence. Jodie flicked a glance at Novak.

'Do we have the email address?'

'Yeah, but it doesn't help. Some anonymous remailer thing, I can't trace it.'

Barrow shook his head. 'It's not valid any more, either. My emails bounce back. He must have shut it down the same time he closed out the account.'

Novak frowned. 'Wait a minute. You never told me he closed the account.'

The banker's gaze shifted, and he looked caught out. 'Maybe I was hoping there was a way you and me could still do business.'

'You were going to lie to me, you mean.'

Jodie looked from one to the other. 'When did he close the account?'

Barrow gave her a direct look. 'When I met with him a couple of weeks ago. He wasn't happy at being called back in, let me tell you. I don't know if that was the reason, but he made a decision there and then to withdraw all his funds and close the account down.'

Jodie squinted. 'Can we just back up a bit? Why exactly did Ethan visit your bank two weeks ago?'

'I instructed him to come in.'

'Why?'

Novak interjected. 'That was my idea. The account had been dormant ever since Ethan died, but then six weeks ago, the transactions started up again. I figured maybe Caruso was behind it. Didn't expect it to be Ethan, back from the dead.'

Jodie turned back to Barrow. 'And you were willing to manufacture some kind of meeting?'

The banker's expression grew cynical. 'What do you think? For a fee, I'm willing to do a lot of things. If you want to know why, just take a look around.'

His gaze roamed the dilapidated quays, with their shabby buildings and littered boardwalks.

'This is a poor city in a poor country,' he said. 'I have a job, but for how long? City's shot to hell. Poverty's hovering over all of us around here.' He glanced skywards. 'Like those vultures up there, just circling, waiting to get us.'

Jodie followed his gaze, and for the first time noticed the dark birds of prey riding the air currents overhead. She suppressed a shiver, and turned her attention back to Barrow.

'So how did you persuade Ethan to come in?'

'I sent him an email, told him the bank was tightening up on our KYC compliance and we needed to meet with him again in person or else we'd be forced to freeze his account.'

'KYC?'

'Know Your Customer. Banks need proof of their customers' identities, no matter how private the account. Due diligence against money laundering, mostly. In Belize, we're not always as strict about it as we should be.'

Jodie darted a look at Novak. 'You didn't come out here to see the account holder for yourself?'

His gaze broke away. 'Something came up. Something I had to take care of.'

He'd turned tight-lipped. Jodie frowned at the sudden buttoned-up look. What could have been so important it interfered with his precious story? Shelving the question for later, she turned back to Barrow.

'So how much money did Ethan have in this account of his?'

The banker shrugged. 'It varied. Twenty-five million at the peak, maybe six or seven years ago.'

168

'Jesus.'

'But the money never stayed still for long. He transferred it around, moved it to his business accounts in the US. Last three years, all he kept here was twenty thousand dollars.' Barrow's expression turned rueful. 'Which he withdrew in cash when he closed out the account.'

Twenty-five million, six or seven years ago.

Jodie's mind reached back. As long as she'd known him, Ethan had always had money, always had investment schemes on the go. Real estate, mostly. And six years ago, he'd invested in a shopping mall in Nashua. She'd never questioned where he'd found the capital.

She leaned forward, hands clenched together.

'Did Ethan mention where he was headed when he left the bank? Or even where he was staying when he was here in Belize City?'

'He mentioned nothing at all, except a flight home that same day. Seemed worn out at the idea of it. He was in the bank for less than ten minutes, and I'm sorry to say I did most of the talking.'

His tone was dry, and Jodie pictured him scrambling, trying to talk Ethan out of closing the account. The loss of a wealthy client couldn't have played well with his standing at the bank.

She slumped back in her chair. 'So you can't tell us anything.'

The banker paused, looked down at his hands. 'I've been thinking. There might be something. For a fee.'

169

He went silent. Jodie glanced at Novak, who was looking sceptical. She ignored him and dug a packet of bills from her bag, slapped it on the table. Barrow eyed it for a moment. Then he nodded and went on.

'I was trying to persuade him not to close the account. I started talking up our services in the bank, even tried selling him on the local tourist spots around here. Anything to try and keep him banking in Belize. I probably sounded like a fool.'

Jodie could well imagine it. 'Go on.'

'I told him about all the usual stuff: the barrier reef, the snorkelling, the islands. He looked as though he'd heard it all before. Then I told him about Ambergris Caye.'

'Where's that?'

'It's one of the islands. My brother runs a hotel there. I gave him my brother's calling card. I expected him to just toss it away. But he didn't.' Barrow dipped a hand into his pocket. 'Here.'

He passed a matchbook over to Jodie. She turned it over in her hands. Its background design was a seductive shot of luxurious villas and glittering, jade-green sea. *Princess Resort, San Pedro, Ambergris Caye.*

'Did he say anything about it?' she said.

Barrow shook his head. 'Not a word. Just looked at the card for a while, then slipped it into his pocket.'

Jodie exchanged a slow look with Novak. He was watching her closely, his eyes narrowed. She pictured Ethan: haggard and tired; cranky at the inconvenient, long-distance trip; twenty thousand dollars in cash now in his pocket.

Water lapped at the quays, and behind her the boats creaked against the jetty. She glanced back at the matchbook, at the enticing, tropical-island image.

It wasn't much to go on. But right now it was all she had.

17

The speedboat smacked against the waves, hissing clouds of spray up over the sides. Jodie clung to the railing. Her lips tasted salty, and pinpricks of seawater stung her face.

She craned her neck to get a better view. By now, they'd left the city harbour far behind, and she could see the low silhouettes of the islands crouching in the distance.

She eyed Novak in the seat opposite. He'd turned his face up to the sun, eyes closed, hair whipped into a frenzy by the wind. He seemed comfortable in the boat, basking in the elements, his complexion taking on a ruddy, weather-beaten look.

Soon, she'd have to ditch him.

She turned away with a twinge of regret. Truth was, she'd grown used to Novak's presence. Revenge and grief were cold companions, after all. But now that she'd met his contact in the bank, she didn't need Novak any more. And having him tag along for the ride didn't fit with her plans. What if she got another chance to kill Ethan? Chances were, Novak would try to stop her.

She had no choice. As soon as Ethan's trail ran cold in Belize, she'd cut loose and go her own way. Self-reliant and solitary. It was what she was used to.

The speedboat pounded against the water, its engine gunned like a revved-up chainsaw. Jodie glanced back at Novak to find him watching her, his expression wary. As though somehow he knew.

It took an hour for the water taxi to reach Ambergris Caye. The boat docked at San Pedro, the island's only town, where Jodie and Novak clambered out onto a wooden jetty.

A trickle of sweat meandered down Jodie's back. The temperature had climbed, felt close to eighty degrees, and the sunlight bouncing off clear water and white sand was dazzling.

She squinted along the pier. A slow-moving pelican was eyeing her from a distance, and beyond him the rows of coconut palms were strung across with hammocks. Already, the island felt more postcard-Caribbean than Belize City.

'Come on.' Novak led the way down the jetty. 'The boat crew say the resort's a short walk from here.'

Jodie followed him along a narrow, sandy road that wound away from the beachfront and into the town.

'So how do we do this?' she said, catching him up. 'Asking about Ethan McCall probably won't get us very far. He'd hardly have gone by the name of a dead man.'

'He did in Belize City.'

'That was different. He'd no choice with the bank account, it was already set up in his own name.'

Novak made a face, conceding the point. Jodie's gaze strayed to the busy cafés and souvenir shops that lined the narrow streets. The paint here was smarter than in Belize City: fresh apple-greens, warm terracottas, crisp yellows and pinks.

She turned back to Novak. 'We'll have to rely on Ethan's photo. Do you have some kind of press pass, anything to make us look official?'

He shrugged, looked away. 'Not one that's current.'

The evasion wasn't lost on her. 'I'm guessing that hasn't stopped you before.'

'We just need to flash it.'

They turned a corner onto Barrier Reef Drive, where many of the larger hotels seemed to be located. Jodie scanned the luxury villas, tuning into the voices of the locals around her: mesmerizing tones of Rasta-tinted English, sprinkled with Spanish and another lilting blend that was probably Belizean Creole.

Novak slid her a look. 'This is a hell of a long shot. No reason to suppose he ever came out here.'

'I know.'

'Chances are he got straight on a plane and headed back home. Wherever home is.'

'I know, Novak, you don't need to tell me.'

He turned to face her, walking crab-wise so he could watch her expression as he talked. 'So what if it's a dead end? We need a plan for what happens next, don't we? Or maybe you've already got one?'

His gaze was challenging, and she worked hard not to look away. He was trying to draw her out, to pick up on her intentions. He knew she didn't need him any more. But he needed her: she was his ticket to his scoop, to the inside track.

Jodie didn't answer. Instead, she pointed over his shoulder. He turned, and together they took in the view of the Princess Resort Hotel.

It was a U-shaped vista, the architecture a blend of Spanish and the Caribbean: pristine white stucco topped with rustic tiled roofs; repeating arches over verandas and balconies; walls festooned with hibiscus and bougain-villea in a tumble of purple and red.

Jodie's skin tingled. She pictured Ethan against this elegant backdrop. The image was more than convincing.

Novak led the way. 'Let's find the bar.'

It was cooler inside, the air sweet with the fragrance of tropical flowers. Jodie slipped off her shades, blinking at the expanse of coral-pink marble, all polished to a wet-look sheen.

Avoiding reception, they veered left across the foyer until they found a poolside bar. Suntanned tourists flip-flopped in and out, ordering fruity drinks to take back to their hammocks. Novak strolled up to the barman, who was leaning against the counter looking bored and checking his phone.

Novak flashed a press card and a fifty-dollar bill in a single, fluid movement. 'I'm a reporter from the *Boston Globe*, mind if I ask you a few questions?'

The barman eyed the fifty, which had fetched up on the counter, half-covered by Novak's palm. He shrugged, and Novak passed him the photo of Ethan.

'Recognize this guy?'

The barman studied the photo, then shrugged again. 'He checked in here a couple of weeks ago.'

Goosebumps crawled along Jodie's arms. 'Do you know his name?'

The barman frowned at the photo. Then his brow cleared and he passed the snapshot back. 'Brown. Joshua Brown.'

He reached for the fifty, but Novak kept his palm down.

'Any idea where he went?'

The barman looked sulky. 'I wasn't here when he checked out. I been on vacation, only came back today.'

The notion seemed to depress him. Jodie leaned in closer.

'Did he ever talk to you about where he was from, or where he was headed?'

'Never talked to me at all, except to order drinks. Only reason I know his name is he charged everything to his room, so he had to sign for it.'

'Was he friendly with anyone else in the hotel?'

176

'Not that I saw. Kept himself to himself, spent most of the time dozing out by the pool. Like he was exhausted or something.'

Jodie's gaze drifted out to the swaying hammocks, and beyond them to the strip of aquamarine sea. She glanced back at Novak, who gave a meaningful look in the direction of the foyer. She nodded, and Novak let the barman have the fifty, then together they headed back out to reception.

The girl behind the desk flashed a welcoming smile. She was model-thin, with straightened hair draped forward over one shoulder, like a swatch of black silk.

'How may I help you?' The badge on her shirt said her name was Daniella. 'Are you checking in with us this afternoon?'

Novak grinned. 'I wish. This is quite a place you got here.'

'The very best on the island. You're staying in San Pedro?'

He made a face. 'The Plaza in Belize City. Next time we'll know to come here.'

Jodie wondered where he was going with the cosy chit-chat, and decided to cut in. 'Actually, we're here to meet a colleague of ours, but I've a feeling we got our wires crossed.'

'Oh?'

'His name is Joshua Brown. It's a couple of weeks since he checked in, so I think we're too late. I believe he's already left?'

Daniella's smile turned sympathetic. 'Oh, what a shame. Yes, I'm afraid you just missed him.'

Something fluttered in Jodie's chest. 'Really?'

'He was booked in till tomorrow, but he got an urgent call. Said he had to leave right away.'

Jodie felt herself grow still. Traces of Ethan seemed to whisper close by, like breath on her cheek. Daniella went on.

'He must have packed in a real hurry, he left a few items behind. If you see him, you might let him know. He can call us with an address and we'll have his things sent on.'

Jodie's spine hummed, the shadowy essence of Ethan lingering like a ghost. She kept her voice neutral.

'When exactly did he leave?'

'About six o'clock this morning. As I said, it's a shame.' Daniella gave a rueful smile. 'Just a few more hours, and you would have caught him.'

178

18

'Fuck!'

Novak slammed the table with his fist, sending the cutlery crashing. Jodie darted a quick look around the beachfront café, a thatched, open-sided pavilion that looked out onto the sea. The young family beside them had turned to stare, and Novak lowered his voice.

'I can't believe we got so close. Where the fuck did he go? And how come he left so suddenly?'

Jodie's fingers tightened around her glass. 'He knew we were coming to find him. Don't ask me how, but he knew.'

'That's impossible.'

'That call he got. It was like someone warned him.'

Novak stared at her. 'Shit.'

'What?'

'Caruso.'

'The sheriff? How could he know anything?'

'He knows you're out. And he's probably heard by now that I visited you in prison.'

'So?'

'Caruso knows who I am.' He swigged at his beer. 'Our paths crossed a few years ago, he knew I was digging. The fact that you broke out of prison right after talking to me may have spooked him.'

'So he called Ethan.'

Novak nodded. Jodie sighed and flopped back against her seat, closing her eyes briefly. Fatigue shuddered through her. She inhaled deeply, breathing in the aroma of sweet coconut and garlic that drifted out from the kitchen.

They had an hour to wait before the next water taxi to Belize City. By now, Ethan was thousands of miles away. According to Daniella, he'd mentioned an 8 a.m. flight back to the US, which meant he could be anywhere.

A cheer went up from the family beside them as a child's birthday cake arrived at the table. Jodie looked away. She fastened her eyes on Novak instead, noting the flush on his nose and cheekbones where his face had caught the sun. It made him look feverish. But his grey eyes were still cool and clear. He leaned forward.

'You know, it didn't sound like him. All that loner stuff, keeping himself to himself.'

'Are you saying it wasn't Ethan?'

'It was him alright, that barman knew him straight off. I'd just pegged him as more of a pack leader, you know? The type that likes to surround himself with lap dogs and bootlickers.'

'You're right, that's how he was, most of the time.'

'But not always?'

Jodie shook her head. 'Every now and then, he'd just take off on his own. Camp out in the backwoods for long stretches, in some isolated cabin. For weeks, sometimes.' Her gaze roamed out across the wide expanse of white, sugary sand. 'He seemed to need the solitude to recharge or something.'

Novak shoved his beer away. 'Great. So now he's feeling all nice and refreshed, but meantime, we've got nothing.'

'We've got a name.'

'Joshua Brown? You know how many Joshua Browns there could be out there?' He raised his voice a little, to be heard over the chorus of 'Happy Birthdays' beside them. 'And maybe that's just a name he used in Belize. Maybe he's calling himself something else by now.'

'You're over-thinking it. Why would he be that paranoid? After all, no one's looking for him. He's been safe for nearly three years, everyone thinks he's dead.'

Novak shrugged. 'Maybe.'

'And if he's been feeling safe, he might have got careless. Maybe somewhere Joshua Brown has left a trail.' Jodie swirled her Coke, sending the ice cubes tinkling. 'I'd like to take a look at that dossier of his.'

'How's that going to help? That file is almost three years old.'

She glared at him. 'Look, I'm trying to stay positive here. We've got to start somewhere.'

Novak sighed and stretched out in his chair, his eye line wandering off towards the beach. 'Maybe. But we need to know where he is now, not where he was three years ago. And we need to know soon. I mean, where the hell do we go when we leave Belize? Back to friggin' Boston?'

He seemed dismayed at the prospect. Jodie followed his gaze, past the thatched canopy to the blue-green sea and the thread of white about half a mile out where the surf line snagged against the reef. A silky breeze drifted over her shoulders. The tranquillity was seductive, and a whisper of temptation breathed through her.

Why not stay here? Why not forget about Ethan, just let him go? You're so damn tired.

Jodie closed her eyes, giving into the notion.

You're free here. You don't ever have to leave. No one knows where you are, apart from Novak.

Jodie dragged her eyes open and flicked him a glance. His expression had turned bleak. He was watching the table beside them, and Jodie followed his gaze. The birthday girl was standing up on her chair, surveying her cake.

Jodie's chest constricted.

Five candles.

Two more than Abby.

She jerked her gaze away. A familiar coldness stole over her, and she felt her jaw tighten. She fixed her eyes on Novak.

'Give me the dossier when we get back to the hotel. I might see something you missed.'

He nodded, distracted, his attention still on the celebrations at the next table. He dragged his eyes away, reached for his beer and took a long, thirsty swallow. Jodie hesitated, then said softly,

'Tell me about your son.'

Novak set his glass down carefully.

'His name's Toby. Greatest little guy. Deserves better parents, the divorce isn't helping him.'

Novak's words were becoming clipped, and Jodie caught herself wondering what kind of woman he'd choose as a soul-mate.

'What happened with your wife?' she said.

'Marriage just fell apart. My fault, I guess. I wasn't much of a provider. Nothing but layoffs and cutbacks in the newspaper industry for the last few years.'

'Your wife blamed you for that?'

'Maybe not that part. But it put a strain on things, and that's when I really fucked up. I was freelancing by then and started taking shortcuts with my stories, anything to try and beat the other guys to a deadline.' He shook his head. 'I was an ass.'

'What kind of shortcuts?'

Novak sighed. 'Didn't verify my sources, didn't check my facts. I rushed interviews, fabricated quotes, you name it. Let's just say, my approach was less than painstaking.' He shrugged. 'You can guess the rest. Newspaper got sued, I got sued. Now I'm broke and no one will touch me. Had to sell every last thing I owned just to trade with Barrow. Even my beat-up old car.'

Jodie made a rueful face. 'Put it like that, I guess you *were* an ass.'

He gave a humourless laugh. 'That's what my wife said. She saw the writing on the wall and bailed.'

'All the way to Florida?'

'She stayed in Boston for a while. I got to see Toby every weekend. Then she married again, moved out to Key West last year.' His jaw muscles tensed. 'I haven't seen Toby in months.'

For the second time that day, Jodie experienced the urge to touch him. She clamped down on it, securing her armour, afraid of what might happen if she let her guard down. After a moment, she said,

'Your wife won't share custody?'

'She doesn't trust me. Can't say I blame her, not after how I screwed up. But it gets worse. Her new husband's in the military. He's being stationed overseas for the next five years, and they're going with him. I'll be lucky if I get to see my son once a year.'

'Can she do that?'

'That's what I'm trying to find out. Had my first joint custody appeal hearing a couple of weeks ago.'

Something slotted into place. 'Is that why you couldn't come out here? Ethan's appointment with the bank was the same time as the hearing?'

Novak snorted. 'May as well have missed it and come

184

out to Belize. Fucking lawyer's no good. I need a kick-ass divorce attorney. Problem is, that costs money. Plus, I need a steady income to prove I have a stable job. What judge's going to award me joint physical custody?'

'But you're his father.'

'I'm a broken-down hack who can't even pay maintenance.' His bright eyes latched on to Jodie's. 'But I can change that. A good scoop, that's all I need. That could be a career-maker.'

She looked down at her hands, and Novak went on.

'It'd give me a fresh start. Put me back in the money. I could take Toby for part of the year, instead of watching some military jock be a father to my son.'

'Okay, I get it.' Jodie had a hard time meeting his eyes. 'You need this story. You need Ethan.'

He leaned forward. 'And I need you. The fugitive wife trying to prove her innocence? Hell, with you, this story could be dynamite.'

It was dark by the time they got back to Belize City.

The sun had plunged below the horizon as though in freefall, with no warning or intervening dusk, and the blackness at Haulover Creek was absolute.

The river was rank with seaweed and decay. Jodie's eyes raked the darkness as they disembarked, scouring for a taxi to take them back to their hotel. The moored boats creaked behind her, and her spine tingled as though she was being watched.

She quickened her pace.

Novak's eyes were restless. 'Let's find a cab, get the hell off these streets.'

Away from the harbour, the city was crowded. Reggae pulsed from the bars, and on every corner men huddled in hostile groups, slouched into dark hoodies pulled up against the evening chill. Jodie felt their eyes tracking her, watching and waiting. Like the black vultures roosting somewhere above her in the trees.

Novak put out a hand to hail a cab, but it sped on by. They picked their way through litter and potholes, past graffiti-branded clapboards and derelict lots. The fetid, muddy smell followed them from the river, blending now with the scent of fried food from the street vendors.

Jodie glanced behind her. A panhandler was stalking them, his eyes trained on Jodie. Novak signalled to another cab. This one stopped, and Jodie clambered with relief into the back seat next to Novak.

She gave him a sideways glance. He looked rugged and sturdy, the sun-reddened cheeks giving him a healthy, outdoorsy look. She tried to picture him with a small son in tow. The image came easily and she instantly buried it, not wanting to dwell on the reason he needed her help. It just made it harder to ditch him.

They reached the hotel, and together rode the elevator to their rooms on the second floor, Novak to grab the dossier and Jodie to pull on a sweater before meeting up again in the bar downstairs.

Novak disappeared into his room. Jodie unlocked her

door, stepped inside, groped for the light switch along the wall. The door swung to behind her, clicking shut, plunging her into darkness. She swore softly.

Then a hand reached out, clamped down over her mouth and slammed her into the wall.

19

Jodie's head snapped back, cracked against cinderblock. Pain splintered through her skull and she tried to yell.

The hand across her mouth smothered the sound.

'I need you to be quiet.' His voice was slow, soft. 'Just do as I say.'

His dark silhouette filled her vision, and his weight pinned her against the wall. The face was featureless, backlit by the window, the head crowned with braided knots that stuck out around his skull like spiders.

Jodie clenched her muscles. Heaved against him. She tried to lift her knee, shove it into his groin. But his bulk immobilized her. His fingers dug hard into her face. Then the cold barrel of a gun jammed into her throat.

She froze. Tried to swallow. Her jugular pounded against the metal, and the hand across her mouth was suffocating. She breathed rapidly through her nostrils, picking up his musty, sweetish smell. Sweat and weed.

'You'll do as I say.'

His features resolved themselves in the dark. Broad cheeks, oily skin. Blank, empty eyes.

Jodie's pulse jackhammered. A jolt of adrenaline shot through her, and she tried to twist away, tried to lash out with her foot, ignoring the burning fire in her stab wound. He stared at her with dead, hooded eyes. Then he raised the gun and smashed it into her skull.

Her head reeled. The floor spun upwards, slammed into her face. The whole room tilted. She tried to stand up, but the world lurched again and she slumped face down on the floor.

He grabbed her arm, yanked her onto her back. She tried to open her eyes. Couldn't lift her lids. A long, ripping noise tore through the room, and she opened her mouth to scream. But her brain see-sawed, and no sound came out.

Scream, damn it!

Something tight pressed down hard against her mouth, pinched her skin. Her lips felt sewn up. Panic choked her. She groped for her face, but he grabbed her wrists, jerked them behind her back. Thin straps lashed them together, wrenched around them so tight they cut through flesh. Jodie worked her throat, but her strangled sounds seemed faraway.

Knuckles rapped on the door. Jodie's eyes flew open. Her heart thudded, and the shadowy form kneeling over

189

her went still. Then slowly, he pressed the gun against her forehead.

'Jodie?'

Her chest squeezed at the sound of Novak's voice. The barrel of the gun dug deeper into her flesh. Jodie's lungs pumped, hyperventilating. A sob welled up inside her but she shut it down, afraid she'd choke against the tape sealing up her mouth. Above her, the guy's vacant eyes shone in the dark.

Novak knocked again, louder this time. 'Jodie? You in there?'

I'm here, I'm here!

'Jodie!'

The door handle rattled. Stayed locked.

'Fuck.' Novak thumped the door, and his footsteps receded down the hallway.

Jodie closed her eyes. Novak probably thought she'd ditched him, thought she'd snuck out of the hotel to cut loose on her own. She felt drained. Used up. It was what she'd planned, after all, and he'd known it.

The pressure of the gun eased off her forehead. She opened her eyes. Her attacker's bulk loomed over her, his braided head cocked as though listening for sounds. Then he got to his feet, grabbed under her arms and hauled her across the floor.

Jodie thrashed with her legs, her abdomen shrieking at the stretch to her wound. Her face collided with something smooth: her carry-on bag, upturned on the carpet. He dragged her towards the bed, and her eyes registered the ransacked room, the clothes dumped out on the floor.

The guy heaved her up, flung her onto the mattress. Jodie lashed out with her feet, but the fight was bleeding out of her. He regarded her with dead, unblinking eyes, the plaits springing out, Medusa-like, around his head. Then he whacked her backhanded across the face.

Her head whiplashed sideways. Dazed, she felt him grip her shoulders, flip her onto her front. The mattress bounced as he clambered up, straddled her from behind, his weight crushing her pelvis.

His belt buckle clinked.

Jodie's blood turned icy.

She flashed on other hands that had held her down, other belt buckles that had clinked and loosened in the dark, in the foster homes where they said she'd be safe.

This is our special secret, Jodie. You tell anyone, I'll make you pay.

She felt the familiar, nameless ache for the scared little girl who couldn't fight back. Jodie's muscles hardened.

The guy shifted against her pelvis, bending low and close, the ugly spider-knots prodding her head. He shoved his hands beneath her, kneaded her breasts. She clenched her teeth, pressed her face deep into the pillow. Then she lunged backwards, arching her spine, and snapped her skull with a crunch into his.

She felt him sway.

'Bitch!'

Jodie writhed beneath him, twisted around. Looked

up to find him two-handing the gun into her face. His nose was bleeding, and the disconnect in his empty, drugged-up eyes told her he was about to kill her.

She held her breath. Stared at the gun. Something clicked, and she flinched. Then a wedge of light slid across the floor.

'Jodie!'

Her attacker swung the gun around. Aimed it at Novak, who stood frozen in the doorway. The guy's finger squeezed around the trigger. Jodie clenched her abdomen, heaved herself upright, muscles screaming, and slammed her head into his arm.

The gun exploded off to the left. The guy swore, jabbed her with his elbow. Then he leapt off the bed, the gun still trained on Novak.

The guy edged around the room. 'Get in here.'

Novak moved closer to Jodie. His eyes sought hers. Locked her gaze. A younger man in a suit followed him into the room, hands raised as he flattened himself against the wall. Jodie recognized him from the front desk downstairs.

The guy with the gun back-stepped towards the door. He paused on the threshold, arms braced, weapon levelled straight at Novak. His eyes flicked to the corridor outside. Then he turned and disappeared down the hallway.

For a second, no one moved. Then Novak strode over to the bed, while the guy against the wall pulled out a cell phone.

Novak's eyes raked her face. 'Jesus Christ.' Gently, he peeled the tape from her mouth. 'You okay?'

Jodie nodded, sucking in deep gulps of air. An involuntary quiver started up in her limbs, and her whole frame trembled. Novak fingered the zip ties shackling her wrists, then disappeared into the bathroom, returned with scissors and snipped through the plastic straps.

Jodie massaged her wrists, not wanting to meet his gaze in case it triggered the urge to sob. She felt him watch her for a moment, then he flicked on some lights and knelt in front of the mini bar, clinking through the bottles.

'Here, drink this.'

She shook her head. 'I don't—'

'Drink it.'

Jodie did as she was told and gulped the brandy down. It scorched through her, and she pictured her interior coated in a fiery glow. She took a deep breath, unsure about the wisdom of mixing alcohol with head trauma, but she had to admit, she felt better.

Novak flopped down on the bed beside her. 'I should have got here sooner.' He shoved a hand through his unruly hair. 'Frankly, I thought you'd cut and run.'

Jodie chewed her lip, and Novak went on.

'Then I wasn't so sure. I had a hunch you were planning to bail out in the morning, but I figured you really wanted to see that dossier first.' He nodded at the guy from reception, who was still on the phone. 'I persuaded him to let me into your room.'

193

She looked down at her hands, acutely aware of his nearness. Eventually, she said,

'Your hunch was right. I *had* been planning to leave.'

He nodded slowly, unsurprised. 'And now?'

She lifted her eyes to his, gave him a steady look. 'Now, I think I'm glad you're here.'

He nodded again. They sat in silence, the air somehow warm and comforting between them. But Jodie held herself rigid, aware she was in shock; aware that might be enough to break down her guard, make her do something reckless. After a moment, the guy from reception stomped over to join them.

'Fucking city. Cops don't give a crap. This place is out of control. Murders, rapes, killers for hire. I'm from Miami, you think I'd be used to all this shit.' He surveyed the room. 'Did he steal anything?'

Jodie shrugged, her eyes straying to the safe in the open wardrobe. She'd locked her cash in there, and it looked untouched. A formless doubt hovered at the base of her brain.

She turned to Novak. 'Give me your phone.'

'Why?'

'Just give it to me. And that business card for the Princess Resort Hotel.'

Novak frowned, and handed them over. Jodie punched in the number and got through to Daniella at reception. After identifying herself, Jodie said,

'Our colleague, Joshua Brown. Did he happen to get in touch with you after we left?'

194

'Yes, as a matter of fact, he did. He called right after you left, about the items he'd left behind. Turns out his flight out was cancelled this morning, he's still in Belize City.'

An icy draught crept down Jodie's spine. She locked eyes with Novak, and Daniella went on.

'I mentioned you'd called in to see him. When I described you, he knew straight away who you were. He was so sorry to have missed you.'

'I'm sure he was.' Jodie's grip tightened around the phone, and beside her, Novak tensed. 'Did you by any chance tell him where we were staying?'

'Yes, I did, The Plaza in Belize City.' Daniella sounded pleased with herself for remembering. 'He said he'd look you up before he caught his flight out this evening. I hope he catches up with you.'

20

They left the hotel without talking to the police.

Snagging their attention seemed like a bad idea to Jodie, considering she was a fugitive. And besides, from the cynical shrug of the guy on reception, she was guessing they'd probably never catch the intruder anyway.

She huddled back against the rear seat of the cab, hugging her chest, unable to get warm. Pain still pulsed to and fro in her skull, like a vicious metronome. Her gaze wandered out to the dark, narrow streets. The city was congested, the air throbbing with yells and catcalls. Packs of men cruised the sidewalks, eyes ever-watchful. The whole place felt on edge.

Novak shifted in the seat beside her. He hadn't spoken much since she'd made the call to Daniella, probably blaming himself for letting their hotel name slip. Eventually, he said,

'Look, we can't be sure Ethan was behind it.'

His face was set in tight lines. Jodie shrugged and said,

'He knew our hotel. It wouldn't have taken him long to find out which rooms we were in, he's a persuasive man.'

'But to arrange all that before we got back from Ambergris Caye?'

'He had plenty of time, easily a couple of hours.'

'And he just happened to know a guy in Belize City who'd do the job?'

Jodie didn't answer. She glanced back out at the seething streets. The cab had slowed for a red light, and a surge of youths were spilling off the sidewalk and swaggering towards the car. They surrounded the cab, jostling each other to get a look inside. A fist banged the roof, and Jodie flinched. The cab driver cursed, the lights changed and he gunned the engine, accelerating away.

Jodie let out a shaky breath. She looked across at Novak, whose face was pale.

'Killers for hire,' she said. 'That's what the guy at the hotel said about this city. You only have to look around to see that it's true.'

Novak's eyes raked the streets outside. After a moment, he said,

'You think Ethan is still in Belize?'

A chill frisked down Jodie's spine at the notion. She shook her head. 'I doubt it. Daniella said he was booked on another flight out this evening. Easiest thing in the world is for him to catch a plane and disappear. Why would he hang around and risk being identified?'

'But if he hired someone to kill you, wouldn't he stick around to make sure the job got done? He wants you dead.'

'Does he? Maybe he just wants me scared. Controlled, like the old days. Maybe dead is just a bonus.'

Novak huffed out a breath, dragged a hand across his face. 'Fuck it.'

'What, you'd prefer he was still out there, waiting to kill me?'

'Well, at least we'd have some chance of picking up his trail. If he's left Belize, how the hell are we ever going to find him?'

Jodie closed her eyes briefly and leaned back against the seat. They sat in silence for a while, and ten minutes later the cab had pulled up at a stylish Radisson Hotel. It was located in the old Colonial area of Fort George and, according to the cab driver, was the best hotel in the city.

Jodie followed Novak across the lobby, eyeing her surroundings: rich mahogany fittings, claret-red upholstery. She shivered, wondering if five-star luxury really meant better security.

They checked in, then made their way to the fourth floor where they'd booked adjacent rooms. Novak paused outside his door.

'You going to be okay?'

Jodie hesitated. Her body felt bruised and cold to the

bone. She stared at the key card in her hand for a moment, then swiped it briskly through the lock.

'Sure. I'll be fine.'

She opened the door, her muscles knotted. Flashed on the last time she'd entered her hotel room. She jerked the door shut, turned back to Novak.

'On second thoughts, I'm sticking with you for a while.' She lifted her chin. 'We need to go through that dossier.'

'It's all in here.'

Novak dumped a dog-eared manila folder on the bed, opening it up to extract two more files: one red, one blue. He gestured at the red one.

'That's just some paperwork from his property transactions. The blue one is his dossier on you.'

Jodie perched on the edge of the bed and eyed the dossier. Her brain signalled at her to pick it up, but her hands wouldn't move. Novak patted it gently.

'The photos are all in an envelope at the back. You know, in case you don't want to see them.'

Jodie bit her lip and nodded. Kept her hands clasped on her lap. Felt paralysed at the thought of stumbling across a photo of Abby. Yet hungry for the sight of one.

Novak turned away and busied himself with setting up his laptop on a table by the window. Averting her eyes from the blue file, Jodie played for time and picked up the red one instead.

She leafed through the pages. They looked like a bunch of conveyancing documents, most of them property transfer affidavits filed in different cities and states. She browsed through the details, noting that ownership of the title deeds was transferred in each case to an entity called PWD Corporation. She glanced across at Novak, who was staring at his screen.

'PWD,' she said. 'That was Ethan?'

He looked up in surprise, his eyes straying to the unopened blue folder on the bed.

'I can't prove it a hundred per cent,' he said. 'Which means I can't write about it without getting sued. But yeah, it's Ethan.'

Jodie flicked through a few more pages, and noticed that some of the documents were witnessed by Zach Caruso. She raised an eyebrow. Typical Ethan. He'd protected his own identity with corporate layers, but had hung his stooge out to dry.

The blue folder snagged at her peripheral vision. She kept her eyes fixed on the documents in her hands, shuffling through them, till another name caught her eye.

Henry Novak.

She frowned, and shot a quick look across the room. Then she read the details aloud.

'Henry Novak, 92 Clarendon Avenue, Boston, MA.'

Novak's head jerked up.

'My uncle,' he said. 'It's how I got started on this whole thing.'

Jodie stared. 'He lost his home?'

'For a while. He was looking at re-mortgaging, and found out he wasn't the registered owner of the house.

200

Hadn't been for years. 'Course he wouldn't *tell* anyone about it, or ask for help. He just worried and stressed out till he had a heart attack and wound up in hospital.' Novak's expression was grim. 'I knew something was wrong, so I badgered him till he told me.'

Jodie could well believe it. Novak went on.

'By the time I checked it out, the title deeds had already been changed back into my uncle's name.'

'How come?'

'Just Ethan covering his tracks. He must've paid off any dodgy loan he'd raised against the property and didn't need the collateral any more.'

'So did your uncle go after PWD?'

Novak shook his head. 'He was pretty frail, he didn't need that kind of grief. I convinced him it was all just some clerical error, no harm done. It got him back on his feet.'

'But you started digging.'

'Yeah, I started digging.' His expression turned sour. 'And I dug us all the way to here.'

He sighed and slumped back against his chair, flipping a hand at his laptop.

'Know how many Joshua Browns there are? Thousands, that's how many. And that's only in the US. Who's to say he hasn't skipped to South America? Or Europe, even?'

He shoved his chair away from the table and wandered over to the window, slouching against the wall, staring out at the dark. 'We've lost him.'

201

Jodie dropped her gaze to the papers in her hands. Tidied them up, slipped them back inside the file. Her gaze drifted over to the slim, blue folder and slowly, she reached out, slid it towards her and opened it.

21

The first thing Jodie saw was the newspaper article recounting her father's death. She extracted it from the folder and scanned the familiar words.

Storms in Ramsey County . . . three men drowned in Devil's Lake . . . Peter Rosen (19).

She felt a tug in her chest. Kept her face passive, aware of Novak's scrutiny. She stared at the article. What the hell was Ethan doing with a copy of it in his file?

She set it aside, then sorted through the next few pages in the folder, working hard to ignore the large white envelope of photos at the back. She flicked through reviews of her art exhibitions, the same ones Novak had read out over the phone. Beneath those lay a stack of envelopes: old letters addressed to her, most of them opened.

Ethan had been intercepting her mail.

She checked the dates on a few unopened envelopes: 2012, late June, early July. He probably hadn't got around to opening them before the day of the fireworks. She extracted a sheet of paper from one already opened, dated February 2012. A rescheduled doctor's appointment for Abby. Jodie went still, a cold wash of time flooding through her. Ethan's voice: *Jesus, Jodie, how could you forget to take her to the doctor? What kind of a mother does a thing like that?*

Jodie scrunched the paper up, shoved the stack of envelopes to one side. Novak wandered over to the bed and picked up the newspaper article.

'So you never knew your father?'

'Nope.'

'What about your mother?'

'Never knew her either.' Jodie removed another bunch of pages from the file, some of them stapled together. 'I was brought up in foster homes.'

She sensed him pause, felt his gaze slide her way. He was silent for a moment, probably re-thinking his view of her. She was used to that. She fixed her gaze on the pages in front of her. People never understood about foster care; they always assumed you'd done something wrong to get there. After a moment, Novak said,

'Wow, that explains it.'

Her head snapped up. 'Explains what?'

'The tough shell.'

Jodie felt her face set. Novak nodded, gesturing towards her.

'There it is again. That *Keep-Out* sign. Well, you know what? I'm a journalist. Trespassing is what I do.'

Jodie broke off eye contact, focused instead on the papers in her hands. Her brows shot up as she took in the details in front of her: dates, times, locations, activities; a diary of her movements in the months before Abby had died. Novak was right. Ethan had hired someone to follow her.

She flicked Novak a glance.

'Have you been through all this stuff?'

'Not really. It's Ethan I've been investigating, not you.' He gave her a steady look. 'Until now, that is.'

Jodie flipped through the pages, trying to ignore him. He sat across from her on the bed.

'Ever try to trace your mother?'

'No point.' Jodie extracted the next set of documents from the file. 'She died in prison soon after I was born.'

That seemed to bring him up short, but not for long.

'What was she in for?'

'Drugs.'

Jodie was aware her responses were becoming clipped, as though shorter sentences would give less of herself away. Her gaze slid over the page in her hand, not really seeing it.

'Sorry,' Novak said. 'I guess that was tough.'

A knot of guilt twisted inside her. The truth was, as a child she'd always hated her mother. Hated her for being a drug addict. Hated her for being in prison, for giving her up.

205

Hated her for dying.

Jodie flashed on the women she'd known in Framingham. Young Nate, hooked on crack; desperate to change, doomed to fail. Bleak-faced Orianne, recently pregnant; forced to desert her baby while she served another seven years. Jodie felt a sharp pang of regret. Maybe she'd never really given her mother a chance.

Novak indicated the article in his hand. 'So you managed to trace your father?'

She gave a curt nod. 'Now I wish I hadn't.'

'Because you found out he was dead?'

'Because it's how I met Ethan.'

He gave her an enquiring look and she started to explain, beginning with how she'd wound up in Carrington, North Dakota, talking to old Mrs Blane.

'She had a contact number for Celine Rosen, my father's mother. My grandmother, that is.'

Jodie paused. She hadn't thought about her grandmother in some time, and felt a sudden rush of empathy for the woman she'd never met; a woman bullied by her husband; a woman grieving for both her son and her daughter. Jodie gave herself a mental shake and went on.

'It was a contact number for her lawyers, Ives and McKenzie, but it was almost ten years old. They'd moved a few times since then, but I finally ran them down in Boston. They'd gone up in the world.' She pictured the imposing, cylindrical skyscraper, forty-six floors of law firms and bankers. 'By then, the original

Ives and McKenzie were dead, and no one had a record of my grandmother as a client. I never found her.'

She could still recall the sense of loss she'd felt as the last link to her family had melted into the past. She shrugged the memory off and said,

'Ethan walked into the building as I was leaving it. Turned out he'd just opened his own law firm there.'

She'd been lingering in the ritzy, impersonal lobby, feeling adrift, when he'd stepped through the revolving doors. She'd looked up. Felt the room undergo a subtle shift. As though the air had been polished. There was a vibrancy about him, an intense energy that contrasted with the casual, undone collar, the barely there beard, the longish hair. He'd greeted the security guard by name, seemed unaware of the man's gratified look as he continued on towards the lifts. Then he'd slowed his pace, and settled his dark eyes on Jodie's. Her senses had prickled with a heightened awareness.

He'd hesitated. Asked if she was okay. His gaze had been probing. Tentatively, he'd offered to buy her a coffee. He'd seemed diffident. Shy, almost. She'd smiled up at him and said yes.

Novak broke through her thoughts. 'That's it? What, he just walked in the door and swept you off your feet?'

She shrugged and looked down at the papers in her hand. 'Something like that.'

She'd never known anything like it before. The bond had been immediate, locking them together like fast-acting glue. Captivating them, almost. At first, she'd resisted, too cautious to share herself or her past. But within a few months they were together all the time, discovering the same likes and dislikes, the same shared gestures, finishing each other's sentences. The way lovers do when their world feels magnetic, every microcrystal aligned just to fuse them together.

But in truth, at times it was overwhelming. A smothering brew of intimacy and claustrophobia that made it hard for Jodie to breathe. Magnets could repel as well as attract. More than once, she'd experienced the urge to surface for air.

But of course, she hadn't. She'd put the urges down to her own hang-ups about intimacy, and shut the warning voices out.

Jodie's gaze refocused on the pages in her hand. She let out a deep breath, expelling the memories. Then she flicked a glance at Novak. His expression looked cynical, and she didn't blame him.

She turned her attention back to the pages, flipping through them, scanning their contents. Then she frowned. Backtracked and read them again. Dates, names, institutions. Jesus. Ethan's investigator had chronicled her pass-the-parcel upbringing. All the residential care centres; the dozen or so foster families; almost as many schools. Strung together it read like the résumé of a juvenile delinquent.

Jodie stared. What had Ethan been planning to do with all this information?

Novak reached ahead of her into the file, extracting the last loose sheet. He perused it for a moment, then handed it over.

'I guess this must be your grandfather.'

Jodie skimmed the single, short paragraph: a death notice dated ten years previously.

Rosen, Elliot (Carrington, North Dakota). Died Feb 1, 2005. Survived by wife Celine, daughter Lily. Father of the late Peter. Funeral service Feb 4, 10:30 a.m., Holy Spirit Church, Fargo.

The wording was stark, devoid of sentiment. No 'deeply regretted'; no 'sadly missed'. A death unmourned. Jodie read it again. *Survived by wife Celine.* So she hadn't divorced him.

She turned the page over, as though hoping for more. There was nothing else about her grandfather, but someone had scribbled an address and phone number slantwise on the back. She frowned at it for a moment, not sure it really meant anything. Eventually, she said,

'That flight Ethan was meant to catch on the fourth of July.'

'What about it?'

'You said there were only a few he could have caught at that hour of the night.'

'Yeah, that's right. Flights to London or Zurich.'

'There was a third one, wasn't there? Some place in Oregon?'

Novak paused, then nodded. 'Yeah, I'd sort of discounted it. Some dinky little airport I'd never even heard of. I looked it up and you can't even fly there from Boston any more.'

'Was it Grants Pass?'

His expression sharpened. 'That sounds about right. Yeah, Grants Pass, Oregon.'

She read out the address. 'Marshall Lake Treatment Facility, Grants Pass, Oregon.'

Novak held out a hand. 'Let me see that.'

'It mightn't mean anything.'

Novak frowned at the scribbled words. 'You think that's where he was headed that night?'

'Maybe.'

'Seems like a long shot. And why does it matter now, anyway?'

'You were the one who said it matters. You said it matters because he lied about it. And I think you're right. If it was important enough to lie about back then, maybe it's still important to him now. Maybe we can get a line on him there.'

Novak's eyes lingered on the address. 'Treatment Facility. Sounds like some kind of therapy centre.'

He moved over to his laptop and hit a few keys, reading aloud from the screen. '*Private residential centre. Depression, addiction, trauma, anxiety disorders. A Safe, Tranquil Place for Healing and Recovery.*' He reached for his phone. 'Let's see if they know anyone called McCall or Joshua Brown.'

'Or Rosen.'

He looked up and nodded, then made the call on

210

loudspeaker, but immediately got stonewalled by the woman who eventually picked up at the other end. Impossible to discuss things of that nature over the phone, she said, and advised them to speak with their Director of Admissions in person in the morning.

Novak cursed and disconnected. 'Predictable, I guess.'

Jodie nodded, and gathered up the documents on the bed, shuffling them together, squaring up the edges. Her eyes strayed to the blue folder. The only thing left was the envelope of photos.

She set the paperwork aside and lifted out the envelope, resting it on her lap.

'You don't need to open that, Jodie.'

Novak's voice was gentle. He watched her from across the room for a moment. Then he moved back to the bed, sat down close beside her. He smelled of the sea and of fresh air, his rumpled hair still windswept from the boat journey.

'You don't have to look at them,' he said. 'Why do that to yourself now?'

Jodie's fingers rested over the flap. She opened her mouth to speak. Got cut off by a sudden congestion in her throat. She stopped and tried again.

'You think I don't already see her every day?' she managed. 'You think an hour ever goes by when I don't picture her face?' She smoothed a hand over the envelope, her fingers still oddly reluctant to open it. 'Photographs can't hurt any worse, can they?'

Novak squeezed her hand. His was warm and strong,

and she resisted the urge to cling to it with both of hers. He brushed a finger under her chin, tilting her face up. His eyes probed hers, as though asking permission for something.

The air between them stirred like a warm current.

His mouth found hers. Light and soft, his lips tasting of salt and beer. A shiver whispered through her, cleaving a wake of long-forgotten stirrings. Her insides melted, dissolved. Instantly felt vulnerable. Her guard snapped into place like a sprung mousetrap and, slowly, she pulled away.

Her cheeks felt suffused with heat. Novak's gaze searched her face, his eyes, always challenging, now filled with confusion.

Jodie set the envelope aside and busied herself with tidying the documents back into the file.

'You're right,' she said. 'Now's not the time. I don't need the distraction.'

22

The view of Oregon from the plane was a lot less colourful than the view of the Caribbean.

Mountains and vast acres of forest blended together under a grey veil of snow and fog. According to the pilot, temperatures on the ground were in the sub-zero range, breaking record lows as a mass of Arctic air hovered across all the northern states.

The plane banked into a steep descent, and Jodie's stomach dipped. They'd been travelling for a gruelling eleven hours, apart from a brief pit-stop in Mexico, and her body dragged with fatigue. She stared at the dark, advancing hinterland, and Reuben's warning about her passport looped through her head:

'Leaving the US isn't a problem. But you try and re-enter, that's when they'll take a closer look.'

She shivered, and glanced over at Novak. He'd been

213

keeping his distance since their encounter the previous night, generating an Arctic air mass all of his own. She suspected it was less about injured feelings and more about a protest at the trip to Oregon.

'It's a waste of time,' he'd said, following her out into the hotel corridor and watching while she let herself into her own room. 'That paperwork of Ethan's was impounded right after his death, it's almost three years old.'

'So?'

'So that address in Oregon is from a few years back. How could it possibly tell us where Ethan is now?'

'Look, if you've got any better ideas, just say the word. I'm all ears.' She'd paused, her door half-open. 'You don't have to come with me to Oregon, you know.'

At that, he'd moved closer, one forearm raised to lean against the wall, his face bending in towards hers. Her insides had fizzed, and for an instant she'd felt reckless. But the impulse had passed, and Novak had said,

'Push me away all you like, Jodie, but right now, you're my story. Where you go, I go.'

The aircraft swooped and Jodie's innards lurched. She felt Novak watching her. His eyes flicked to the window. Back to her face.

'You think we'll have a problem down there?' he said.

Jodie averted her gaze. 'Why would we? It's not like anyone's looking for me in Oregon.'

'Show me your passport.'

'What for?'

'Just show it to me.'

She rummaged in her bag, handed the passport over. He flicked to the photo page, examining her new identity of Clara Philips.

'Where'd you get this?'

'Friend of a friend.'

'Will it get you through immigration?'

She looked at her hands. 'It got me out.'

He riffled through the pages, then handed it back. 'Just how well did you cover your tracks before you got to Logan Airport?'

Jodie flashed on her drive through the snow in Reuben's truck, and on the cab driver who'd sounded the alarm not far from Reuben's place. For all she knew, Reuben was known to the cops in the area. Maybe they'd already talked to him. Maybe by now she had bigger problems than the risk of immigration spotting a forgery. Maybe by now, airport security around the country was on the lookout for Clara Philips.

She stared at the looming, grey terrain, her pulse racing. 'Nothing's foolproof.'

Novak rolled his eyes. 'Shit.'

Jodie shuffled along the packed queues at immigration, holding herself rigid against the crush around her. Passengers were crammed together like fish in a dragnet, and beside her, Novak was using his elbows to carve out a space.

From the plane, Portland Airport had looked small

215

and compact, too modest to handle a crowd of this size. People started bellyaching, and behind her, somebody complained to one of the ground crew.

'Holiday weekend, sir.' The steward looked tense, trying to herd in the swarm of passengers. 'Lots of delays with the snow, too, bunch of arrivals all in at the same time. Keep moving, sir, please.'

The queue pressed forward, carrying Jodie with it. A holiday weekend. She flipped through a mental calendar. Presidents' Day? Her gaze drifted across the hemmed-in crowds. These people were travelling home to share a family weekend: squabbling kids and in-laws; fancy dinners and leftovers; bedtime stories and kisses.

Normal lives.

Jodie's chest felt hollow. She looked across at Novak, at his woolly hair and burly frame. She recalled his touch, his soft kiss. Felt a whisper of regret. She smothered it and dug her passport out, clutching it tight.

The queue stalled. Immigration checkpoints barred the way ahead, and the crowd jostled towards the glassed-in cubicles, security guards snapping at them to get back in line. Jodie craned her neck, her heartbeat jumping. The area beyond the checkpoints was just as congested, passengers cleared for entry still clogging the way through to baggage claim.

Novak squeezed in beside her, his bulk reassuring. 'You okay?'

Jodie nodded, stiffening against the pack of bodies. New arrivals were still flooding in from behind, jamming the crowds tight. Novak stretched his neck, watching the checkpoints.

'They're just waving a lot of people through,' he said. 'With this mob, maybe they won't check you out too closely.'

Jodie stood on tippy-toe. Novak was right. Most passengers were just attracting a cursory glance: a flick through the passport; a signal to proceed. She pushed forward with the crowd. Behind her, someone shouted, 'Hey, quit shoving!' In a few minutes, it'd be Jodie's turn.

Up ahead, one of the security guards spun away as though summoned. He peeled off from the queue, strode up to one of the cubicles. The passenger at the desk had a stricken look, and the guard led him away by the elbow, hand hovering over his holstered weapon. Jodie's stomach plunged.

She inched forward to the head of the queue, and leaned in to Novak.

'You go first. It's me they're looking for, not you.'

'But—'

'And when it's my turn, you've got to create some kind of diversion.'

'What? How?'

'I don't know. Use the crowds. It's all we have.'

Novak opened his mouth to argue, but a testy security guard was motioning him on to the next vacant cubicle. Novak edged away, glancing back over his shoulder. Jodie nodded, and waited her turn at the red line. Her skin felt clammy.

Novak reached the cubicle. The immigration officer flicked him a brief glance, checked his passport, waved him through. Novak sidestepped towards the throng on the other side, his eyes pinned to Jodie's.

The officer beckoned her forward. She hesitated. Made herself move. Stepping up to the cubicle, she handed over her passport. Up close, the immigration officer looked strained and tired. He sighed, and riffled through the pages of her passport, tapped at his keyboard. Then he frowned. Glanced up. Checked back to his screen.

Jodie's adrenaline surged. She shot Novak a look. His eyes widened. Then he broke into a run, jabbed the air with his finger in the direction of the red line and yelled,

'*Gun! Gun! Man has a gun a gun a gun a gun!*'

For an instant, the world froze. Then a scream ripped through the silence, then another, then more. The officer in Jodie's cubicle leapt to his feet and Novak kept on yelling.

'*Gun gun gun gun!*'

The queues churned and erupted. Guards drew their weapons, eyes darting, uncertain of their target. Jodie edged away. The immigration officer snapped his gaze to her face. Then the crowds boiled over, heaving en masse across the red line. Novak was still yelling over the screams.

'*Gun gun gun gun!*'

Passengers surged towards the checkpoints, bearing down on Jodie. Guards hustled to block them, yelling over the din.

'Back! Step back, sir! Back, everybody back!'

The guards stemmed some of the torrent, but a wave of passengers spilled around them, flooding towards Jodie. The officer in her cubicle narrowed his eyes, shot a look at his screen. Reached for his phone. But the deluge had already poured around her, and was sweeping her along like a tide. She half-toppled in the crush, got squeezed as more guards barricaded the way past the checkpoints.

But the panic was contagious. Passengers already cleared for entry had started a stampede of their own, and there weren't enough guards to go around. Jodie scrambled through a gap with the panicky mob, half-carried, half-dragged, her stab wound biting into her gut. Someone grabbed her arm.

'This way!'

Novak hauled her through the tightly packed bodies. An alarm wailed overhead, just another shriek in the chaos. They shoved against the crowds, ploughing through to customs. Everywhere, security guards yelled into radios, weapons raised, faces creased with indecision. One of them turned his gaze on Jodie, stared at her hard. He spoke into his radio, rapid-fire, then levelled his gun at her face.

'Freeze!'

Jodie went still. People bumped her as they charged past. The guard was close, maybe ten yards away. She couldn't see Novak. The guard's eyes slid left and right, and she could almost see his brain working, weighing up the wisdom of shooting into a crowd. The guard shifted his stance, ran a tongue over his lips. Then a frenzy of passengers body-slammed into him, knocking him off balance.

His gun skittered to the floor, spinning away from him, and instinctively, Jodie lunged. She scrabbled on her hands and knees, ignored the trampling crowd, stretched her fingers, reached the gun. She grabbed it and leapt back to her feet, shoving the weapon down the back of her waistband, underneath her jacket.

The guard was yelling into his radio. Jodie's heartbeat hammered.

Move!

She bolted through the crowds, barging out of customs and into the main concourse.

Where the hell was Novak?

She raced towards the exit, feet slapping hard against the tiles, blood drumming through her electrified limbs. Finally, she spotted him, pacing near the doors, his expression panicked.

When he saw her, he yelled, 'Jesus!' and grabbed her hand, and together they burst through the airport exit and out into the biting snow.

The taxi swished through the slush at breakneck speed, the cabbie on a promise of extra cash for making the long trip and in double-quick time.

Jodie twisted in her seat, peered behind at the squall of snowflakes that gusted like smoke in the dark. Her limbs felt rigid, every nerve in her body on heightened awareness. Beside her, Novak's grip on the hanging strap was white-knuckle tight.

They'd already switched cabs a couple of times, first in Salem, then again in Eugene, each time making the trek worth the driver's while. They'd opted for back routes wherever they were passable: dark, deserted roads, bordered by looming redwoods and firs that guarded a vast stretch of backcountry. It would help to cover their tracks. For a while, at least.

Jodie hugged her chest, fingers digging hard into her arms. Adrenaline still blazed a trail through her veins. She flashed on the gun she'd snatched at the airport, now safely hidden from Novak inside her bag. If she ever found Ethan, at least she'd be ready for him.

She shot a glance at Novak, at the tiny muscle that pulsed near his temple. He looked as if his heartbeat was pounding as hard as hers. They locked eyes for a moment. His gaze was full of fire and speculation, and it sent a ripple of heat along her frame.

The cab scrunched to a halt and Jodie refocused, squinting out through the dizzy whirlwind of snow. A neon sign sputtered in the dark: *Riverside Inn, Grants Pass*. She couldn't see any river. Just a U-shaped motel on the side of the road, backing onto dense forest.

Jodie paid the fare, plus bonus on top, then clambered out of the cab. Blistering cold bit into her cheeks, and she scurried, head down, towards the motel office. Behind her, Novak's feet crackled over hard-packed snow.

They paid upfront for the room, a seventies throwback furnished in brown and avocado. Novak closed the door behind them, dropped his bag to the floor. He held her gaze, his face filled with a mute hunger. Her skin tingled. Then he reached out and lifted the bag from her shoulder. Set it down next to his. Moved closer.

She felt suddenly breathless, all the fear transformed into an explosion of longing. He leaned into the kiss, his mouth hard, urgent, hands pulling her close. She moved into him, pressed herself against him, felt his heartbeat thudding, clashing against hers. A craving for him consumed every cell in her body.

They fumbled with each other's clothes, fetching up on the bed where they clung together. The first touch of skin against skin was electric. A low moan escaped Novak's throat.

He moved over her, and the world became nothing except heat at her core, a spilling of need and vulnerability, every secret touch tender, even in its urgency, until finally the heat exploded in an intoxicating rush, over and over, smashing through fear and hate and pain until there was nothing left but her trembling body fused together with his. With their limbs still entwined, intimate and trusting, she fell into a deep sleep.

23

The room was dark when Jodie woke up.

Her head was pillowed against Novak's chest, her body bathed in warmth. She floated for a while, sedated, almost. Something pricked at her brain, but she couldn't catch hold of it. Didn't want to.

Half-asleep, she raised her head and glanced at Novak. His rumpled hair looked tough and vigorous, but his face was calm, the dogged intensity under wraps while he slept. Crinkles fanned out around his eyes, the kind people got when they usually smiled a lot.

Something quickened in Jodie's chest: the same sensation she'd get when choosing what to paint; the same fluttering that used to tell her she'd found something worthwhile.

Still drowsy, she lay back on the cushion of his chest. Her consciousness gave another jab, and a formless dread seeped over her. Then cold knowledge slammed into place, an avalanche of recall. Crushing her, pounding her.

Abby is dead.

Her brain shut down, buried in a silent, visceral scream.

no no no no no no no

Her intestines churned, rejecting reality, processing the unthinkable all over again.

My Abby is gone. My Abby, my Abby . . .

Soft, round face, dark curls; sturdy little frame, always dressed in the favoured dungarees, the ones with the pink rabbit on the bib.

Or was it blue?

Jodie squeezed her eyes shut.

Why can't I remember!

Novak stirred in his sleep. She lifted her head to look at him again. Last night, she'd chosen to obliterate pain, to block it out for a while. Had she betrayed Abby? It felt disloyal not to hurt, disloyal to forget even for a moment that Abby was gone.

Jodie eased herself gently away from Novak, slipped out from the warm lair of the bed. He grunted, then rolled over like a slumbering bear. Satisfied he was still asleep, she padded towards the bathroom, pausing to pick up Novak's bag along the way.

She closed the door behind her. Snagging a towel from the rail, she wrapped it around herself for warmth. Then she perched on the cold edge of the bath and rummaged in Novak's bag until she'd pulled out Ethan's dossier.

The envelope of photos was still tucked in the back.

Jodie plucked it out, opened the flap. Her hands were steady, no hesitation. The pain would be annihilating. But grief allowed her to stay close to Abby. She could never give that up.

She slipped out the photos. The first few were shots of Jodie herself, walking through Peterborough, browsing through shops. She flicked on through them till she found a photo of Abby.

Jodie drank in the sight of her. She was standing beside a picnic bench, feet planted wide apart, arms spread out, palms upwards. Daubs of paint matted her hair, smeared her cheeks, and her hands were coated Smurf-blue from fingertip to wrist.

'*Look what I can do, Mommy!*'

The memory ripped through her: Abby setting a jumbo sketch pad down on the grass, then standing over it, squirting paint straight out from the tubes. Blobs, splats, snaking lines. A giant splash of primary colours.

'*Don't forget your sandwich, Abby.*'

'*Look, Mommy, I can smush it round with my hands!*'

Abby on her hunkers, kneading the paint; then marching solemnly around the pad, not sploshing the paint on any old place, but thoughtfully deciding what colour went where.

'*Careful, Abby, we can't get paint on the bench.*'

'*Watch this, Mommy!*'

Abby dipping her hands in a pot of blue, surveying the pad, selecting the right spot, then clapping from a height over the page, spattering out a web of speckles and strips. She'd turned to Jodie, plump arms spread out in triumph.

'*Finished, Mommy. Look!*'

Jodie touched a fingertip to the little girl's image, tracing around the dark curly hair, the curve of her cheek, the dungarees with the rabbit motif on the bib.

Jodie peered closer, her heart congesting.

Pink. She hadn't forgotten. The rabbit was pink.

She clasped the photo to her breast with both hands, shut her eyes tight. Then slowly, she slid to the ground. She rocked back and forth on the cold tiles, over and over, backwards and forwards, hugging Abby close.

She stayed like that for a long time, unaware of Novak till he'd sat down beside her, pulling her to him, gathering her wordlessly into his arms and rocking in rhythm alongside her.

24

'I still think this is a waste of time.'

Jodie looked up from the map, keeping her finger on the location for the Marshall Lake Treatment Facility. 'I told you, Novak, you don't need to come.'

'We don't even know what questions to ask when we get there.'

'I'm not arguing the point.'

'Or even who we're looking for.' Briefly, he lifted both hands from the steering wheel. 'I mean, are we looking for someone who was a patient there, or what?'

'Possibly.'

'Who?'

Jodie hesitated. She dropped her gaze back down to the map. 'I've no idea.'

But internally, she was racing through the possibilities, aware she might finally come face to face with a member of her own family. She was strangely reluctant to say that out loud.

The car tyres crackled and popped over the grit that had been spread by the snow ploughs earlier that morning. The blizzards had abated, temporarily at least. Jodie glanced out at the deep mounds of snow, piled into drifts by last night's wind.

She'd painted a lot of snow scenes over the years. Normally at dusk, starting with a base of purple-grey shadow, shaping it with graded shades of white. But for a morning like this, she'd reverse the process: start with the light, add in the shadows. She eyed the towering Douglas firs packed shoulder to shoulder along the road. Frosted sentinels on the edge of wilderness, stonewalling trespassers. Jodie shuddered.

She stole a glance at Novak, who was concentrating on the road. The desk clerk at the motel had put them in touch with a local car rental. *Morley's Motors, Cheap Dealz on Wheelz*. From the dust on the dashboard and the stale smell of ash, she could see where Morley cut on costs.

The car slewed, and Jodie tensed. Novak drove into the skid, recovering his course with nuanced corrections at the wheel. He grinned across at her.

'Don't worry, I got this.'

'You're used to driving in snow?'

'Hey, I'm from New England, remember?'

She tried to smile back, tried to relax against the seat. She glanced at his profile. Sunlight glinted off his stubble, drawing out reds that weren't apparent in his hair. She pictured it on canvas: stippled pigment, dappled over his jawline from dark to light with a small, hard-edged brush.

He must have felt her gaze. He turned and flashed another quick smile. His eyes were clear, a soft grey. Light paint strokes: liquid silver, cool green, layering the irises with radiating colours.

Jodie looked away. 'You should go back.'

'To that crummy motel? We're almost at the treatment centre.'

'That's not what I meant.'

'Hey, look, I'm just a pessimist. Maybe you're right. Maybe we'll find something useful here.'

'I meant, go back to Boston.'

He shot her a startled look. She fixed her eyes on the road, and pressed on.

'You shouldn't be mixed up in all of this.'

'What are you talking about? It's my story.'

'Don't you get it? You're an accomplice now. A fugitive, just like me. Is that what you want?'

'I know what I'm doing—'

'It's not too late. If you go back now, you can talk your way out of it. Say I forced you into it.'

'Look, what is this, Jodie?'

'It's dangerous, can't you see that? The police must know you're helping me by now, and with Caruso in the mix, that means Ethan knows too.' She felt her muscles tense. 'If Ethan came after me, he could come after you.'

'Bullshit, I can look after myself.' His eyes switched

between her and the road. 'What's this really about, Jodie? Is it about you and me? Because if you're regretting last night—'

'No!' The response was instinctive, flew out before she knew it. She hesitated, allowing her gaze to linger on his face. Then she added gently, 'I don't regret it.'

His eyes probed hers, his pupils flaring, the dove-grey irises turning smoky and intense. He glared back at the road.

'I'm not going anywhere.'

Jodie closed her eyes briefly. Was she glad or sorry? Hard to tell. Hard to know what it meant that her chest squeezed slightly, or that a seductive whisper had started up inside her head.

You could have a second chance. Why don't you take it?

Jodie stared out the window. Another snowfall was starting.

Find Ethan just to prove he's still alive. Then you're free.

Hard, icy flakes ticked against the window.

No more prison, no more killing. A second chance.

She glanced at Novak.

A future, even?

She recalled how Novak's arms had felt around her; how he'd sat with her on the floor, holding her, rocking her. Regret crushed at her insides, and she stared back out at the relentless snow. There could be no future. Not even with Novak. Her grief for Abby was an over-whelming tide. It would drown them both.

She felt herself shut down. Groped for something to steel her resolve even more. Hating was so much easier than grieving and longing. Feed one, starve the rest. Annihilate one with the other.

Her brain seemed to shift. She frowned, turned back to Novak.

'That term people use. About Ethan.'

'What term?'

'Family annihilator.'

He looked at her for a moment. 'That's what your attorney called him.'

'I know. I want to hear more about it.'

'Didn't he go over this with you before the trial?'

'I tuned him out, most of the time. But now I want to know more.'

Novak shook his head. 'No, you don't. Believe me, Jodie, you don't want to go there.'

'It's part of your story, isn't it?'

'Maybe, maybe not. It's tough for people to read shit like that. Disturbing as hell.'

'But you know about it, don't you?'

He hesitated. 'I looked into it.'

'So tell me.'

'Jesus, Jodie.'

She fixed him with a stare. 'I need to know.'

Novak's expression looked pained. He took a moment, rasping a hand over his face. Outside, the wind was picking up, spattering pellets of ice against the car like buckshot. Eventually, Novak said,

231

'It's a criminologist's term—'

'For fathers who kill their children. Yes, I know.' Jodie looked straight ahead. 'Is it just fathers?'

'Mostly, yeah. It's rarely the mothers.' He went silent for a moment, coaxing the car out of another skid, probably using the opportunity to stall a little.

'Go on,' Jodie said.

'The cases I read about . . . Jesus.' His knuckles whitened on the wheel. 'I can't talk about those, I really can't. How any father can look at his own child's face and then just . . .' He shook his head, swallowed hard.

Jodie closed her eyes. Heard Ethan's voice.

'*She didn't wake up once . . . it was all over.*'

Jodie's blood vessels turned icy. She went still, letting the coldness seep back in. They sat in silence for a moment. Then Jodie said,

'Why do they do it?'

Novak flicked her a look, shifted in his seat. 'They say there's two types. There's the so-called altruistic killers. You know, they leave bullshit notes about how they're sparing their children pain and taking them off to a better place.'

'And the others?'

He hesitated. 'They're much more common. They're the revenge killers. The trigger is usually the breakup of the marriage.'

He slid her a glance as though to check how she was taking it. She tried to keep her face composed. She must have pulled it off, for he went on.

'The children become pawns, a way of punishing the wife for leaving. Murdering them will cause her maximum pain, so that's what he does. Nothing altruistic about the notes those fuckers leave. Spite, pure and simple.' His fingers tightened on the wheel. 'One guy put his children's bodies in his wife's car, then texted her saying he'd left her a present. Sick, twisted bastard.'

Jodie inhaled a sharp breath, for a moment feeling the other woman's pain as well as her own. Her head felt dizzy. She managed a whisper.

'These men are not sane.'

'That's what we want to believe, right? We want to believe they're psychotic, mentally ill. They must have snapped, lost their mind. Makes it easier for us to bear, I guess. I mean, Jesus, who wants to believe a sane man could murder his own children?'

Novak paused, shook his head, then continued.

'But it doesn't happen in a fit of rage. These are method-ical, pre-meditated murders, committed by rational, loving fathers. These guys are as sane as you and me.'

Jodie whispered, 'Ethan was so proud when Abby was born. He loved her so much.'

'All these fathers do. It's the typical profile: loving father, devoted family man, good provider. They're not drinkers, they're not drug addicts, no criminal record. But underneath, they're controlling and possessive as hell.'

Jodie felt her jaw clench. 'Ethan certainly fits the profile.'

Novak shot her a quick look. 'You think so?'

'Revenge? Control? Of course. Don't you?'

Novak turned away. 'Hey, I'm no expert, what do I know.'

Jodie opened her mouth to pursue it but he switched tack.

'These aren't just isolated cases, either, it happens a lot more than people think. Fact is, if you leave your husband, your children are more likely to be killed by him than by a stranger.'

Jodie closed her eyes briefly. Jesus Christ. How many more women like her were out there? Then she shook her head.

'That doesn't seem possible.'

'We don't hear about it much, media coverage tends to be low. People can't bear to think about it, for a start. And plus, no one can ever prove what really happened.' He paused. 'These cases almost never get to court.'

'How come?'

'Because the father usually kills himself as well. These are murder-suicides, Jodie. It's rare for the guy to stick around afterwards.' He flicked his eyes between her and the road. 'But Ethan didn't kill himself, did he?'

Jodie frowned. 'What's your point?'

'I'm just saying he doesn't fit the profile, that's all. Something's off.'

'Meaning what?'

Novak looked away from her. Then he opened his mouth to speak. Closed it again.

234

'Come on, Novak, spit it out.'

He shook his head. 'It's nothing.'

'Look, you told me you believed that he was a monster.'

'I do. He is.'

'He's a monster, just like these others.' She fought a catch in her throat. 'He *boasted* about what he'd done, for God's sake.'

Jodie clamped her mouth shut, her mind lurching back to that day before the fireworks. Her gut swirled with nausea. When she could trust her voice, she said,

'I'd packed a bag. Told him I was leaving, going ahead with the divorce. Abby was gone, there was nothing left to stay for. He raged at me, went on and on, just wouldn't stop. But I told him he didn't have the power to hurt me any more.' She swallowed, shook her head. 'Big mistake.'

She flashed on Ethan's face: the eyes wild with impotent rage; the split-second shift to something more cunning. She suppressed a shudder.

'That's when he told me. No remorse. No pain. He took pleasure in telling me what he'd done.'

'Jesus.' Novak stared at the windscreen, now caked with snow.

She felt her jaw set. 'He killed my Abby to exact revenge on me. Well, now it's my turn.'

He cut her a sharp look. 'Your turn for what?'

She glanced away, tight-lipped.

'Jodie? Your turn for what? Revenge? Is that what you're saying?'

'No.' She fixed her gaze on the swirling flurries outside. 'I don't know.'

'What's that supposed to mean? Look, this is going down the way we said, okay? We find Ethan to prove he's still alive. We prove you didn't kill him, your conviction gets overturned. That's what we said, right?'

When Jodie didn't answer, he barged on.

'Look at me, Jodie. Tell me that's what you're going to do.'

She nodded and tried to meet his eyes. But her gaze slid away. Novak thumped the wheel with his fist.

'Goddamnit!'

He slammed on the brakes. The car scrunched into the snow, skidded to a halt. Jodie's seatbelt yanked her backwards, the map slid to the floor. She turned wide eyes to Novak. He'd twisted around in his seat to face her. The green-grey irises were almost black.

'Don't bullshit me, Jodie. You think I don't know what you're planning to do? I've known it from the start.'

She shook her head, but he cut across her.

'You think I don't know about the gun in your bag?'

She stared. Couldn't answer.

'Jesus, Jodie, I don't believe this. You're going to make the same mistake all over again?'

She folded her arms tight across her chest. 'There'll be no mistake.'

'What are you going to do, just walk up to Ethan and pull the trigger?'

'I've done it before.'

'Are you crazy? They'll dump you in prison until you rot. Is that what you want?'

'That's not how it'll be.'

'You can't do it!'

'Why not? Think of the story it'll make.'

She regretted the words as soon as they were out of her mouth. Novak's eyes flared.

'You think that's all I care about now?'

'Look, I didn't mean—'

'Listen to me!' He grabbed her by the arms, pulled her round to face him. 'You've got a chance here. A chance at a life. You want to throw that all away?'

Something inside her turned rigid. Hard and inflexible. 'You don't get it.'

'I won't let you kill him.'

'It's none of your business.'

'You think he's just going to stand there and let you shoot him?'

'Novak—'

'What if something goes wrong? What if he kills you first?'

'I don't care!' She glared at Novak. 'Don't you get that yet? It doesn't matter what happens to me. Ethan is a monster, you know he is. A monster that needs to be slayed.'

'And you have to be the one to do it?'

She locked eyes with his, searched deep. 'Tell me, Novak. What if it was your little boy he'd killed? What if it was Toby?' She sensed him flinch, pushed on regardless. 'Think about it. What would you do then?'

His eyes stayed fixed to hers, slowly losing focus as his gaze turned inwards, examining some cruel, interior landscape. His expression grew bleak, and instantly Jodie regretted inviting him to try on the pain. But she'd had no choice.

'Ethan killed my little girl and now he's going to pay for it.'

Novak refocused. He fixed her with a long, hard look. 'I won't let you do it.'

Jodie shook her head, heard the sadness in her own voice as she whispered,

'You can't stop me.'

25

The Marshall Lake Treatment Facility was located far outside the town, pocketed among colonies of looming redwoods made white and ghostly by the snow. Jodie eyed the building, a jarring stucco-and-glass-block design, and wondered what the hell she'd say when she got inside.

Novak parked near the entrance. They hadn't spoken for the last few miles, the silence erected like a barricade between them. He glanced up at the building.

'We could show them Ethan's photo,' he said. 'See if they recognize him.'

'And flash your expired press card?' Jodie shook her head. 'This isn't some laid-back bar, Novak. That's not going to work in a place like this.'

Her tone had more bite than she'd intended, but something had shifted between them, setting them at odds. No longer fully on the same side.

She wrenched the car door open. Wind and snow lashed at her face, and she hunched against it, ducking out into near-blizzard conditions. She pushed through the glass double doors, aware of Novak following close behind.

Inside, the warm air made Jodie's skin tingle. She paused to stamp the snow off her boots, stalling just long enough to take in her surroundings: spacious reception area, furnished in cream; empty, except for the girl at the desk.

The receptionist glanced up, the enquiry already forming on her face: *What do you want?* Jodie made her way towards her, scrambling for an answer in the few strides she had left.

She reached the desk, got a reprieve while the receptionist answered the phone. The girl was probably in her mid-twenties, short brown hair framing a discontented face, pug-like features clustered close together. Her white coat had a nametag that read Samantha Hynes.

Samantha banged down the handset, turned back to Jodie. 'Can I help you?' Then she frowned, her focus suddenly sharpened. 'Hey, wait a second.'

Jodie went still. The girl squinted at her face. Stared hard.

Shit. Had she recognized her from some news bulletin on TV? Jodie darted a glance at Novak, who looked ready to edge away. Then Samantha clicked her fingers and pointed.

'Got it.' She sat back, her expression smug. 'Let me guess, you're here to see Lily Rosen. Am I right?'

Jodie stared. Beside her, she sensed Novak's sudden alertness, and she groped for the right response.

'That's right, I'm Lily's niece.' Jodie's heartbeat felt fluttery. Her father's sister. Lily was here? 'How did you know?'

'The eyes, mostly.' Samantha squinted some more. 'It's not an obvious likeness, I can see why you wouldn't realize. Especially being family. Too close to it, I guess.'

Novak stirred beside Jodie, and she felt his curious glance. He leaned a casual elbow on the desk.

'They say outsiders can often see these things better,' he said.

Samantha shrugged. 'Maybe. People always say I look just like my older sister, but personally I can never see it.' The discontent flitted back over her face, some sibling rivalry evidently souring her mood. Jodie cut back in, trying to salvage the chatty tone.

'So you think I look like Lily?'

'Oh no, you're nothing like her. No, it's her mother you remind me of. Mrs Rosen.' Samantha snorted. 'Not now, of course, she's ancient now. But I've seen photos of her when she was young, about your age.' She gave Jodie another long look. 'You can see a likeness. Comes and goes, if you know what I mean.'

Jodie stared. Mrs Rosen. So she looked like her grandmother, Celine. Old Mrs Blane in North Dakota had said it too. Somehow, the corroboration made it real, and the knowledge of it almost physically clicked into place. Missing pieces snapping together. Finally, Jodie knew she looked like someone.

The desk phone rang. Samantha flashed it an irritated look, then dealt with the call in snippy tones. When she'd finished, Novak said,

'Does Lily get many visitors?'

Samantha shook her head. 'Just her mother, no one else.' She looked back at Jodie. 'If you're her niece, that makes you Peter Rosen's daughter, right?'

Jodie nodded, puzzled by the girl's knowledge of her family tree. Samantha went on.

'Lily told us about you. Though I thought you'd be younger, but then she gets confused at times.'

Jodie took a moment to process the information. So the Rosens had known about her? Yet they'd never made contact. Just like her mother's family.

Novak leaned in closer over the desk. 'You seem to know a lot about the Rosens.'

'Don't look so surprised.' Samantha drew herself up, casting a disdainful look at her surroundings. 'Despite appearances, I'm an intern, not a receptionist. I'm training to be a mental health counsellor, and I sit in on most of Lily's sessions.'

Jodie's eyebrows shot up. She tried to picture Samantha dispensing sympathy and guidance, but the image wouldn't come. The phone rang again, but Samantha ignored it. She waved a dismissive hand around the empty reception.

'Look at this place.' The pug features grew pouty. 'I'm supposed to be getting supervised clinical experience, but I don't see much supervision going on here today. I'm the only one who bothered to slog in through this crazy

242

snow, and now they expect me to cover for everyone. For intern, read dogsbody.'

Jodie murmured in sympathy, and after a tactful pause added, 'Do you think I could see my Aunt Lily?'

Samantha shot her a look. 'That's what I'm trying to decide. She only ever sees her mother. Is she expecting you?'

'No, but I'll only stay a minute.'

'You haven't cleared this with Dr Bauer?'

Jodie was tempted by the lie, but it was too easy for the girl to disprove. 'Frankly, I didn't think it was necessary. I am family, after all.'

'I'd really need to check this with my supervisor.'

'I thought you were in charge here today.'

'Yeah, right, like we both believe that's true.'

The phone was still ringing, and Samantha flung it a look of loathing. She chewed her lip, tapped a pencil on the desk. Then she lifted her chin.

'To hell with it. If you ask me, another visitor will do Lily good.'

She checked her watch, then got to her feet, beckoning them down a hallway and talking over her shoulder as she went.

'Lily gets worse after her mother's been in to see her sometimes. Only to be expected, given the circumstances, but maybe a new face will help.'

Given the circumstances. Jodie curbed the urge to quiz her more, afraid to draw attention to her ignorance of Lily's situation. Samantha flung her a quick look.

'I'll supervise the visit, if you don't mind.' Then as if

reading Jodie's thoughts, she added, 'How much do you know about Lily's condition?'

'Only a little.'

'Well, you've caught her on a good day. She slept through the night last night, first time in a while.'

Samantha rounded a corner and headed for a door marked *Art Therapy – Studio 4*.

'Her art class finished fifteen minutes ago, but she always stays long after the others have gone.' She paused, her hand on the door knob. 'Wait here please.'

She disappeared inside the room, leaving the door open a crack. Jodie peered in, but her view was obstructed. She leaned in to listen, and when Samantha spoke, Jodie almost didn't recognize her voice.

'Hey, Lily, you still painting?' Her tone had softened, mellowed by a surprising note of kindness. 'There's someone here to see you.'

There was a pause, then the sound of a pencil clattering to the floor.

'Come on now, Lily, don't give me that face. It's not your mother this time.' A chair scraped along tiled flooring. 'Mind if I sit with you a minute?'

Jodie closed her eyes briefly, trying to picture Samantha and Lily side by side. A profound, biological curiosity stirred through her. What was Lily like? And what had happened to her that she'd ended up in a place like this?

'Peter's daughter is here, she wants to visit.' Samantha's voice was gentle. She paused, then added, 'Would that be okay?'

244

Jodie strained to hear more. Could only make out murmurs. Finally the room was silent altogether. She flashed a questioning look at Novak, who made a helpless face and shrugged.

Then the door swept open and Samantha said,

'Lily wants to see you.'

26

Jodie hovered on the threshold, taking in the everyday art-room clutter: wall-to-wall paintings and messy collages; chairs and easels strewn about.

A young nurse sat by the window, thumbing her phone. Jodie's gaze settled on the only occupied easel, and on the woman who was leaning out from behind it, watching her closely.

Jodie shot Samantha a look, got a reassuring nod, then, slowly, made her way towards Lily.

The woman regarded her with bright eyes. She was a curious mix of young and old: steel-grey hair done in schoolgirl plaits; frumpy housedress with ankle socks and Mary Janes. Her sagging skin put her unmistakably in her mid-fifties.

Jodie held out her hand. 'Lily?'

The woman nodded, wiping her palms on a paint-stained

cloth, stirring up the punchy smell of turps: pine trees and liquorice. They shook hands. Jodie scoured Lily's features, searching for some likeness. Aware she was searching for herself. But Samantha was right, they looked nothing alike.

Tentatively, Jodie said. 'I'm Peter's daughter.'

Lily frowned, looking back to the doorway as though expecting someone else. 'No, that can't be right.'

Jodie's eyes flicked to Samantha, who was watching with interest. Then back to Lily.

'My name is Jodie.'

'No, that's not right either.' Lily seemed quite definite this time. 'I don't remember the name, but that's not it. And no offence, but you're way too old.'

Lily picked up a brush and turned firmly back to her painting. Jodie blinked. As a long-awaited meeting with her own flesh and blood, the moment felt anti-climactic.

Samantha chipped in. 'Hey, Lily, you told me you didn't even *know* her name.'

'I couldn't *remember* it, is what I said. Anyway, whatever. The name doesn't matter. She's too old.'

'So she's all grown up now. Come on, Lily, you've got time-warp issues, you know you do.'

Lily rolled her eyes, like a surly adolescent. She flung Jodie a cynical look.

'Arrested psychological development, is how Dr Bauer puts it.' She indicated her plaits with the end of her brush. 'I like braids and warm socks, and suddenly I'm a retard.'

Jodie felt a smile tug at her mouth. The woman's

truculence was oddly appealing. Setting her parentage aside for the moment, Jodie gestured at the canvas.

'Mind if I take a look?'

Lily shrugged, then slid a coy glance at Novak, who'd been keeping a tactful distance over by the door. 'Maybe Grizzly Adams there would like to see it too?'

Novak hesitated, then started across the room, while Jodie edged around the easel to view Lily's work.

The bleak canvas made her catch her breath. Dark rectangles, expertly distorted, converged to depict the interior dimensions of a room. At its centre stood an open closet, bare except for a blanket and pillow on the floor. The shadows were skilful: gloomy purples, sombre browns. But the absence of light was oppressive. Jodie's eyes lingered on the single window. It was bricked up.

Mrs Blane's words echoed through her.

'Lord knows what he did to Lily, but I can guess . . . she tried to run away . . . he had the windows in her room permanently bricked over. Like a dungeon.'

A shiver skittered down Jodie's frame.

Lily's gaze was pinned to her face. She must have liked whatever she read there, for she nodded and smiled, then turned to Novak.

'What do *you* think, Grizzly?'

He looked taken aback. 'Is that a real room?'

'Sure it is. It's where I slept as a child.'

'In a closet?'

Lily shrugged. 'I was trying to feel safe. I told Peter he should do the same, but he said it didn't help.'

248

Jodie's chest turned over at the reference to her father. And at the notion that as a child he might have felt afraid.

Lily eyed her painting, reaching out with a brush to blend in a shadow. For the first time, Jodie noticed the skin on her arms. It was criss-crossed with scars and lacerations. Like Nate's, only deeper.

A faint beep sounded across the room. Samantha cursed, pulled out a pager. She got to her feet.

'I'm needed elsewhere.' She drilled Lily with a look, though when she spoke, her voice was kind. 'Behave, okay? I won't be long.'

She hurried from the room, and when she'd gone, Lily turned mischievous eyes to Jodie.

'Would you like to see more of my paintings?'

With a sidelong glance at the nurse by the window, Lily set the painting of the closet on the floor. Then she reached into a bag slung on the back of her chair and extracted a rolled-up tube.

'We're meant to destroy them.' She unravelled sheets of soft canvas, her fingers scrabbling to stop the edges springing back. 'They make us pour all our bad memories into these paintings, then they tell us to rip them up. Can you believe that?' She clipped the sheaf of canvases to her easel. 'Cathartic and cleansing and all that jazz, but mine are works of art, you know?'

She stood back and regarded the first painting.

It depicted another stark interior, the proportions cleverly distended to give a fisheye view. A rusted old bed took centre stage this time. Soiled blankets lay dishevelled across it. Dark, foreshortened walls crushed the room inwards, and the low ceiling gave the sense of being buried alive.

Jodie took a deep breath, fighting off an inexplicable tide of desolation. Beside her, Novak had gone still.

Lily twirled one plait around her finger. 'My father called it his special room.' Her voice was matter-of-fact. 'He used to take us there, one at a time. As soon as we'd turned eight years old. First me, then Peter.' She faltered slightly. 'Then later, my sister, Anna.'

Jodie's insides felt cold. She traded looks with Novak. His expression was bleak. She turned back to Lily.

'What about your mother? Didn't she try to stop him?'

Lily gave a scornful laugh. 'Not that I ever saw. Peter tried to stand up to him, but he was just a kid. My father used to beat him, kicked him on the ground till he bled, sometimes.' Jodie flinched at the image. Lily went on. 'Then as punishment, there'd be extra visits to the special room.'

Jodie closed her eyes briefly. Couldn't bring herself to look at the painting any more. Lily was still talking.

'Dear old Dad dragged us to church every Sunday, made us sit up at the front like a normal family. My mother pretended as much as he did.'

Jodie felt her jaw set. How could Celine have stood by and done nothing? How could a mother fail her children like that? A jeering voice started up inside

250

her head: *What about Abby? You failed her too, didn't you?*

She caught her breath. Ethan had never abused Abby, she was certain of that. After all, she'd know the signs better than anyone. But if he had, she'd have stopped him. She'd have killed him sooner.

You still failed to protect her.

Jodie groped for a way to drown the voice out. 'Did my— did Peter paint, too?'

'No, he studied all the time.' Lily reached up to unclip the painting from the easel, revealing another one underneath. 'He worked hard at school, said that'd be his escape.'

'And painting was yours?'

Lily shrugged. 'I just played dead. It was never really me in that room.'

She stepped back, gesturing at the easel, sliding an arch look at Novak. Jodie glanced at the painting and felt herself recoil. Beside her, Novak inhaled sharply.

Jodie made herself look. Same room, same bed. This time with a self-portrait of Lily sprawled naked on the sheets. Her aging flesh was pale and flabby, the grey plaits coming undone. Her legs were spread in a pornographic pose, her eyes dull and staring, mouth curled in an expression of self-disgust. Razor cuts scored every inch of her skin, like a body-suit of bleeding tattoos. Jodie narrowed her eyes. Most of the gashes resolved themselves into words; the same words carved over and over: *sick of me, sick of me, sick of me.*

251

Jodie dropped her gaze, couldn't look any more. Even Lily appeared disconcerted this time. She'd shrunk down into her chair, her shoulders hunched over.

'I tried to throw myself through a glass door once.' Her voice wavered. 'So that I'd look like how I feel on the inside, you know? Cut to ribbons. But the nurses stopped me, so I painted this instead.'

Lily's expression turned blank, her gaze locked inward. She folded her arms tightly, her fingers kneading and pinching at her own flesh. 'Cutting makes the other pain weaker for a while. Drugs do that too. And sex.' She attempted a lascivious look at Novak, but her heart wasn't in it.

She rocked to and fro, blinking rapidly. Jodie reached out to take the canvases down.

'Maybe we've seen enough.'

'Wait!' Lily jerked to her feet, smacked Jodie's hands away. 'There's still one more.'

Lily whipped away the disturbing self-portrait, then gestured at a half-finished sketch underneath. It depicted a small boy, maybe nine or ten years old. Dark-haired, untidy. He was huddled on the floor, hugging his knees, his face buried in his arms. Desolation seeped from every line in his body: the cowering shoulders, the bowed head.

Jodie swallowed hard. Lily stumbled back to her chair, started to rock.

'Poor Peter,' she whispered. 'I couldn't help him.'

Jodie stared at the portrait of her father. Her chest ached. She thought of her grandfather, Elliot Rosen, and a sickening wave of revulsion swept through her. She'd finally come face to face with her own family, and she wished to Christ she hadn't.

She inhaled deeply through her nose. Fuck Elliot. He had nothing to do with her.

She glanced at Lily, then back to the portrait. 'So that's why Peter ran away to Ireland. Because of your father.'

Lily shook her head, kept on shaking it. Her breathing was rapid. 'He didn't run away. My mother *sent* him away. To protect him, she said. But he was seventeen by then, it was too late. And what about me? Why did she never try to protect *me*?'

She plucked at her clothes, couldn't seem to sit still. Then she leapt to her feet, snatched the painting off the easel, as though she couldn't bear to look at it any more. In a frenzy, she rolled up the sheets of canvas, snapped an elastic band around them with a twang.

'Here.' She thrust the rolled-up tube at Jodie. 'You take them.'

'I can't, they're yours—'

'Take them! Dr Bauer's right, I shouldn't look at these again, I shouldn't look, I shouldn't look . . . You need to go now.'

Reluctantly, Jodie took the paintings. Lily huddled back in her chair, rocking and staring. Trapped in some black cave of her mind. Novak flicked an uncertain glance at Jodie, then stepped in closer.

'Lily? Can we ask you a question before we go?' He

253

hesitated. 'Does the name Ethan McCall mean anything to you?'

When Lily didn't respond, Novak added, 'Or Joshua Brown?'

Lily's eyes had glazed over. It was hard to tell if she'd even heard. Novak reached into his pocket and drew out Ethan's photo, holding it up so that Lily could see.

'Has he ever been in to visit you?'

She stared at the photo, but made no move to take it. Her expression was vacant. Catatonic. Jodie's insides sank.

Then Lily nodded.

'Once,' she whispered.

Jodie went still. Then she touched Lily's arm. 'Where is he now? Did he say what his name was? Please, Lily, it's important.'

Lily shook her head, still rocking. 'Some fake name. Said he didn't want people here to know who he was.'

'Was it Joshua Brown?'

Lily ignored her. 'He said he knows all about playing dead. He said he's playing dead too.'

Her gaze zoned back out, her lips curled in self-loathing as she seemed to trawl inward over some kind of vile terrain. Small mewling sounds escaped her throat. Jodie felt a flash of alarm, and shot a look at the nurse, flagged her attention. The woman set her phone down and got to her feet.

Jodie turned back to Lily. She was clawing at her stomach, as though something grotesque was erupting inside it. Jodie knelt down beside her.

'Lily? Can you hear me?'

Lily's hands scrabbled upwards, gouged at her own chest, at her throat, her mouth, until finally whatever torment was inside her spewed out in a strangled, harrowing scream.

Hairs stood erect on the back of Jodie's neck. The nurse took one look at Lily and slammed the alarm.

27

'You need to leave.' Samantha's heels snip-snapped along the corridor ahead of Jodie. 'Now!'

'Wait! What about Lily? Is she okay?'

'Lily is never going to be okay.'

Jodie's step faltered. 'Jesus, I'm sorry.'

Novak cut in, trailing from behind. 'What *was* that back there? What just happened?'

Samantha halted, swung around to face them. 'She had a flashback.' Her close-set features were tight with fury. 'And when I say flashback, I don't mean some hazy memory. I mean a full-blown panic attack that wracks her with physical and mental anguish until she feels like she wants to *die*.'

She glared at them both. Jodie broke eye contact, and Samantha went on, her voice low with suppressed emotion.

'If we don't get to her in time, she starts hurting herself. Self-mutilation, suicide attempts. She's tried overdosing, wrist-slashing, slitting her own throat. She's even tried to hang herself from the pipes of a state hospital. Some day, she's going to succeed.'

Jodie's insides shrank. She thought of her own occasional flashbacks, recollections of episodes in the foster homes she'd rather forget. She bit down hard on her lip, then said,

'Do the flashbacks ever stop?'

'With counselling, maybe after a few years. When all the memories have come back. But that's the problem with Lily. She keeps remembering more.' Samantha cast a withering look at the canvases under Jodie's arm. 'Those paintings triggered it, she should never have kept them.'

Novak held up Ethan's photo. 'We showed her this, too, she said he came to see her. Do you know him?'

Samantha stared at him for a moment. Then she glanced at the photo. Stared at Jodie. Her gaze was flinty, full of reproach.

'Why did you really come to see Lily?'

Jodie scrambled for an answer. Couldn't find one. Samantha turned on her heel and marched on down the corridor.

'I don't know who that is, I've never seen him.'

Novak strode after her. 'When can we talk to Lily again?'

'You can't. She's been sedated, and after that she'll need intensive therapy, a lot of care.' She stopped to glare at them again. 'She's a survivor of child sex abuse and she's severely traumatized. She probably will be for the rest of her life. As her brother would have been, if he'd lived.'

'And her sister, Anna,' Novak added.

Samantha's gaze flickered away. Jodie stared, and felt a sliver of something cold. She hesitated, then said in a low voice,

'Anna wasn't her sister, was she?'

Samantha didn't answer. Jodie made herself go on.

'Anna was her daughter, wasn't she? Elliot's daughter.' Jodie worked it out. According to Mrs Blane, Anna had been seven or eight years younger than Peter. 'Lily must have had her when she was what, twelve? Thirteen?'

Samantha didn't contradict her.

Novak half-turned away. 'Jesus.'

Jodie felt like her insides were caving in. Why the hell had she ever come here?

Samantha was still silent. Then she blew out a long, defeated breath and slumped back against the nearest wall.

'Christ. Look, this is all my fault, not yours. I screwed up, I should never have let you in.' She closed her eyes, pinched the bridge of her nose. 'Shit.'

She huffed out another breath, then jerked her head up.

'I just get so impatient, you know? The treatments here are outdated. There are better ways. Better dialectical behaviour therapy, better cognitive analysis, more advanced psychoanalysis . . .' She pulled herself up, shook her head. 'Forget it, it doesn't matter.'

Jodie regarded her for a moment. 'Will you get into trouble?'

The girl shrugged. 'It won't be the first time. Probably won't be the last, either. Unless they kick me out.'

'Tell them we forced our way in, if it helps.'

Samantha looked glum. 'Nope. It won't.'

Jodie gave her a reassessing look. She was an odd mix: vocational passion alongside downright rudeness; intolerant of ordinary people, yet kind to those in her care. Maybe Jodie was wrong. Maybe she'd make an excellent counsellor.

Jodie's thoughts strayed back to Anna, to what Mrs Blane had told her.

Sickly all her life, some lung disease.

'I was told Anna died young,' Jodie said.

'When she was ten. Cystic fibrosis.' Samantha looked weary, her truculence giving way in the face of her mea-culpa admission. 'A result of her parents being first-degree relatives. Both were carriers of the gene. Another tragic side-effect of incest. It's why nature usually guards against inbreeding.'

Novak shook his head in disgust. 'Well, nature spectacularly failed this time, didn't it?'

'The rules of nature don't apply to the likes of Elliot Rosen.'

Samantha pushed herself away from the wall, started slowly down the corridor.

'For the rest of us, it's different,' she said. 'We all have a natural tendency to mate with our own tribe, nothing wrong with that. A normal human desire to be with our own. But sometimes it can be overwhelming. Primordial, even.'

Novak shot a wary glance at Jodie, looked braced for something else he'd rather not hear. Samantha went on.

'Sexual attraction between family members isn't unheard of. When siblings have been separated by early adoption, for instance, and don't meet until adulthood. Genetic sexual attraction, to use the mumbo-jumbo.'

Novak was looking queasy, and Samantha gave him a sardonic glance.

'Don't worry, it's rare. For most of us, it's wiped out by living together as a family. Close proximity desensitizes us to sexual attraction. Reverse sexual imprinting, to go back to the mumbo-jumbo. They call it the Westermarck effect. It's what prevents inbreeding.'

Novak clenched his fists. 'Whatever they call it, it didn't stop Elliot Rosen, did it?'

Samantha looked grim. 'Like I said, the rules don't apply to people like him.'

Jodie watched Novak's jawline bulge, sympathizing with his need to take refuge in anger. Sometimes, other emotions were just too harrowing to process. He jutted out his chin.

'Sounds to me like that sick bastard warped everything he touched.'

Samantha nodded. 'He had problems of his own,

according to his wife. Celine said he was beaten and abused by his own father, too.'

'Pardon me if my heart doesn't bleed.'

Jodie shook her head, taking in the legacy of repeating patterns. So who was the first culpable abuser? How far back in the chain did a person have to go? She brushed the thought off, and pointed out in flat tones,

'Most survivors of abuse don't go on to become abusers.'

'No, of course they don't. Most are like Lily: trauma-tized to varying degrees, and no danger to anyone except maybe themselves.' Samantha halted for a moment, and gave them a steady look. 'But sometimes, the trauma takes a different form. It gets imprinted on the child's brain as a kind of attachment, a way of relating. The behaviour is hard-wired in and they go on to re-enact it, just repeating what seems familiar and normal.'

Hard-wired.

Jodie recalled Momma Ruth's theory: that our mistakes are hard-wired into our DNA; that we never really have any choices. Then Nate's response: '*That's bullshit, right?*'

Jodie's fists closed over. 'Celine should have stopped him.'

'That's what Lily thinks. She's angrier with her mother than she is with her father.' Samantha trudged towards the exit. 'But Celine had her own limitations, she did the best she could do at the time. Don't get me wrong, that doesn't make it okay. It just makes it human.'

By now, they'd reached the double glass doors. Beyond

them, the snowstorm was still blowing hard and the vast stretch of whiteness made Jodie's eyes water. She squinted over at Novak, who was shoving Ethan's photo back in his pocket. Jodie turned back to Samantha. Kept her voice casual.

'Maybe you're right about Celine. Maybe I should have a talk with my grandmother.'

The family term didn't sit well with her. Neither did the prospect of meeting the woman who'd betrayed both Lily and her father. But if Ethan had come here, then maybe Celine knew where he was.

Jodie made her face bland. 'Can you tell me how to contact her?'

Samantha paused, one hand on the door. Jodie could see the debate teeter-totter behind her eyes. Finally, the girl shook her head.

'Sorry. Can't give out that kind of information.'

She opened the door, admitting a frigid blast of wind that whipped in around their legs. Jodie groped for a way to change the girl's mind, came up with nothing. Novak was already out the door, impatient to be gone.

Belatedly, Jodie remembered the canvases under her arm. She held them out, tugging up her hood with her free hand.

'Here, you'd better take these back.'

Samantha shook her head. 'Keep them. Lily wanted you to have them, and besides, she can't look at them any more.'

Jodie nodded, stepped outside, head bent low against

the battering gusts. She crunched across the snow, following Novak back to the car. After a moment, Samantha's voice came hollering over the wind.

'Celine visits alternate days. If you really want to talk to her, she'll be here tomorrow at noon.'

28

Jodie and Novak didn't speak much in the car. Outside, the snow was dazzling white, but the light felt brittle, as if talking out loud might snap it in two and leak in more of the foul darkness already seeping into Jodie's bones.

She glanced at Novak. His jaw was tense, loosening up now and then to expel long, defeated breaths. Jodie huddled into her seat. Shadows stirred in the cracked light: wraiths of her family; monstrous and grotesque.

The muteness stretched on for the next hour while they relocated to another motel, both to cover their tracks and because the way back to the Riverside Inn was now impassable. They signed in silence for separate rooms. Jodie lasted ten minutes alone in hers before joining Novak across the hall, fleeing the creeping demons of her own family.

He let her in without comment. Just a flicker of something bright behind his eyes to say he was pleased to see her. He moved to the table over by the window, took a seat in front of his laptop. The heating was on and the curtains were drawn, blocking off the too-crisp light outside, a lamp spilling amber to warm up the room. The effect was soothing, like a fireside thaw.

Jodie helped herself to coffee while Novak hunched over his keyboard, then she drifted towards the bed where Ethan's dossier was spread out. She sat down to leaf through it one more time; re-reading the log he'd kept of her movements; opening some of her letters that he'd intercepted. Bills, circulars, bank account statements. Evidence that he'd been spying, having her followed. Was that why he'd tracked down her family, too? Knowledge was power?

She frowned at the explanation, tried to make it a smooth fit. But something snagged at the edges.

'Bingo!'

Jodie's gaze whipped up. Novak was sitting poker-straight in his chair. He jabbed at the screen, shoved a hand through his hair, crackled with an energy that punched leftover ghosts from the room. She shot to her feet and strode over, while Novak read aloud from the screen.

'*Missing. Keith Daggett. Last seen leaving a Shell gas station in Marlborough, Cheshire County, at 9 p.m. on July 4th 2012.*' He broke off to flick her a meaningful look. 'Fourth of July. And Marlborough puts this guy

265

maybe ten miles from you and Ethan that night. Look: *Sales Manager, forty-five years old, five foot eleven,* yada-yada, doesn't matter what he looks like. Here we go: *Daggett's car, a red Honda Accord, was found abandoned two weeks later at Logan Airport, Boston. The car had sustained front bumper damage, and police are appealing for the public's help in tracing witnesses to any accident* . . . blahdy-blahdy-blah.'

Novak flashed Jodie a look of triumph. Switched to impatience when she didn't respond right away.

'The second car?' he prompted. 'The one Ethan swerved to avoid that night, the one that sent him into the ditch? It was this guy,' a finger-rap at the screen, 'Keith Daggett. Had to be. I've been searching all week for a missing-persons match. This is it. Fits the time, fits the place. Too much of a coincidence otherwise.'

Jodie leaned over his shoulder to scan the article, aware of Novak's soap-scented heat radiating against her skin. She stared at the screen.

'So Ethan crashed into Daggett, switched places, then took off in the red Honda and headed for the airport?'

'Exactly. Maybe he even lived as Keith Daggett for a while. Used his credentials to set up a new identity, left a trail we could follow. The guy must've had a wallet. Driver licence, credit cards. Pieces of his life that Ethan could've used to build a new one for himself.'

Jodie fired him a scornful look. 'He wouldn't have risked it.'

'Why not? You were the one who said he wouldn't be

paranoid, that he'd feel safe because people thought he was dead and no one was looking for him.'

'No one was looking for *Ethan*. But if Keith Daggett was missing, then people were looking for *him*. Not to rain on your parade here, but Ethan wasn't dumb. If he really used Daggett's identity, someone would've closed in on him before now.'

Novak glared. 'Look, we've got to start some place. The guy's out there living as somebody somewhere. Keith Daggett, Joshua Brown, who knows. Having a life, with people in it. Friends, colleagues, neighbours. Maybe even a family.'

As soon as he'd said it, his gaze skidded away.

Maybe even a family.

The room shimmered. Zoomed in and out. Abby's name hung like a hand-grenade between them.

In a rush, just for a second, Jodie pictured her little girl. She let herself imagine that Abby was there in front of her, the air warm with her sweet vanilla scent. Dark-eyed, serious. Hopping on one leg. The image began to fade, and Jodie felt a sudden, spinning panic, a tightness in her head. Then a grey hollow as Abby slipped away.

The empty space she'd left behind was unbearable. Jodie shut her eyes, felt the room sway. Then she clenched her fists, tried to unplug her emotions, and spun away from Novak.

'Okay.' She made it as far as the bed, her legs too shaky for pacing the room. 'So maybe you've found a

267

name for the body in Ethan's car. But searching for traces of Daggett seems like a dead end to me.'

Novak didn't respond. Jodie exhaled a long breath, relenting a little. In truth, she didn't think the discovery helped them that much, but at least it corroborated Novak's theory about a second car. She tried a more conciliatory tone.

'Look, suppose we search instead for Joshua Browns here in Oregon?'

'Why, because he came here once to see Lily?' Novak's turn to be scornful. 'Not sure I see the link. It doesn't mean he ever lived here.'

'It's a place to start.'

'I mean, Jesus, we don't even know *when* he visited Lily. Chances are, it was years ago, when he was still Ethan McCall. It'd make more sense, wouldn't it? That he'd try to trace your family when he first knew you? Why wait till he'd disappeared and left his life with you behind?'

Jodie shrugged. Novak was right, it made more sense. Ethan spying on her when they were married, tailing her movements, digging up her past, hoarding secret knowledge for some future tyranny. That was the rational explanation. Yet the fabric of it still snagged on something.

Something Lily had said?

Jodie squinted, trying to reel the memory in. Lily rocking, zoning in and out. Huddled in her chair, eyes vacant.

Jodie stared at Novak. 'Remember what Lily told us? *He said he's playing dead.*'

Novak stared back, worked it out. 'So he didn't go to see her till *after* he'd faked his death?'

'Sounds like it.'

'But why? You were in prison by then, or about to be. He'd dealt with you already. Why would he care about finding your family?'

Slowly, Jodie shook her head. 'I don't know.'

The warm air in the room seemed to quiver, rippling with something dark and furtive; something cunning that scurried underground before she got a closer look at it.

Another one of Ethan's secrets.

Novak had turned his attention back to the screen. Jodie reached out for the dossier, browsed through it for a while. Presently, Novak said,

'That lawyers' office you went to look for, when you first bumped into Ethan. Was it Ives and McKenzie?'

'Yes, in Boston. Why?'

Novak opened his mouth to explain, then flicked her a look and seemed to think better of it. 'Not sure yet.'

He said nothing more. The silence between them stretched on, threaded with occasional small sounds: the rustle of paper, the clack of keys. Finally, when the light cracks in the curtains had darkened, and Jodie's bones were aching with tiredness, she gathered up the dossier and got ready to return to her room.

'Jodie, wait.'

She paused by the door. Novak moved towards her,

stood so close she could make out the kaleidoscope of greens and cool greys in his irises. He didn't touch her, but her skin fizzed as though he'd laid a bare arm on hers.

'You could stay,' he said.

The air thrummed with a low-level charge. Novak's cheeks looked suffused beneath the stubble. More beard now than bristle. Grizzly Adams, Lily had called him. The nickname seemed to fit.

Jodie blinked, and gave herself a mental shake, then she reached for the door. Novak made no move to stop her, just said,

'Why not, Jodie? What are you afraid of?'

Her fingers tightened around the handle.

Jesus Christ, couldn't he *see*? Didn't he know that if she opened up even a crack, she'd splinter into a million tiny pieces? And never have the strength to pick them all up again? Couldn't he see she was afraid of *feeling* something?

The flash of anger drained away, a weary residue silting along her bones. She made her face a blank, stepped out into the hall and pulled the door closed behind her.

29

A furious gust snatched at the car, shook it like an enraged child with a toy. The back wheels slid sideways and Jodie stiffened. She steered into the skid, somehow regained traction. Inside her gloves, her palms were clammy.

The wind roared like a deafening tide, whipping up ground snow into huge waves of white. Novak had said it was too dangerous to drive and she had to admit, he was probably right. So she'd left without telling him. He'd have tried to talk her out of it, making what's-the-point arguments against chasing down long-lost grandmothers. Maybe he'd have been right about that, too.

Jodie eyed the swirling tornados of snow. Temperatures had plummeted overnight. The radio stations were issuing wind-chill alerts, warning of ground blizzards and deadly sub-zero conditions.

Jodie flexed her gloved fingers on the wheel. Would Celine venture out to the Marshall Lake centre in hazardous weather like this? An elderly woman? Probably not. But maybe if she'd heard about Lily's condition. Maybe then.

But suppose she didn't show?

Jodie tried the what-if on for size, not sure whether she'd be relieved or disappointed. Celine's link to Ethan's trail was thin, after all. And did she really want to meet the woman who'd been a bystander to her father's pain? Yet she had to admit to a primal curiosity about the woman she was meant to look like.

She peered into the white gauze ahead, recognized the clearing in the shadowy redwoods. She made a right into the clinic driveway, sticking to a set of tyre tracks already carved through the snow. The wind raged outside and Jodie shivered, thankful for the padded jacket she'd got from Dixie's brother.

The car park was mostly deserted, apart from a handful of vehicles up near the door, topped with thick pillows of snow. Jodie inched along the avenue, her back wheels losing purchase every few feet, sending the car fishtailing on slick patches. Jodie kept the gears low, and tried not to gun the engine.

Up ahead, a slight figure emerged through the doors. A woman bent against the wind. Puffy full-length parka, hood up; scarf wound balaclava-style around her face. Jodie stared. Saw nothing to indicate the woman was elderly. No arthritic gait, no tentative steps. Yet something in her neat carriage resonated. Stirred up an odd sense of the familiar.

The woman headed towards a small red Toyota, tucked in between a van and a black jeep. For a moment, she disappeared, obscured by the other cars, and Jodie risked accelerating to close the gap between them. Bad idea. The engine whined, the back wheels slewed. Then the car shimmied and lodged with a jolt into a snowbank.

'Shit!'

Jodie geared down, coaxed the accelerator. The wheels spun, but the car didn't move. Up ahead, the red Toyota was cruising towards her down the driveway.

Jodie snatched at the gearstick. Flung it into reverse, nudged the accelerator, rammed the gears back into first, coaxed some more. Kept switching gears back and forth, trying to bump the car out of its logjam.

The red Toyota drew level. Jodie paused to stare as the car sailed past. Glimpsed a small-boned face, no scarf muffling it now; crêpey skin; cheekbones still proud under up-tilted eyes.

Something hummed along Jodie's bones. Some kind of whispering déjà vu. She knew she was looking at her grandmother.

She jammed the gears into first, juiced up the engine. The tyres gripped, and with a lurch, the car dug itself out of the snow. By now, the black jeep was crunching down the avenue, and Jodie whipped at the wheel, anxious not to let anything come between her and the Toyota. She heaved the car into a one-eighty turn, bumping

273

into the tracks that had guided the Toyota and followed it out onto the road.

The wind was still shrieking, whisking up a hurricane of snow from the ground, sending it hissing against the car. Jodie tightened her grip on the wheel, kept the Toyota in her sights. The jeep fell into line behind her.

She drove on straight for half a mile, then followed the Toyota round a slippery bend, branching off into a narrower road on the right. Movement caught Jodie's peripheral vision: Lily's canvases had rolled from the passenger seat onto the floor.

She'd brought them with her to give to Celine. The paintings didn't feel rightfully Jodie's, though she doubted Celine would take them either. What mother would want mementos of her child's pain? Or of her own negligent hand in it, for that matter?

Jodie eyed the rolled-up paintings. Their bleakness seemed to soak right through the canvas and bleed out onto the floor. Lily could paint, no doubt about that. Not mindless copies, but honest images that exposed how life felt from the inside. Jodie had painted like that at one time. Not her *Wizard of Oz* pictures, as Novak had called them, but other works she'd mostly done for herself. More abstract and elemental. She'd shown them once to Lucas, the Danish architect who'd commissioned all the paradise colours. He'd stared at them for a long, quiet moment, then turned his thoughtful gaze her way.

'They're powerful,' he'd said. 'Disconcerting. Probably the

best you've ever done.' His look had been penetrating. Then he'd given her a fond, rueful smile. 'Of course, they'll never sell. They don't make people feel good, do they?'

A blast of wind battered the car. Jodie clenched the wheel, kept her course steady, following the diffused, red blur of the Toyota's rear lights. She checked her mirror. The black jeep had disappeared, and by now the Toyota was the only other car in sight. Jodie glanced at the line of shivering firs crammed along both sides of the road. Frontiers into dense, impenetrable forest. Like the primitive backwoods encroaching on Ethan's house. Jodie shuddered.

The Toyota's rear brake lights flared, and the car slowed. Jodie hung back, watched it make a careful turn into a laneway. She peered after it, saw its tail lights disappear through a gateway on the right. Jodie hesitated for a moment, then followed it up the laneway, cruising on past the gate, glimpsing a house half-buried under snowdrifts.

Jodie rounded a corner out of sight. The laneway looked deserted, no signs of life in the neighbouring houses. She pulled up near the kerb, letting the engine run. Switching it off would mean a decision. And she still wasn't sure.

She debated the wisdom of getting out. Of walking through that gate and knocking on the door. Was she still just following some dubious link to Ethan? Or was she pursuing something else? Some longing for wholeness? What missing part of herself was she hoping to find, for God's sake?

Jodie swore softly at herself. Then she killed the engine, grabbed her bag and the roll of paintings and climbed out of the car. The wind slapped snow into her face, stung her eyes. She snatched at her hood, pulling it tighter. The cold sliced deep into her lungs, freezing the breath inside her chest. She kept her head low, started back towards the gate. Across the road, another car door opened. She glanced over.

Black jeep.

Jodie felt a small hitch in her step. A twist in her gut. No idea why.

Then a man stepped out of the jeep's passenger side. Solid, compact. Unrecognizable in hooded winter gear. Yet a familiar undertow pulled at Jodie, dragging the twist in her gut even tighter.

He stalked towards her. Blocked her path. Close enough now for Jodie to see his face.

Fleshy and dark. With watchful eyes.

Sheriff Zach Caruso.

30

'Don't look so surprised.' Caruso levelled a gun at Jodie's face. Her gut lurched. 'You musta known we'd find you sooner or later.'

Jodie stared at the pistol. Felt the weight of her own weapon buried deep inside her bag. Snow burned her cheeks, froze on her eyelashes. Caruso shifted his stance, and had to yell to be heard over the thunderous wind.

'Put your hands up where I can see them!'

Slowly, Jodie raised her arms, still holding Lily's roll of paintings in one hand. Icy gusts battered into her, almost toppling her. Caruso gestured with his chin.

'Toss the bag on the ground, far away from you.' He nodded at the canvases. 'And whatever that is, too.'

Jodie scoured her surroundings for someone to help, for some way out. But the laneway was deserted. Not that it mattered. All he had to do was pull out his badge. *Fugitive under arrest, nothing to see here.*

Caruso adjusted his sights on the gun. 'Toss it!'

She dropped the roll of canvases to the ground, pitched her bag on top. Still hoping she might get to it. Her arms felt heavy as she raised them back up in the air.

Caruso motioned with the gun.

'Now move over towards the jeep.'

His two-handed grip on the weapon looked solid, his boxy frame braced firm against the blizzard. But in spite of the snow, Caruso's face was sweating. Jodie's heart kicked up into high gear. He wasn't here to take her into custody. He was out of his jurisdiction. No backup, no squad car. No official arrest.

'*Move!*'

She edged towards the jeep. Recalled how Caruso had stepped out of the passenger side. Which meant he had a driver. Jodie squinted at the dark, tinted windows. Couldn't see through them.

Small hairs rose on her skin. Whirlwinds of snow gusted around her, like white ghosts sweeping the terrain. She took a deep breath, called out over her shoulder,

'Still doing Ethan's dirty work for him, Zach?'

'Just keep moving!'

'Real estate fraud, falsifying evidence. And now what? Accessory to murder?'

Caruso didn't answer. His footsteps crunched close behind her. The jeep was only a few yards away, and she peered at the driver's side, looking for shadows. Icicles formed at the base of her spine. Whose face would she see?

The tide of snow swirled around her, stung her eyes. She half-turned her head back to Caruso.

'How did you find me?'

'You're all over the news, people snitch. Now get over by the trunk.'

Jodie plodded on towards the rear of the jeep. Her arms were getting tired, and snow was leaking an icy trickle into her sleeves.

Something shifted in her peripheral vision. A stirring of the darkness inside the car. Jodie's bones felt chilled. She swallowed, raised her voice.

'That you in there, Ethan?'

For an instant, the screeching wind lulled. Caught its breath. The Arctic air almost crackled in the silence. Jodie squinted, made out a silhouette.

'Come on, Ethan. Don't you want to talk to me after all these years?' She came to a halt at the rear of the jeep. 'Or maybe I should call you Joshua Brown?'

She sensed Caruso falter behind her. Then the wind gathered up, surged to a roar, and the blow to her head came fast and hard and drove her spinning to the ground.

Something thrummed against Jodie's cheek, buzzed along her frame.

An engine rumbling. Juddering through her. She felt herself sway, pitch from side to side.

She dragged her eyes open. Blinding pain lurched

through her skull, reached down and swirled her gut. She let her eyelids close.

The pain staggered back and forth. Kept tempo with a background thump of wipers. Her shoulders ached, and she tried to move her arms, but her wrists jammed, pinched by metal. Her hands were cuffed behind her back.

Jodie opened her eyes. Stared at the roof. At the thick, snowy fir trees flashing past the windows. She was lying in the jeep's trunk.

Her head swam. She explored with her legs, nudging them up against car-trunk clutter: maps, ropes, carpet remnants. Paper rustled near her feet. She frowned. Not paper. Something thicker. Sheets of canvas? Lily's paintings. Caruso must have unrolled them to take a look.

Jodie slid her gaze to the front of the car. The rear seats were down, giving her an uninterrupted view of Caruso in the passenger side. Next to him, the driver was mostly obscured by the high, wide seat and the headrest shielding his face.

She craned her neck, and a surge of pain flooded her skull, dragged her under. She felt herself spinning. Sinking, drifting. Skimming consciousness, in and out.

Suddenly, Ethan's face was hovering close to hers. Tender and passionate. The way he'd been when they'd first met. The air between them was heady, magnetic. She could feel it vibrate, drawing her into his orbit like a lodestone.

Then the air changed. Became dense and suffocating. *'You've been seeing someone else, haven't you, Jodie?'*

Her lungs squeezed. She felt stifled, smothered. Ethan's face was transforming, shape-shifting into something cruel. Dr Jekyll and Mr Hyde.

'*If Mommy leaves, we can't be a happy family any more, Abby.*'

She tried to open her eyes, willed herself to resurface.

'*How do I even know that Abby's my daughter?*'

Jodie tried to scream, but no sound emerged. Ethan turned away, his features melting. But his hard eyes still watched her in the rear-view mirror. They were back in the Bentley, the night air fizzling, fireworks exploding, filling her brain with sparkling parachutes of light.

'*I warned you over and over . . . if you try to keep her from me, I'll take her away . . .*'

Jodie couldn't breathe. *Open your eyes, Goddamnit!*

'*I picked a pretty spot . . . The water wasn't cold.*'

Ethan twisted back around in his seat to look at her. Jodie gasped. His face had changed again. So much older, more haggard. All the vibrancy leached out. His expression looked bleak. Numb, almost. As though he was trying hard not to feel any pain. Something in his inward-looking gaze reminded her of Lily. Self-loathing? He turned away, back to the road. To the thick wall of snow closing in on the jeep.

Back to the snow.

Jodie held her breath. Not sure if her eyes were open or closed. If Ethan was real.

His image blurred. Her head was still reeling. The jeep bumped her back and forth, tilting, rolling, until her brain staggered punch-drunk down into freefall, and her world tumbled end over end.

The bumping stopped. The engine idled, throbbing along her bones.

Jodie forced her eyes open. Her vision was still filmy. Behind her, the trunk door groaned on its hinges, and a vicious slash of cold air whipped into her like a blade.

Strong hands grabbed her, dragged her backwards out of the jeep, hauled her onto her feet, wrenching at her healing stab wound. Her legs buckled. Caruso hoisted her up, hustled her forwards. Jodie squinted. The whole world had plunged into a blinding whiteout. Shrieking wind screamed through her, and she staggered against it, hands still cuffed behind her back. Then Caruso shoved her face-first into the snow.

Jodie lay there, stunned. The cold scorched her cheeks like fire, numbing her against any pain from the fall. Behind her, the trunk door creaked and clunked and out of nowhere, her bag catapulted to the ground in front of her. Sheets of canvas tumbled after it, thrashed along by the gale.

'Get up!'

Caruso wrenched at her arms, yanked her upright onto her knees. Jodie opened her mouth to scream, then felt the hard barrel of a gun press against her skull.

Caruso yelled over the banshee wind.

'Don't waste your breath! No one's gonna hear you way out here.'

282

The cold squeezed tears from her eyes, clearing her vision. Faint shadows traced contours in the whiteness: tufts of undergrowth; fanned tips of conifer branches.

Jodie stared. Made out the flock of snow-laden trees. Heavy firs, soaring redwoods. Packed in, stretching back, closing in on all sides.

Dear Jesus. They'd driven her out into the wilderness.

Jodie's whole body trembled. Her legs ached as she knelt there with her hands behind her back, Caruso's gun pressed to her skull.

Execution-style.

She bowed her head, felt the numbness creep in and claim her shivering body. Cold desolation bled through her. A week ago, she'd craved death. Thought it would bring her closer to Abby. Now it was here. And all she felt was waste and regret.

The jeep revved up somewhere behind her. She sensed Caruso stiffen, felt the gun bore into her. She squeezed her eyes shut, saw her little girl's face. Dark eyes, round cheeks.

'*The water wasn't cold, she didn't wake up once.*'

Jodie's heart pounded, fist-pumping warm blood into her veins. Her eyes flared open. She took a deep breath, twisted her head, screamed out over the wailing wind.

'*Ethan!*'

The jeep's engine idled behind her.

'I know it's you in there!'

Caruso jabbed the gun into her head. She winced. Screamed again.

283

'You bastard, Ethan, I'll see you in hell!'

Jodie was sobbing now, hot tears coursing down her cheeks, warming her face. The engine growled, revved a warning. Caruso swore. He dug the gun into her skull, thrust her head forward.

Click-snap.

Jodie flinched. *Sweet Jesus*. Her body went rigid, braced for the shot.

sweet jesus sweet jesus sweet jesus

Caruso tore at her wrists, ripped off the cuffs. Jodie's head felt dazed. What the hell? His footsteps slushed away through the snow, and she whirled around in time to see him climb back into the jeep. The engine roared, tyres chirruping. Jodie clambered to her feet.

'*Ethan!*'

The jeep took off. Jodie stared. They were leaving her here alive?

She staggered after them, not caring if they shot her, not caring as she scrambled and slid in the snow, screaming at the jeep, yelling at Ethan till her throat was blood-raw. Then the white blizzard swelled and closed in like a whirlpool and swallowed the jeep up.

31

Jodie opened her eyes, lifted her head off the ground.

Couldn't remember falling.

Her body felt icy. The ground was deadly cold, and her temperature was plummeting.

Get up!

Slowly, she heaved herself onto her knees, shivering violently. A lasso of wind whipped at her face and she blocked it with her forearm, managed to drag up her hood, pull her scarf over her nose. She strained through the blizzard for sounds of the jeep.

Nothing.

Her heart knocked against her chest, and the shivers grew convulsive. Jesus, how long had she lain there?

Keep moving!

She dragged herself to her feet, knew she had to keep her circulation going. Snow slapped into her face, burned her eyes. Then she blinked, disoriented. The world had disappeared. No shapes, no shadows; no contrasts, no horizon. Just an eternal wall of white.

Jodie stretched out a hand in front of her. Could barely see it. She smothered a growing sense of panic, blindly groped her way forward. Felt as if someone had thrown a white hood over her head.

People got lost in their own front yards during a whiteout. Had to feel their way back, though their doors were only feet away.

The wind bludgeoned into her, an invisible force. She cast about with her arms, scrambling for a reference point. Out of nowhere, Momma Ruth's voice drifted back to her.

'*Last woman who tried to escape died of exposure in the blizzards . . .*'

Jodie flailed around, desperate to connect with something.

'*. . . Days later, they were still trying to thaw her out.*'

Jodie's breathing grew rapid, stoked up by a screaming rush of panic. She stood still. Took a deep breath. Made herself control it. Understood now why Caruso hadn't pulled the trigger. He knew she'd freeze to death out here. No unexplained bullet wounds. No need for an investigation. Just another dumb fugitive who didn't make it.

Jodie forced her legs to move. Baby steps. Left, right. Her muscles ached, contracting painfully in the cold.

Just find the trees, get some shelter.

She inched one foot in front of the other. Left, right. Left, right.

Then the ground gave way.

Her foot plunged through it, found only air.

Jodie screamed, lurched, fell backwards onto the ground. Snow *whumped* somewhere far below her, as though dumped from a great height.

Jesus Christ.

She stiffened, paralysed. The white blindness crowded in. Where to now? Backwards, forwards? Left, right? How could she tell the difference any more? How could she tell safe ground from the edge of a cliff?

Sweat flashed along her back, conducting precious heat away from her body. The cold crept closer to her bones.

Jodie struggled to her feet, her movements slow and laboured. By now, she'd lost all feeling in her toes, and her shivering was uncontrollable.

Nearby, something snapped back and forth in the wind. She squinted, sightless. Then she closed her eyes, shutting down her vision, channelling everything into the senses she had left.

The sound was coming from her right. She reached out, shuffled sideways. Something poked her gloved fingers. She grabbed, tugged, felt the heavy swing and give of a bush. Jodie opened her eyes, tugged again. Snow dropped away, exposing dark branches, the sudden contrast giving definition to the whiteness. Her eyes focused on the thorny shrub. And on the sheets of canvas snagged among its brambles.

Lily's paintings.

Four sheets. Waterproof. Insulating.

Jodie snatched at the canvases, then hunched against the wind and stuffed them inside her jacket. She zipped up, patting the sheets in place around her chest. As a thermal layer, it wasn't much, but it might just help to brake her plunging temperature.

She hunkered down, the canvases crackling. What were the chances her bag was around here some place? She stretched out her arms, made wide breaststroke-sweeps, scuffling along in small steps until her fingers tipped something soft. The cushiony leather of a bag.

She hauled it towards her, fumbled with the zip, raked through its contents. No phone. No gun. No surprise.

But everything else was there. Money, fake passport, motel room key. Other handbag-clutter stuff. Caruso hadn't wanted any of her belongings. Hadn't wanted any incriminating links to her corpse when it was found.

Jodie zipped up the bag, tested its weight in her hand. Then she pulled herself upright, her limbs stiff and clumsy. She tossed the bag forward into the whiteout, holding onto it by the strap. It plopped onto snow, breaking up the camouflaged surface of the ground, temporarily splintering the illusion of blindness. She stepped up to the bag in one stride, then flung it again, repeating the process. Step, toss, step, toss. Revealing the ground a few feet at a time.

The wind ripped through her, and the shivers wracked her frame, a last-ditch attempt by her muscles to generate heat. Her head was starting to feel sluggish and woolly. She couldn't even feel the throbbing in her stab wound any more.

Keep moving!

She summoned up Ethan's face. Waited for the surge of hate that would stoke her forward.

It didn't come.

Step, toss. Step, toss.

She gave up on Ethan and pictured Novak. Grizzly Adams, hunting down Joshua Browns from his cosy motel room. Would Ethan go after Novak too? Her chest turned over. She wished she'd listened to Novak. Wished she hadn't slept alone the previous night. All those walls of self-protection. What use were they to her now?

Jodie blundered forward, her head drowsy and clogged. Then she stumbled, and fell on all fours to the ground. She stayed there for a moment. Couldn't remember what she was doing. Or why she needed to get up. Puzzled, she clambered unsteadily to her feet, her brain cloudy. Then she saw her bag and remembered.

Step, toss.

She dragged herself on. The wind stampeded into her, and she floundered sideways, stumbled again. Then stepped out into nothing.

For an instant, she was weightless. She thrust out her hands, pitched forward. Sailed through the air. Hard vertical ground slammed into her shoulder, bowled her over, sent her tumbling, rolling, plummeting, until finally she slammed to a halt on level ground.

Jodie lay there, winded. The world see-sawed. Meltwater trickled down her neck and spine. Any body heat she had left was leaching into the ground. She lifted her head.

Couldn't feel her limbs. The strap of her bag was still wound around her arm. She peered through the whiteout. Grey shadows flickered through it this time, looming nearby. Clusters of trees? She sank back, exhausted. Closed her eyes.

She should probably get up.

Maybe in a moment.

Just a short rest first.

Her brain floated and slid. Cold pain pierced her ears, but the shivering had stopped. Had her body finally abandoned the urge to get warm? She snapped her eyes open.

Get up!

She tried to fight the stupor. Raised her head to see the trees.

You can crawl, it's not far.

She fell back against the snow. *In a minute. Maybe in a minute.*

She couldn't remember why she'd come here. Why she felt so cold.

Think of some place warm!

Ambergris Caye.

Hot and fragrant. Hibiscus and frangipani, pink and purple. Beachfront villas, sugary sand, crystal waters lapping at wooden jetties.

She'd go back there some day.

Jodie felt herself drifting. Letting go. Then her floating brain faltered. Got snagged on something, brought up short.

Ambergris Caye.

Luxurious villas, jade-green sea. The Princess Resort brand. And the matchbook that was still in her bag.

Adrenaline trickled through the ice in her veins. She could light a fire. If she could just get to the damn trees, she could light a fire!

She hoisted herself into a sitting position, ignored the screaming pain in her limbs. Then she toppled over onto all fours and dragged herself inch by inch towards the shadows. The wind screeched, and she ducked her head against it. Her arms quivered. Buckled and gave way. She rested her forehead against them for a moment, eyes closed. Saw an image of cold stone. Momma Ruth's angel statue in the cemetery: perched on a column, balancing a ledger; tallying up sins, accounting for souls. Jodie opened her eyes, straightened up.

Fuck him and his ledger.

She braced her muscles, slogged on through the snow, kept going till the shadows resolved and separated. Tall redwoods, Douglas firs, dense enough to block some of the wind-chill out.

Jodie crawled under the canopy of the nearest tree, a half-fallen conifer laden with snow, and collapsed against the trunk. The sudden shelter was a blessed relief. Pain cramped her stiffening body. She rested, breathless. With the blizzard half-muffled, it felt like she'd gone deaf. A spicy, pine fragrance threaded the cold air and she drank it in, willing her eyes to stay open.

A low-grade pain twisted in her stomach. Pangs of hunger. She hadn't eaten or drunk since early that morning. Jodie stared at the snow, considered sucking down a handful. But something told her it would lower her body temperature even more.

Dehydration versus hypothermia.

For now, the priority was warmth.

She fumbled for the bag still wrapped around her arm. Her hands were trembling. She struggled with the zip, upended the bag's contents onto the ground, scrabbling till she found the matchbook from the Princess Resort. She clutched it to her chest, sent up a quick prayer of thanks. Then she unzipped her jacket and tugged out the canvases. They crackled in her hands. Perfect for tinder. Somewhere there had to be half-dry twigs and foliage she could burn.

Her eyes skimmed over the familiar paintings, their bleak colours blurring together. All except for one. Jodie frowned. Yellows and blues jumped off the page. Vibrant paint-bursts, as if splashed from a height, trails of colour squirted straight from the tubes.

Jodie's vision swam. She blinked, swallowed. Spread out the canvas for a closer look.

Gemstone colours, speckled and drizzled. Sapphire sky, emerald trees, topaz sun. Globs of paint hand-clapped into familiar spatters.

'*Look what I can do, Mommy.*'

Jodie's hand flew to her mouth. *Dear sweet Jesus.*

Her throat closed over, her chest squeezed to near-suffocation. She made herself look at the bottom corner of the page.

Abby Brown Age 6

Abby! Abby Brown?

Joshua Brown.

Impossible. *Impossible!*

Jodie's head reeled. *Think, reason it out!* Where had the canvas come from? Not from Lily. She pictured Caruso flinging paintings into the wind.

Ethan's jeep. It had come from the trunk of Ethan's jeep.

Jodie brushed her fingers along the canvas.

Abby Brown Age 6

But her Abby had only been three. Never six, never even four or five.

Only three, only three, only three.

Jodie rocked to and fro, smoothing her hand over the canvas.

Only three, only three, only three.

Abby Brown.

Age 6.

Jodie stopped rocking. Stared at the painting. Saw Abby's flair, familiar and unmistakable. But with less scribbling. More awareness of space.

The refinements of an older child.

Jodie's breathing stopped. Her head swirled, and her eyes flared wide open.

Abby Brown.

Age 6.

Her little girl was still alive.

32

Jodie's heartbeat raced. She clasped the painting close to her chest. Abby's painting.

But how could that be true?

Something leaden seeped through her; something insidious and bleak. The threat of false hope.

She clenched her jaw. Stupid to believe it. It was impossible. Impossible! She'd buried her precious little girl three years ago.

A whisper trickled into her head.

Her body was never found.

Jodie went still. Then she shook her head. The current had taken Abby, that had never been in doubt.

But they searched for days, and they never found her.

Memories flashed: helicopters thudding over the Contoocook River; frantic searches in the dark.

Jodie shook her head again, over and over. The current had taken Abby, it had swept her away!

What if it hadn't?

Jodie caught her breath. She snatched the painting away from her chest, pored over it again. Recognizable shapes emerged from the splatters: finger-daubed trees, fat yellow sun-blob, dollops of white for a roly-poly snowman.

Abby Brown Age 6.

Jodie squeezed her eyes shut. The wind roared around her. Bullets of ice burned her skin, stung her eyelids. She surrendered to the pain, relished it, even. Anything to drive out the torment of hope.

It was only a painting. Her daughter was dead.

The whisper persisted. *But Ethan loved Abby. How could he have killed her?*

He was a monster, a family annihilator!

Novak didn't think so.

Jodie snapped her eyes open.

Novak said Ethan didn't fit the profile, something was off.

She recalled Novak's hesitation, the unnamed doubt he wouldn't put into words. Was this what he'd meant? Had he believed there was a chance that Abby was alive?

Jodie held herself rigid, trembling with the cold and with the effort of fighting off hope. She clamped her mouth shut, flatlining her emotions. Ethan had boasted about killing Abby, for God's sake.

But he wasn't like other family annihilators. He hadn't

295

ended his own life to duck the consequences. *Would he really have killed Abby, then chosen to live on?*

Jodie's whole body clenched, a barricade against feeling. The blizzard was ice and fire on her skin, the wind a white noise. She tried to block the voice out, but it whispered on.

He'd loved Abby. How could he have faced all that pain, all that remorse?

She yelled into the white emptiness. 'Because he was a monster! He told me what he did, there was no pain, no remorse!'

Because Abby wasn't really dead.

'Jesus Christ.' Jodie choked back a sob. 'Why would he lie about something like that?'

To punish you. That had always been the reason. To cause you maximum pain. But this way, he could hurt you and still keep Abby for himself.

Jodie hugged the painting close to her chest. Was it possible? Then she gazed at the picture again, stroked the signature. Allowed herself to believe it, just for a moment.

Abby Brown.

Joshua Brown.

He faked his own death at a moment's notice. You think he couldn't have faked Abby's, too?

Jodie closed her eyes, and this time, Ethan's voice filled her head.

'*If you try to keep her from me, I'll take her away.*'

Ethan always lying. Always in control.

'I'll take her some place where you'll never see her again.'

His words sliced into Jodie, back and forth like a switchblade. She hugged her arms tight across her chest, warding off the lacerations. Then the whispering was back.

What's more likely? That he killed the little girl he loved so much? Or that he told you he did, just to watch you suffer?

A memory cut in: Ethan boxing up Abby's stuff after she died, refusing to say where he'd sent it. Toys, clothes, favourite blankets. Things little Abby wouldn't sleep without.

Dear sweet Jesus.

Sudden hot tears spilled down her cheeks. For an instant, she felt insulated against the cold, oblivious to the snow, to the raging wind. Ready to risk the penalty of hope.

Joshua Brown.

Abby Brown.

Age 6.

It was true. It *had* to be true!

Warm blood rushed through her veins in dizzying, wondrous, breath-taking relief.

Abby was alive!

Alive, alive, alive, alive.

She was six years old and she was alive!

33

A gust of wind snatched at the painting.

Jodie hugged the canvas close, jarred back into an awareness of her surroundings: the one-sided shelter from the half-broken fir; the snow hissing through it, blasting against her like crushed glass in the wind.

The jolt galvanized her limbs. She shoved all the canvases back inside her jacket, stowed the matches into her bag for safekeeping. Adrenaline had thawed her, but she knew it was temporary. The rush would soon evaporate, hypothermia would creep back in.

Think!

Jodie peered out into the flat, diffuse light. The whiteout still clung like an opaque veil, obliterating even the nearest trees. She twisted around where she sat, examined the broken fir. The trunk was splintered in two above her head, jack-knifed down into an inverted V, the low overhang of branches a welcome roof. Shivers juddered along her frame, her adrenaline almost spent. She stared up at the thick umbrella of branches.

Shelter and fire. Survival priorities.

She struggled to her feet, stretched up an arm to the nearest branch and pulled. Snow dumped away to the ground, exposing wide conifer fans. She brushed at the sprays, examined the needles. Stiff and crisp. Near-water-resistant, packed with flammable pitch. Better than wet grass or moss. She groped along the stem, searching for a weak spot. Found its attachment to the main branch. Twisted and tugged, wrenched it away, tossed it on the ground near the base of the tree to protect it from the blizzard. Then she reached up and grabbed again.

Jodie battled on until her arms ached, breaking stems where she could, chafing at thicker branches with her motel key. When she'd collected a high, springy pile, she hunched against the blizzard, left the shelter of the overhang and draped the largest branches either side of the trunk.

The wind charged into her, whipped at the firs. Somehow she managed to interleave the fans, twisting them together, knotting them with low-hanging canopy stems to fix them in place wherever she could. Then she crawled on all fours into her makeshift shelter, huddled against the trunk, teeth chattering. The crude screens thrashed in the blizzard, flailed back and forth. Held together. Rudimentary breakers. Jodie basked in the blessed respite from the wind and snow.

She rested for a moment, catching her breath. Then

she clambered back to her feet and reached up to the fractured joint of the tree, scrabbling inside the broken trunk for treasure: shredded bits of dry, inner bark; woody splinters protected from the wet. Stashing her tiny haul in her pockets, she hunkered down at the shelter's entrance, shoved at the snow till she'd cleared a wide circle, and began to build her fire.

Canvas for tinder; pine needles and dry inner bark for kindling; then a pyramid of stems and woody splinters, with a tepee of thicker branches on top.

Jodie struck her first match, bending low to shield it from the wind. She touched it to a peeping corner of canvas, hands trembling. The flame snacked on the edge of Lily's painting, lapped along towards the kindling. Then it fluttered and spread into the heart of the tepee. An orange glow flickered, drying out the damper stems on top, then it blazed up in a crackle and hiss of sap. Jodie crouched in close, bathing in the warmth.

She gathered up the remaining fir stems and spread some of them beneath her, insulating herself from the icy ground. Then she eyed the dwindling heap of stems. It would last maybe another twenty minutes. After that, she'd brave the blizzard and hunt for more.

The flames spat and quivered. Her face tingled. She closed her eyes, savoured the warmth, the thaw, the sweet piney scent. The air felt light and clear. Full of magnificent relief. Glorious reprieve.

Abby was alive. She hadn't drowned, Ethan hadn't killed her. None of it had been true.

Jodie opened her eyes, watched a dark curl of smoke get shredded in the wind. What had Ethan told Abby? Had he told her Jodie was dead? Or just that she'd left, happy to abandon her little girl? Jodie's heart shrank, feeling every drop of Abby's hurt.

So Novak was right. Ethan was no family annihilator. Not that particular brand of monster. But still a monster. Still hurting Abby, still punishing Jodie with a diabolical lie.

What had he been planning when he'd faked Abby's death? Had he intended to keep her hidden forever? Or maybe he'd harboured some twisted fantasy that some day they could still be together again as a family. A fantasy that had shattered when Jodie had said she was going ahead with the divorce. That had been the trigger. For his final, vindictive lie.

Maximum pain.

But Abby was alive. Another of Ethan's secrets unravelled. Was this the last one? The last secret?

Jodie leaned in closer to the flames, relishing the heat, the smoky scent of charred wood. Conifer needles flared and fizzed like tiny firecrackers.

Jodie watched the sparks, recalling how Ethan had once been: a captivating lover, proud adoring father. At what point had he turned into a monster? All those lies, those twisted secrets. The more he'd indulged them, the more he'd seemed to forget he had a better side.

Had his dark nature slowly transformed him? Had his shape-shifting so imprisoned him, that in the end he'd been unable to change back?

Dr Jekyll, Mr Hyde.

She added another conifer stem to the fire, recalling Ethan as she'd seen him in the jeep, real or imagined: his shattered look of suffering and self-loathing. Which part of his dual nature did that belong to?

The fire spat and snapped. Jodie's extremities fizzled in the warmth. Then she realized Novak was right about something else, too. She couldn't kill Ethan. Not now. He was the only one who knew where Abby was.

She caught her breath, a sudden cold realization sucking the air from her lungs. What if she'd succeeded that night of the fireworks? What if she'd really managed to kill Ethan? To kill herself? Never knowing that, all the while, Abby was still alive.

The blood roared in Jodie's ears. She hugged her knees, felt the crinkle of Abby's painting against her chest. Her body trembled, shivers of icy, shocked relief. She bowed her head. Sent a heartfelt prayer of thanks for her last-minute salvation. For the grace of deliverance.

Resin spattered and crackled in the flames. She lifted her head, stared at the fire. Felt a slow burn of exhilaration as the heat repaired her, made her whole. The fire blazed into her bones, every cell in her body tingling with renewal. Fresh beginnings.

What's worth living for, what's worth dying for?

Her muscles glowed in the reviving heat. Killing Ethan no longer mattered. Revenge and hatred weren't enduring. But her love for Abby was.

And Jodie intended to find her.

34

The ground blizzard raged long into the night.

Hour after hour, Jodie nursed her fire, feeding it, coaxing it, stockpiling fuel for it. Darkness seeped in, reversing the whiteout like a photograph negative into a cold, inky fog.

Her body grew rigor-mortis stiff. At regular intervals, she pushed through the fatigue, pumping her arms, stomping her feet, fighting an irresistible urge to close her eyes.

Sleep would kill her. Lure her, oblivious, into profound hypothermia. So she kept on the move, tended her fire, until eventually the wind abated, the blackout dissolved, and, drop by drop, the world bled back through.

Immense trees. Shadowy backcountry.

To her right, a steep, rising ridge. To her left, a sloping descent. She was on some kind of forested mountain, had fallen down a near-sheer ravine. Without the snow to break her fall, she'd probably be dead.

Moonlight leaked through the sky, and the snow glowed like phosphorous in the dark. Visibility restored.

Jodie's extremities tingled. She got to her feet, edged away from the fire and stared at the brutal wilderness below her.

Ethan was out there somewhere, his trail already growing cold. Only one place left she knew to look. What if he disappeared before she had the chance? What if he whisked Abby off some place new, obliterating his tracks for good this time?

Tendrils of panic snarled up inside her chest. It was time to move. She shot a glance at the overhang above her, darted her gaze back to the slope below.

Down, not up. Up was prehistoric mountain. Down meant valleys. Civilization.

Dousing her fire with snow, she grabbed her belongings and headed down the ravine. The terrain was treacherous. For what felt like hours, she slid and scrambled, zigzagging between trees, clambering through undergrowth and rocky outcrops. The snow was deep, and sometimes she plunged into it up to her knees, blundering into invisible potholes. She scrabbled on, kept her eyes down, intent on the next immediate obstacle. Refusing to contemplate the vast wilderness ahead.

And through all of it, the same whirling thought. *Where is Abby? What if I can't find her?* Then a countering whisper. *But what if you can? Think of that! What if you can?*

Bit by bit, the terrain levelled out. The darkness thinned to a grey chiffon light. She dragged herself on. Heard the trickle of water. The delicate chimes of waking birds. Then the blessed sound of tyres swishing in the wet. She emerged, exhausted, onto a dark, winding road.

It didn't take long to hitch a ride. The truck driver who stopped watched her clamber into his cab, stared as she sank back against the seat, then wordlessly handed her a flask of coffee and half a Hershey bar.

After she'd thawed, he told her she'd emerged from Mt Hood National Forest, three hundred thousand acres of designated wilderness about twenty miles east of Portland.

Three hundred thousand acres.

If she hadn't fallen into that steep ravine, who knew what deadly direction she might have taken?

The trucker was headed north, so he took her as far as the next highway service stop, where she disembarked and managed to negotiate the rental of an old Mazda for a cash deposit far exceeding the car's value. She tried calling Novak from a pay phone in the store. He didn't pick up.

Following the salty scent of fried food, she found a diner at one end of the service station, where she stoked up on energy with bacon and eggs and three mugs of scalding-hot coffee. She availed herself of the single-occupant bathroom, then grabbed a sandwich and coffee to go for the long drive ahead.

Firing up the rental, she navigated her way to Interstate 5, heading south towards Grants Pass. The journey took hours. She slogged on through heavy rain and hail, icy pellets peppering the car like bullets. By the time she reached the motel, her head was thick with fatigue. She killed the engine, climbed out of the car, ducking through the sleet as she raced for cover.

'Novak!' She rapped on his door. 'Novak, open up!'

No answer.

She pounded again. Felt the door give. She paused, hand still raised in the air. Then she eased the door open, peering in from the threshold.

'Novak?'

The bed was unmade, the single chair knocked over. Papers were strewn across the floor.

'Novak!'

She reached the bathroom in four quick strides.

Empty.

Jodie's chest hammered. She snatched up the phone beside the bed, called Novak's number. Got his voicemail. *Shit!*

She sprinted the thirty yards to reception, found a matronly-looking manageress huddled over coffee, eyes glued to a TV behind the desk. The woman seemed half-asleep, and it took a while to get the message through.

'Room 34? He's still here, honey, hasn't checked out yet, far as I know.'

'Have you seen him, do you know where he is?'

'I don't keep track of comings and goings.' Her eyes strayed back to her TV screen.

'What about visitors? A black jeep, did a black jeep pull up here?'

'Well now, I do recall a black jeep. I noticed it on account of my brother-in-law wants to buy—'

'Did you see who got out? Did my friend go with them?'

'I couldn't tell you, hon, my favourite programme was on.' The woman turned up the volume on her TV. 'I hate being interrupted when my programme is on.'

Jodie cursed, spun away, scudded back over the snow to Novak's room. She rifled through his things. His clothes were still there, but his laptop was gone. Had he taken it with him on some routine errand? Or had Ethan taken it, disposing of Novak's files in case they pointed his way?

Her stomach churned. She set the chair back on its legs, then gathered up the papers from the floor. Tried not to read the mess as signs of a struggle. But a merciless image shoved into her head: Novak being strong-armed into the jeep, abandoned some place remote where he'd disappear. Jodie clapped a hand over her mouth, shook her head.

No! Not Novak!

Maybe he was just out somewhere following a lead, maybe he'd found Joshua Brown. Jodie scoured the papers she'd picked up from the floor, searching for something to say where he'd gone. The pages were mostly blank, just doodles and scribbles. The last one had a single list of handwritten names.

Peter Rosen
Mrs Blane
Ives and McKenzie
Celine Rosen

Jodie frowned. She paced the room, dragging her hands through her hair. The list made no sense.

Where the hell is he?

Another brutal image: Novak handcuffed, on his knees; Caruso's gun pressed to the back of his head.

Jesus! Think!

She had to get help. Maybe the cops could find the jeep, maybe they could stop Caruso. She could make an anonymous call. Jodie grabbed the phone, began to dial 911. Caught sight of the motel caller ID on display. Her finger hovered over the last digit.

What if the cops came after her instead? Her description of Novak might just trigger an alarm, linking them both to the breach at airport immigration. As soon as she dialled, they'd know where she was. They could probably have a patrol car at the motel in five minutes flat. A description from the manageress would confirm their suspicions: that she was the Framingham fugitive they'd all been looking for.

Jodie slid the phone down from her ear, clutched it to her chest.

Novak needs help!

But they'd find her, no question. And they'd lock her up, snatching away her only chance to find Abby.

Jodie bowed her head. Her innards felt shredded,

ripped in two. She pictured Novak's sun-burnt face, the grey-green eyes.

I'm sorry I'm sorry I'm sorry I'm sorry

Slowly, she returned the handset to its cradle. Then sank to the floor, slumped back against the wall. Spent, empty.

No luxury of tears.

Would Novak understand? She had to believe he would. Had to believe that in her shoes, he'd make the same choice. He'd choose to find his son.

35

'Samantha, please! I need to talk to Lily.'

'And I told you, you can't.'

Jodie gripped the phone hard. 'I only need a minute—'

'You're not listening. I told you, she can't talk to you. She's out of it.'

'You're still sedating her?'

'This isn't sedation. She's turned catatonic. Mute.' Samantha's tone was accusing. 'No movement, no eye contact. Just stays crouched on her hunkers, palms pressed up against the wall. Same rigid position for thirty-six hours now. She's shut herself down, and you won't get a word out of her.'

Jodie sank down on Novak's bed, closing her eyes against the image: feisty Lily, with her braids and her knee-highs; frozen and silent.

Jesus.

'I'm coming out there.'

'You won't get in. We've got security guards on the door. If you show up, they're under orders to call the cops.'

Jodie tensed. 'Under orders from who?'

'From Celine. Seems she doesn't want to see you either.' The girl paused. 'I'm sorry, but there's nothing I can do.'

'Samantha, wait!'

But the girl had already hung up.

Shit!

Jodie slammed the phone down. Now what? Ethan's visit to Lily was the only lead she had. She cast a desperate look around Novak's room. Couldn't bear the reminders of him, of the choice she'd had to make. She got to her feet, strode towards the door. She'd camp outside Celine's house if she had to, stay as long as it took for the woman to talk to her.

She made a quick detour to her own room, where she dropped Novak's list of names on the bed, then rifled through her bag for a set of dry clothes. She unzipped her parka, and the canvases fluttered to the floor. There were only two left: Abby's painting, and the sketch of her father as a boy.

Jodie bent to retrieve them. The sketch was topmost. She took in the figure of the cowering child, huddled in bleak misery on the floor. Like Lily's catatonic crouch. A cold churning started in her gut. What kind of monster did this to his own children?

Averting her eyes, she set the canvases on the bed.

Harrowing as the sketch was, she was glad she hadn't burned it. It was the only picture she had of her father.

She kicked off her boots, peeled off her cold, damp clothes and scrambled into dry layers. A hot shower would've eased the stiffness in her bones, but she didn't have time. She bent to lace her boots, then straightened up, reaching for her coat.

A sudden dizziness swirled through her. She groped for the bed, perched on the edge, dipped her head low between her knees.

Damn it!

Muggy heatwaves flashed over her skin, hot and cold at the same time. Slowly, the blood drizzled back into her brain. She took a minute, then eased herself upright, her gaze unfocused as she waited for the giddiness to pass. Her eyes came to rest on the bedside table. On Ethan's dossier.

Jodie stared. She'd forgotten she still had it. She'd assumed Caruso had taken it from Novak's room. Not that it mattered any more. She'd been through the damn thing so many times, there was nothing left to find.

She groped behind her for Novak's list of names, then reached for the dossier and slotted the sheet inside. The movement stirred up another dizzy rush, and the folder spilled to the floor. Shit. Her skin felt clammy. She gripped the mattress, tried not to move. Stared, unblinking, at the scattered paperwork on the floor. Two of her letters were still unopened.

The faintness subsided. With slow-motion movements,

Jodie took the two envelopes onto her lap. Opened the first one. A credit card statement, dated a few days before the fireworks. No activity on the account. No surprise. After Abby's funeral, she'd hardly ventured out of the house.

The second envelope was plain and white. Discreet-looking. Unmarked, apart from her address and the date stamp of July 4th 2012. She slid her thumb under the flap, extracted the contents. Three pages, stapled together. She took in the headed paper and frowned.

Boston Biolabs.

A dim memory stirred. Echoes of recurring, age-old arguments.

'*You want me to arrange a paternity test, Ethan? Is that what you want? I'll do it, I'll prove it to you!*'

And Ethan's smug look, the one that said he was baiting her. He'd known without doubt that Abby was his. Her likeness to him was unmistakable.

Jodie had forgotten. She'd forgotten the same old row they'd had the day before Abby died. Forgotten that, unknown to Ethan, she'd made good on her threat and finally sent the samples off. But with everything that had come after, it had no longer mattered.

She scanned the cover letter.

'*. . . apologize for the delay . . . unforeseen backlog . . . Overleaf are the results of your DNA Paternity Test . . .*'

Jodie flipped over the page, aware of an unexpected flutter in her chest. She stared at a complicated table of numbers, its columns headed with obscure terms: STR

Locus, Allele Sizes, Paternity Index. Row after row, column after column, of meaningless numbers and codes.

She turned to the last page which showed a boxed-in section labelled *Statement of Results*. She read the summary. Frowned at the page. Read it again.

She shook her head. That wasn't right. *Couldn't* be right. There had to be some mistake. The words seemed to flicker and lift off the page.

'. . . *alleged father . . . Samples A and C share insufficient genetic markers . . . Probability of Paternity is 0% . . . excluded as the biological father . . . Sample B . . . Combined Direct Index . . . Probability of Paternity greater than 99.999% . . . is therefore the biological father . . . conclusive results . . . conducted in accordance with the standards set forth by . . .*'

Jodie shook her head, over and over. They'd got it wrong, mixed up the samples. She'd labelled everything so clearly, how could they have made such a ludicrous mistake? She noticed her breathing was ramping up, and she thrust the pages away from her onto the bed. What did it matter? They'd screwed up the tests. So what? It didn't matter, not any more.

But a nagging, sickening voice in her head told her that it might.

She made herself look at the report again, and located the contact number on the first page. She hesitated for a moment, then lifted the phone and dialled. A low charge frizzled along her skin.

This is pointless! It doesn't matter!

'Good morning, Boston Biolabs, how may I help you?'

Jodie explained, and got put through to a senior manager in the lab, who searched his archives, double-checked the results, then assured her with conviction that all was correct. No confusion was possible.

'We don't make those kind of mistakes,' he added. 'Frankly, if we did, we'd soon be out of business.'

To prove it, he stepped painstakingly through the records of Jodie's samples, confirming the labels noted at the time, detailing the chain of custody within the lab and the provenance for each sample as it passed through the DNA tests.

'We run a tight ship here, Ms Garrett. No room for error.'

Jodie hugged an arm around her waist, started to rock back and forth on the edge of the bed. 'But that result, it's all wrong, it's just not possible.'

The lab manager paused. When he spoke again, his tone had softened. 'I appreciate this is difficult for you. Finding out something like this. It's . . . well, it's an abnormal case, no doubt about it. The tragedy is, it's not the first time we've seen it. I'm very sorry.'

An abnormal case.

Sudden nausea lurched through her. A boiling sickness. She dropped the phone, staggered to the bathroom and vomited violently into the sink. Her legs almost buckled. Her torso convulsed, gut-clenching heaves that wracked her body, purging, disgorging, on and on. She couldn't breathe.

It isn't true!

The churning wouldn't stop. Jodie retched and strained until the cords in her neck felt like they might break. She shut her eyes, blocking all thought, blanking it out. Yet remembering, remembering.

Jesus Christ!

She gagged, almost choked, the truth reaching deep down into her gut, ripping her insides out through her throat. Reaching far back into her childhood, plunging, eviscerating, spinning her into a vile, sickening place.

DNA . . . mistakes are hard-wired . . . imprinted on the brain.

She dry-heaved, her throat raw, until at last, the convulsions released their grip, melted away. Jodie clung to the cold enamel of the sink, her body spent. She glanced at the mirror. Her face looked clammy and white with shock. Bloodless, like a wraith. She didn't recognize herself any more. But then, everything was different now.

Everything had changed.

And she knew where Abby was.

36

The Mazda swivelled on black ice. Jodie snatched her foot off the accelerator, curbed an urge to slam the brakes.

She held her breath. The car coasted sideways, skating till it found traction. Her third skid in less than a mile. Jodie peered through the windscreen, coaxing the car forward. Faint lights glowed in the distance, leaden clouds darkening the day to dusk.

She'd eventually found the strength to leave her room. She'd cleaned herself up, rinsed her mouth, held her wrists under cold running water till an icy rush streamed through her veins. Then she'd packed up her belongings and left the motel behind. Time to leave this godforsaken wilderness.

Her heart lifted at what lay ahead. She'd get to Abby, take her away. Take her some place safe and warm, where no one could find them.

Hibiscus and frangipani. Hot and fragrant.

Rain hissed against the car, crackling as it froze on contact with the roof. The pewter sky was spitting an ice storm. Not a violent squall, but a steady downpour of freezing rain. She stared at the icy glaze on the road, formed by super-cooled drops that froze on impact. The glossy sheets were lethal.

Jodie's limbs twitched with the need for action, the need to cover ground and get to Abby fast. She nudged her speed up a few notches. Outside, the world seemed made of glass, every object encased in its own crystal membrane: branches, cars, gates, pylons. The rain spilled over every surface, following contours, staying liquid till the last second before freezing solid, dripping icicles down like an icy fringe.

She focused on the road, on where she was going. So many things had fallen into place. She knew now why Ethan had been to see Lily. Why he'd travelled to Grants Pass, why he'd collected so much information on Jodie's family. She knew everything now. Down to his last monstrous secret.

A sickening coldness slopped into her gut. Jodie inhaled through her nose, breathing against it, not sure she had the strength to survive what she'd found out. Her fingers tensed on the wheel. She'd deal with it later. All that mattered now was getting to Abby.

She groped for a distraction to quell the nausea. Latched on to Novak's list of names. Even that was starting to make sense now. *Peter Rosen, Mrs Blane, Ives and McKenzie, Celine Rosen.* Had Novak figured it out, too? Had he somehow arrived at the truth from another angle?

318

The queasiness slithered.

Focus!

She allowed her thoughts to linger on Novak. Grizzly Adams. Broke, sued, unemployable. Recalled how she'd wanted to ditch him in Belize. How glad she'd been in the end to have him there. She pictured him beside her on the bathroom floor, rocking her gently in his arms.

Grizzly Adams. Her only ally.

I'm sorry, so sorry.

The rain popped and crackled on the roof. Stranded cars stood angled into the berm, coated in a smooth, frosted sheath, ice hanging from their wing mirrors like frozen drool. Jodie averted her eyes from the swirl of skid marks, risked another nudge of acceleration. Not long now. She was almost there.

Her mind skipped ahead. What would Abby look like now? Were her cheeks still plump, her hair still curly? Jodie ached to see her, to hold her little girl.

Then she felt her heart trip. Would Abby even know her? Would she know Abby? She caught her breath, balked at the notion that she mightn't recognize her own child. Abby a stranger? Jodie shoved the thought away. She'd know her little girl no matter what.

A sharp crack splintered the air. Jodie flinched, the car swerved. She straightened the wheel, gaped up ahead at a dormant tree, at the large branch that was wrenching itself free from the trunk. With a slow-motion crunch, it ripped away, weighed down with a build-up of ice. It crashed across the power lines, dragging them low, bouncing to and fro in a hammock-swing. Nearby lights flickered and waned. Flickered again, then blinked out. A synchronized shutdown.

Jodie gripped the wheel, coached herself on. Nothing to get spooked about. The Mazda skidded on another patch of glaze, and she followed the slide, willing herself to stay calm.

Just keep going, no need to panic. Abby would be waiting. Ethan had no reason to uproot her now, no reason to move and hide away. He'd be feeling safe. After all, as far as he knew, both Jodie and Novak were dead.

A whispering charge prickled down her spine. A niggling doubt about her phone call to Samantha. It had been a risk, she'd known that at the time. A risk that the girl might alert the authorities to her whereabouts. But Samantha hadn't sounded any different. Hadn't sounded like she'd known that Jodie was a fugitive.

Caruso's voice sneered inside her head. '*You're all over the news, people snitch.*'

But not Samantha. Samantha hadn't known. Who, then?

Jodie's eyes flared wide. Her heart slammed into her chest as she realized the terrible mistake she'd made. She thrashed the gears, revved up the engine. Ignored the treacherous slick on the road, pushed the Mazda to reckless speeds.

She had to get to Abby. Had to get to her before Ethan found out she was still alive.

37

The clapboard house was set back from the road at the end of a long, grit-covered driveway.

Jodie paused by the gate, her heart hammering high in her chest. She stared at the house. A two-storey A-frame, steeply pitched roof. Snowdrifts sloping in undulating mounds against the windward side. Like white sand dunes.

Icy rain pelted her face. Ducking her head, she shoved the gate open, made her way through. Rock salt popped and crunched beneath her feet. Ahead of her, lights glowed in a downstairs window. Someone was home.

Jodie reached the front door. Everyday noises seemed to recede, leaving behind a silence as deep as a well. Occasional sounds dropped into it: frozen rain ticking against the windows; branches creaking under burdens of ice. Loudest of all was the blood pounding in her ears.

She rang the bell, tensing her muscles, ready to react. Her ears strained for new sounds. Tuned into distant threads from neighbouring gardens: a dog barking; light, young voices. Then finally, slowly, the front door eased open.

A slight, elderly woman stood on the threshold. Mid to late seventies. Silver hair cut short as a pixie's. Oversized cream sweater and slacks. Her head was cocked to one side in enquiry.

Jodie stared at the face she'd glimpsed once before: the fine-drawn features; the tilt of long, upper eyelids, partially obscured by drooping brows; the high cheekbones, scaffolding now for loose, wrinkled skin.

Reality shifted for an instant, pitching Jodie into free-fall; stirring up scattered pieces of herself, lining them up, snapping them together. She took a deep breath, found her voice.

'Celine Rosen?'

The woman gave her a blank look. Then briefly, her eyes flared wide, a puzzled leap of near-recognition. But it flickered out and the moment passed. She frowned at Jodie in confusion.

'Yes?'

It was all Jodie needed. She shouldered the door wide, shoved past Celine.

'Where's Abby? Where's my daughter?'

She didn't wait for an answer. She raced down the dimly lit hall, ignoring Celine's look of alarm.

'Abby? Abby?'

She barged into rooms, sending doors crashing and banging off walls.

'Abby? Abby! Where are you, Abby?'

Warm fug, amber-glow. Living room. Empty. Vaulted ceilings, cold black stove. Dining room, empty. Kitchen, pantry, utility. All empty.

Celine had followed her down the hall. 'He told me you wouldn't come. He spoke to you, he said you agreed—'

Jodie swung round to face her. 'Where is she? Tell me where she is!'

Celine lifted her chin and glared. Her skin was like cracked plaster. 'She isn't here.'

Jodie whirled away, shoved open the door to another room. TV, footstools, leather-glove smell. Secluded den.

Empty.

Blood stormed through her veins. She brushed past Celine, took the stairs two at a time.

'Abby, are you up here?'

She swung the first door open. Vintage fragrance, rose-heavy. Celine's bedroom. Jodie kept going. Marble bathroom, storage box room. Windows black against the growing darkness.

Empty, empty.

Dear Jesus.

Was she too late? Had Samantha already told Celine about her phone call, just like she'd told her about Jodie's visit to Lily? All along, it had been Celine who'd passed the information on to Ethan. Had she inadvertently let him know that Jodie was still alive? Had he already taken Abby away?

Jodie fought the surging panic, crossed the landing to the last room, dimly aware that Celine was no longer following her. She opened the door wide. The curtains were drawn, but she could tell the room was large and spacious. She groped for the light switch, flicked it on.

Jodie caught her breath. She took in the chalky, poster-paint smell; the riotous mess of vivid colour. A patchwork of paintings covered the walls. Cornflower blues, fire-engine reds, forest greens. A plastic dust sheet protected part of the carpet, splattered with the same vibrant shades.

Slowly, Jodie moved into the room, past a rickety shelf stacked high with books, past a conversational grouping of teddy bears on small chairs. She touched her fingertips to their fluffy heads, then picked up a stray sweater from the floor, pressed it to her face. Inhaled its vanilla-honey scent.

Her skin tingled. The air felt soft and alive around her, swirling with warmth and crazy colours, lifting her, spinning her, breathing sweet life back into her little girl.

It's real, she's real, she's alive, still alive.

Jodie clutched the sweater to her chest. Abby was close. She felt it like the hum of an electric current. Her gaze flashed around the room, scouring for traces. Unwashed brushes, jars of water, open tubes of paint on the floor.

Artwork interrupted.

Her heart did a quick flip. Interrupted for what? For

Celine's recent visit to Lily? The woman went on a regular basis. So where did Abby go when Celine wasn't here?

Think!

Iced raindrops cracked against glass. Jodie stared at the curtains drawn across the window. Beyond them, presumably, lay the garden, adjoined to a neighbouring lot. Her eyes widened.

A dog barking; light, young voices.

Air seemed to lift inside Jodie's chest. She flew to the curtains, reached up to snatch them open.

'Get away from the window!'

She jerked her head around. Celine was standing on the threshold, a hefty, ancient-looking hunting rifle aimed at Jodie's face.

Jodie didn't move. The woman looked frail and her hands were shaking. Jodie eyed the long, wild-west rifle. Celine held the butt propped against her shoulder, one hand on the grip, the other further out along the stock. Her back was straight, her gaze unwavering. But the rapid tremors in her hands betrayed the strain.

Jodie held her breath. The damn rifle could go off by accident as much as by design.

Celine took a step forward. 'I said, move away.'

Her voice didn't seem much steadier than her hands. The woman sidestepped around the room towards the window, gesturing with the rifle for Jodie to back off. The light gleamed on her silver hair, exposed the tracery of cobwebby lines on her face.

Jodie's eyes strayed to the curtains. What if she opened

them? Would she see a small dark-haired girl next door, with baby-round cheeks and paint-smeared hands? The image almost broke her in two.

Celine hefted the gun higher on her shoulder. Her arms were trembling. The old varmint rifle had to weigh maybe eight or nine pounds. With effort, Jodie dragged herself away from the window, backing up against the wall. She watched the rifle. Made her voice calm.

'Look, why don't you just put the gun down? I'm not here to hurt anyone, I just want my daughter.'

'You've already hurt people.'

'That's not my intention.'

'You tried to kill your own husband. Sounds like an intention to me.'

'I just want my daughter.'

'He's told me all about you, you're not fit to be a mother.' Celine adjusted her jittery grip on the gun. 'Make no mistake, I'll use this if I have to. I may be old, but I know how to shoot. No one's going to hurt my little Abby.'

Jodie felt her jaw tighten. 'The lioness protecting her cub? It's a bit late for all that, isn't it?'

'Put your hands up where I can see 'em.'

'You couldn't protect your own children. What makes you think you can protect mine?' The words came out hard and flat and Jodie couldn't stop them.

Celine's gaze shifted. 'I said, put your hands up!'

'You're the one who's not fit to be a mother.'

'I'm warning you—'

'Your own children. You stood by, you let it happen!'

326

'You don't know anything about it.'

'Don't I?'

Jodie felt as though her blood vessels were boiling over. She wanted to lash out, to rail against all failed mothers. Against Celine, against herself, against her own dead mother.

Celine was shaking her head. 'My husband . . . You don't know what he was like.'

'You should have protected them.'

Celine's eyes lost focus. Something clouded them over, something shadowy and dark. Her jaw turned slack and the muzzle of the rifle dipped. After a moment, she whispered,

'You think I didn't try? But Elliot . . .'

'You could have stopped him, got help.'

Celine shook her head again. 'No one believed me. He was Elliot Rosen. People looked up to him.'

'You could have left, taken your children away.'

The old woman's eyes looked blank and watery. 'You didn't *leave* Elliot. If you tried, he'd find a way to hurt you. To hurt the children.'

'You don't seem like such a pushover to me. Didn't you ever challenge him?'

Even as Jodie said it, she could hear an echo of Novak's words: '*You don't seem the type to fall for such a take-charge kinda guy.*'

Celine was looking at her as though she'd lost her mind. 'Challenge Elliot?'

She paused, and was quiet so long Jodie thought she was done. Then finally, Celine spoke into the silence.

'He fractured my leg once. Smashed it with a baseball bat because I'd overcooked his eggs. That was to be expected. But you know what he said as they wheeled me off to surgery? *Now I get the children all to myself for a while.*' Her voice dropped back to a whisper. 'He was alone with them for three whole days.'

Jodie felt her fingers curl into fists. Celine was still whispering.

'He never showed remorse. He acted like he was indestructible. Divine, almost.' She stared at Jodie, her eyes bleak. 'My husband was a monster.'

The word whisked a chill along Jodie's arms, sent it shivering down her spine. She tensed against it.

'If it was me, I'd have killed him.'

Celine's eyes locked with Jodie's. They traded looks for a long moment, and the older woman seemed to have nothing more to say. Eventually, Jodie said,

'You betrayed your own children.'

Celine's knuckles whitened, and the gun barrel wavered. 'Do you think I don't know that? Do you think I don't know that Lily will never forgive me?' She paused. 'And my son, my poor son . . .'

Jodie looked away. Queasy waves rolled in her gut.

A small boy, cowering on the floor, head bowed.

'He was so young,' Celine whispered. 'I was so afraid for him, afraid he'd . . .'

She seemed unable to go on. The butt of the rifle slipped from her shoulder, and she hiked it back up, her thin arms quivering. Jodie swallowed against the cold

328

swill in her stomach. If she didn't say the truth out loud, was there a chance it wouldn't be real? She fixed her gaze to the floor. Made herself speak.

'It affected them differently, didn't it? Lily and Peter.' If she kept Celine talking, she might get the gun away from her. 'Lily retreated into her own head, but with Peter it was something else, wasn't it?'

'He . . . I worried about him so much.'

'So you sent him away.'

'Yes, but he came back. He couldn't abandon us. But he couldn't protect us, either. Or himself.' Her voice cracked. 'He always worked so hard, always tried to better himself. He wanted to study law, but Elliot wouldn't allow it.'

Jodie clamped her mouth shut. The nausea surged, radiating out to her skin in prickles of sweat. She opened her mouth to speak. Closed it again.

Don't say it!

Slowly, she raised her gaze from the floor, fixed it on Celine. She took a deep breath.

'When did you find out that Peter hadn't drowned?'

'The very next day. He couldn't let me go on thinking he'd died.'

The queasiness sloshed around in Jodie's stomach. She inhaled through her nose, clenched her teeth. Faced the truth head-on and said,

'So he faked his death, and you went along with it.'

'It was the only way he could escape Elliot. He saw his opportunity and he took it. A do-over, he called it. A chance to start his life again.'

'He was nineteen years old. Couldn't he have just left?'

Celine looked at her. 'I already told you. You didn't *leave* Elliot.'

'But you did. You left him in the end.'

'There was no one left for Elliot to hurt. Lily was mostly institutionalized by then, he couldn't get to her any more. Peter was out of his reach.' The woman's skin sagged. 'Anna was dead.'

Celine's voice trailed away. Then she roused herself and went on.

'But Peter got his life back. He went into hiding for a few years, worked menial jobs. He tried to help me, but with Lily's medical expenses . . . So he decided to study law, like he always wanted . . .'

A light-headed buzz sounded in Jodie's ears.

'. . . wasn't a real student, he couldn't afford it, but he sat in on lectures, worked harder than anyone . . .'

Novak's words were a whisper inside Jodie's head. '. . . *he wasn't a real lawyer . . . Never graduated, never sat the bar exam.*'

Celine was still talking.

'. . . difficult, with no real qualifications. But he always found a way to make money. Real estate investments, he said . . .'

Fraudulent loans. Even then.

'. . . he went to Boston, got a job with a fancy law firm . . .'

The room flickered in and out. Here was the truth, here it was now, spoken out loud.

'. . . started up his own firm, took an office in the same building. Said he liked the prestige of it . . .'

Jodie swallowed at the memory. *Cylindrical skyscraper, forty-six floors. Ives and McKenzie.*

'. . . got married and started a family of his own.'

Jodie shut her eyes, longed to block out her ears. The room spun, and she opened them again to find Celine's gaze fastened to her face. The woman's expression was an odd mix of anger and pleading.

'He was having a normal life,' Celine said. 'That's all I ever wanted for him. A normal life.'

Jodie couldn't speak. Celine went on.

'He's a good man. He loves his daughter, loves his family. Why are you trying to hurt him?'

Jodie blinked. She stared at the woman for a long moment.

Celine didn't know.

Her own grandmother didn't know.

Jodie's head reeled. She opened her mouth to speak, but Celine's gaze had shifted off to the side, her expression crumpling in sudden relief. Celine sank back against the wall.

'Peter! Thank God.'

Jodie snapped her head around, her heartbeat hammering.

Ethan was standing in the doorway.

38

'You shouldn't have come here,' Ethan said.

He stood slumped against the doorjamb, his expression bleak. His eyes looked full of anguish. Jodie stared, transfixed. It was Ethan, yet not Ethan. His face was ashen, more lined than she remembered. The trademark beard looked thin and neglected, his longish hair coarsened with rough, grey strands.

He held a gun straight down by his side, pointed at the floor. As if he was too weary to lift it.

Jodie felt herself shrivel, every particle recoiling. She wanted to curl up, huddle on the floor. Catatonic, like Lily. Instead, she took a step forward.

'I want my daughter.'

The gun jerked up in line with her chest. Jodie froze. Held her breath.

Ethan pushed himself off the doorjamb, kept the gun

aimed her way while he moved towards Celine who was looking at him with hollowed-out eyes.

'Sit down, Mom. Come on, you're shaking.'

His voice was gentle. He took Celine's rifle, placed it carefully on the floor, keeping his own gun on Jodie as he settled his mother on the bed.

Jodie's brain raced. She stared at Celine, at the quivering folds of skin, the tired, slanted eyes. The woman didn't know. What if she did? Was there a chance she might help?

Jodie lifted her chin. 'She doesn't know who I am, does she?'

'Leave it, Jodie.'

'She knows I'm your wife, that I'm Abby's mother. But she doesn't know what else I am, does she?'

'Don't listen to her, Mom. I've told you how she lies.'

Ethan locked eyes with Jodie. His gaze looked tortured, and shaded with a note of something else, something unexpected. A note of pleading?

Jodie looked away. Focused on Celine.

'Ethan is . . .' She took a breath, tried again. 'Peter is my father.'

Celine blinked, puzzled. Jodie's lungs felt congested, suddenly choked with the enormity of saying the truth out loud. She went on.

'Tell her, Ethan. Tell her I'm your daughter.'

He two-handed the gun, steadying his aim. A clammy heat flashed over her. Would he really shoot her in front of his mother? Had he ever actually killed anyone? Zach did most of his dirty work. Even Keith Daggett had probably already been dead when Ethan switched his body into the Bentley.

Iced rain tick-tacked against the window. Jodie took a deep breath, kept her eyes fixed on Ethan.

'Peter met my mother in Dublin. When you sent him away.'

Celine frowned. 'But you're his wife. I don't understand.'

'It's a lie, Mom.' Ethan's face was slick with sweat. 'None of it's true.'

'I can prove it, Ethan. I've got DNA results.'

'Bullshit.'

'I sent off for a paternity test.'

'Mom, this is all horseshit.'

'I told you I'd do it, Ethan. To prove Abby was your daughter. The lab did a full genetic reconstruction.'

Celine looked up at her son. 'Peter, what's she talking about? What's going on?'

Jodie stared at Ethan. 'Your genes and mine. Conclusive parent-child match.'

An abnormal case.

The lab manager's words stirred up a queasy shudder. She suppressed it and tried to catch Celine's eye.

'I'm your granddaughter, Celine. Peter is my father.'

The woman stared, shook her head, over and over, kept on shaking it till the movement became robotic. Ethan shifted beside her. Horizontal lines cut deep into his brow, and his skin was glistening with sweat. He looked a decade older than his forty-two years. But then again, he was. He'd been lying about his age ever since he'd reinvented himself as Ethan. Peter was fifty years old.

A slurry of nausea slid around in Jodie's gut. She'd spent so much time longing for her father. But not this. *Not this.*

She managed a whisper. 'What kind of monster marries his own daughter?'

Celine flinched on a sharp intake of breath. She clapped a hand over her mouth, looked repulsed. Beside her, Peter shook his head, pinned his gaze to Jodie's. The torment in his eyes seemed to strum the air in the room.

'It's a lie,' he whispered.

'You sought me out.'

'No!'

'You followed some sick, twisted urge and sought your own daughter out. You engineered our meeting—'

'No! Jesus, Jodie, how could I? I never knew about you, I never knew she was pregnant. Our meeting, it was . . . it was freakish. A coincidence.'

'I don't believe you.'

But even as she said it, Jodie realized it was probably true. She'd been looking for Celine's lawyer in Ives and McKenzie. But Peter had been her lawyer. He'd worked there, then started up his own firm in the same building. Not so improbable that they'd bump into each other there.

Peter's breathing grew rapid. He adjusted his grip on the gun.

'That cold wall you have, so fucking remote all the time. You never told me about your past, not for months! You never told me who you were looking for that day. You never opened up!' His voice dropped to a hoarse whisper. 'By the time you did, it was too late, we were . . . I wanted . . .'

Celine made a faint, horrified sound. Jodie's gut turned over. Early memories swirled up inside her, like a sickening fever: the heady attraction, profound and magnetic; the shared gestures; shared intimacies; the instinctive sense of belonging together. Samantha's words seeped through the vile delirium.

'*Genetic sexual attraction . . . a natural tendency to mate with our own tribe . . . attraction between family members separated until adulthood . . . overwhelming . . . primordial . . .*'

Jodie shuddered, repelled.

'You should have stopped it,' she whispered. 'When you knew, you should have stopped it.'

Peter's gaze shifted, slid sideways. Something dark crept into his eyes. Something furtive and cunning. A flash of the monster.

Jodie felt herself shrink. 'You didn't *want* to stop it, did you? You discovered you liked it, was that it? Got some sick charge from being with your own daughter. Just like Elliot.'

Celine gasped as though she'd been whipped. She stared at her son, her face white with shock. 'Peter?'

He wouldn't look at her. Jodie went on.

336

'It's your worst fear, Celine. It's what you were always afraid of, isn't it? That he wouldn't be normal. That he'd turn into his father.'

Peter jerked up the gun on a level with Jodie's face. His eyes looked stony. 'Don't ever say that!'

Her heart jolted. Samantha's voice drifted on through her head.

'. . . *trauma imprinted on the child's brain . . . hard-wired in . . . they go on to re-enact it, just repeating what seems familiar and normal.*'

Peter's knuckles whitened. The anguish in his face was haunting. Jodie flashed on the sketch of the damaged little boy. Blanked it out.

'It's why you sent him away, isn't it?' she said to Celine. 'You were afraid he was turning into his father.'

Peter's jaw tensed. 'No!'

Celine was silent. She looked old and shrunken, and her colour was ghastly. Peter took a swift step towards Jodie.

'Go get Abby, Mom, we're leaving. I'll deal with this.'

Panic swooped up inside Jodie's chest. 'Don't let him take her! She's not safe with him, you must know that!'

Celine gaped at her son, looked half-dazed with shock. Peter stepped closer to Jodie, loomed over her, blocking her view of his mother. Jodie flattened herself against the wall, her chest pumping.

'Think about it, Celine! Elliot went on to abuse Lily's daughter. Little Anna. When she turned eight years old, just like the others.'

337

No answer.

Please God, let her listen!

'Peter will do the same to Abby, can't you see that?'

Peter's eyes flared. He shot out a hand, grabbed Jodie by the throat, slammed her head back up against the wall. She gagged, choked, felt her eyes bulge. Harsh breaths tore past her throat. She gaped at Peter. Saw up close what his hair kept covered: a deformed right ear, its outer edge jagged. As though a bullet had once torn it, just missing his head.

She forced out a strangled whisper. 'You're going to hurt Abby, aren't you?'

Dark colour suffused his face. She waited for his denial, for his fingers to tighten. Her jugular throbbed high in her throat. Then Peter went still. His eyes turned glassy. Vacant. The blood leached from his face, left it deathly grey. Jodie could almost see his mind locking in, reaching back, reliving past horrors. Horrors that likely shaped every thought, every action, every yearning, every minute of his life.

Jodie matched his stillness. Watched his mouth turn ugly with disgust. Self-loathing? Then his eyes sharpened, fixed back on Jodie. They were black, impenetrable. He shoved the gun into her face.

'This is all your fault.'

Dr Jekyll, Mr Hyde.

'If you hadn't tried to leave,' he went on, 'if you'd just stayed with me, we could've worked things out.'

His fingers dug into her throat. Jodie gasped for air.

338

Tiny sips. The gun was a whisker away from her eyes, and she stared, mesmerized, down the barrel, unable to look away. Her vision flickered, the room seemed to quiver.

Don't faint, not now!

The light waned. Flickered again. And suddenly, an image replayed in her head: a large branch, weighed down with ice, crashing across power lines. She held her breath. Clenched her fists. The light fluttered in snatches. Dimmed again. Then the room snapped into darkness.

Jodie lashed upwards, connected with the gun in a two-handed punch, jerked it skyward. A shot tore through the ceiling. Peter cursed, Celine screamed. And somewhere in the dark, the gun thudded to the floor.

Jodie struggled, twisted free, dived, scrambled. Peter grabbed her by the hair, yanked her head back. Pain screamed through her scalp, her neck, her throat. She ignored it and stretched along the floor, scrabbled with her fingers. Felt hard, blessed metal. Then in a single rolling movement, she wrenched her head around, flipped onto her back, arms fully extended, and trained the gun upwards into Peter's face.

He went still. Released his grip on her hair. Slowly, he straightened, took a step back.

'Don't do it, Jodie.'

Her eyes adjusted to the dark. Shadows shifted, resolved into the gaunt hollows of his face. Celine was moaning somewhere behind her. Peter whispered,

'You won't do it, you can't.'

339

'I did it before.'

'They'll put you back in prison. You'll never see Abby again.'

Novak's words floated into her head. '. . . *you're not a murderer . . . start over.*'

She couldn't go back to prison, she had to take care of Abby. Jodie gripped the gun tighter.

Just do it!

For an instant, she was back in the Bentley: the flicker of headlights, the screaming engine. '*I die, you die.*' Jodie groped again for that dead, flat place, that cold zone where she stored up her hate. She couldn't find it. Instead, felt an eerie awareness of Peter's pain.

Do it! It's what you're here for, to kill him again!

The gun felt heavy. Her head buzzed with voices: Nate's, Samantha's, Momma Ruth's.

'. . . *if you had the chance to do it over again, would you really do anything different?*'

'. . . *our mistakes are hard-wired into our DNA . . .*'

'. . . *imprinted on the child's brain . . . hard-wired in . . .*'

'. . . *wasn't in my blood to make different choices . . .*'

'. . . *I got choices. And I choose to call that bullshit . . .*'

Jodie clenched her jaw. *Pull the damn trigger!*

Peter held out a hand. 'Come with us. You, me and Abby. We can start again, can't we? That's what I'd always planned. When I took Abby away. I thought maybe some day . . . But then you chose to leave.'

Jodie glared up at him. Adjusted her sights on the gun.

340

He peered at her face, and whatever he read there made him falter. Slowly, he let his hand fall back. When he spoke again, his whisper was cracked.

'All I ever wanted was for us to be together.'

Then, like a doused light, his expression went blank. Fatalistic. As though he'd checked out. As though he knew he'd lost everything.

Jodie stared up into the shadows of her father's face. Squeezed her fingers on the trigger.

The shot, when it came, exploded into his chest.

39

Jodie's eardrums pounded, hammering with hard, bullet-crack echoes.

She gaped at Peter's motionless body. Felt deaf, sluggish. Drowned in sound. Dazed, she turned her head to look at Celine.

The recoil from the rifle had jolted the woman backwards. She was listing to one side, still sitting on the bed, her right shoulder dipped as though in pain, the gun held loosely across her arms. Her face was a mask of resignation. Of hopeless loss.

Jodie blinked. Her ears were still ringing, the hum weighing her head down. With slow, small movements, she struggled to her feet, still holding on to Peter's gun. She backed away from his body. Stared at Celine. The woman hadn't moved.

Jodie inched towards her, her shoes shushing on the

342

dust sheet as she crossed it. Her limbs felt so heavy. It took effort to put one foot in front of the other, as though she was walking underwater.

She stopped by the bed. Time had dilated, slowed right down, and the hush in the room felt eerie. Celine's eyes looked glazed, her face slack. When the woman finally spoke, her voice was faint and hoarse.

'I gave him life. My burden to end it, not yours.'

She was staring at the floor, arms trembling from the weight of the rifle. After a moment, she went on.

'You were right, Elliot twisted him. There'd been incidents . . . young girls . . . I had to send him away.'

She looked up at Jodie. The anguish in her eyes was harrowing. 'But Abby . . . I couldn't let him . . .'

Celine's mouth trembled. She seemed unable to go on. Then she clutched at Jodie's arm, her gaze full of pleading.

'He was in such pain,' Celine whispered. 'Did you see that? My boy was in such pain.'

Jodie nodded slowly, her head still heavy. She glanced at the rifle that was now resting on the woman's lap. Jodie held out her hand for it, but Celine shook her head.

'No, you mustn't touch it.'

She released Jodie's arm, clasped both hands around the muzzle. Jodie watched the woman's fingers, afraid she might turn the weapon on herself. But Celine showed no signs of ducking her pain.

Jodie eased herself down on the bed beside her, her limbs still leaden. Celine scanned her face, and Jodie recalled Lily's words: '. . . *you're way too old.*' The only child of Peter's they'd known about was Abby.

Celine whispered into the dark.

'Peter never showed me photos of his wife. You look . . .' Her gaze held Jodie's. 'You look like my mother.'

The room felt shadowy, insubstantial. Celine went on.

'Her name was Mai. Her father came from Nishio, in Japan.'

Jodie stared at her grandmother. Flimsy shadows hovered in the room like smoke. She exchanged a long look with Celine. A look of mutual recognition. Acknowledgement of shared pain. Both married to abusers, both grieving over children. Both ready to slay the monster.

They stayed like that for some time. Then a door crashed open somewhere below them. Jodie caught her breath, dragged her focus back. Footsteps pounded on the stairs, racing, urgent. Cold air seeped all around her, washed into the room from the ice storm outside. She whipped her head around, in time to see Novak skid to a halt in the doorway: stocky, dishevelled; cheeks ruddy from the freezing cold; woolly cap jammed over wild hair; eyes shining, dogged, vigorous, brimming with life.

The shadows vanished, and the room became solid and real.

PART FOUR

PART FOUR

40

They wouldn't let her see Abby.

The police had crashed up the stairs after Novak, weapons drawn, radios squawking, and had hustled her away to a holding cell in the county jail. Celine and Novak were arrested too, and no one listened when Jodie begged to be allowed next door to see her daughter.

Celine had collapsed in custody soon afterwards. According to Jodie's lawyer, she wouldn't live long enough to stand trial. But Celine had made a full statement, confessing to the murder of her son, Peter Rosen, and confirming his previous identity as Ethan McCall.

'Your conviction's being overturned,' Jodie's lawyer told her, a dry, cynical man by the name of Finch. 'Just a matter of red tape. Since your husband was alive for the last two and a half years, they can hardly uphold a conviction that you murdered him.'

'What about Abby? I want to see my daughter!'

Finch looked uncomfortable. 'Let's just get you out of here first.'

'How long will that take?'

'Well, there's a wrinkle. The New Hampshire Attorney General is considering another indictment. Attempted murder, this time.' Finch lifted a wry eyebrow. 'On the basis that you wrote a letter that fourth of July clearly stating your intention to kill your husband.'

Jodie stared, and Finch went on.

'Don't worry, I'm cutting a deal.'

'What kind of deal?'

'You've served over two years for a wrongful conviction. I've threatened to sue—'

'I don't want to sue—'

'They don't want you to either, believe me. They're falling over themselves to settle. I've made it a condition that no other charges are brought.'

'Can you do that?'

'No jury would convict you, and they know it. The mitigating circumstances are far too emotive.' He started blocking out headlines in the air. '*Attorney General hounds heroic young mother after wrongful conviction.*'

Finch gave a sardonic smile and got up to leave.

'They tell me the AG's seeking reappointment at the end of his term. Last thing he needs is a media witch hunt.'

*   *   *

The days went by.

Jodie paced the cold, dank cell, blocking out the familiar clatter of deadbolts, the din of clamouring inmates. Why wouldn't they let her see Abby?

Novak had been charged with harbouring a fugitive, despite the fact that it was he who'd called in the police. He'd arrived at the truth through a circuitous route of his own, though Finch wasn't clear on the details.

Novak made bail and came to see her. He wasn't allowed inside the holding cell, so they stood either side of the wire mesh screen, Jodie's fingers hooked through it. Novak looked bedraggled, but his eyes were quick and bright. Jodie whispered,

'Have you seen Abby?'

'She's fine, don't worry. Celine's neighbours are looking after her.'

'Why won't they let me see her?'

'She's . . .' He hesitated, broke eye contact.

Jodie raked his face. 'She's what, Novak? Tell me!'

'She's confused. Upset.' He touched her fingers through the mesh. 'She doesn't want to see you. Not yet.'

Jodie closed her eyes, a ripping sensation tearing through her. Novak squeezed her fingers.

'Just give her time.'

Jodie managed a nod. Then she gave him a searching look.

'Did you know all along she was still alive?'

'No! Of course not, how could I know that?'

'But it crossed your mind?'

349

He hesitated. 'Maybe, after a while. Like I said before, something was off.'

'Why didn't you tell me?'

'Jesus, Jodie, how could I tell you something like that? Raise your hopes on a dumb hunch? What if I was wrong?'

Jodie bowed her head, conceding the point. No one spoke for a few minutes, then Novak said,

'Finch tells me he's getting you out of here, real soon.'

'Don't worry, I'm okay.'

'Should you . . . Will you go and see someone? You know, about all this?'

Jodie looked away. Felt the crawling dizziness that seized her body whenever she thought about Ethan. About her father. In a tight voice, she said,

'You mean, like a shrink?'

'Asking for help doesn't make you weak.'

The dizziness spread, washed into her gut. An image cut across it: Lily's flashback at the clinic; Lily clawing at her own stomach, as though something grotesque was erupting inside it.

'. . . *a full-blown panic attack that wracks her with physical and mental anguish until she feels like she wants to die.*'

Jodie shuddered. Maybe Novak was right. Maybe she wasn't quite as strong as she thought. She took a deep, steadying breath, then raised her gaze to his. His eyes were full of concern.

'How did you find out the truth?' she said. 'About Ethan?'

350

Novak hesitated, watching her carefully. As though on the lookout for signs of disintegration. After a moment, he said,

'That law firm of Celine's. Ives and McKenzie? I discovered Ethan used to work there.'

'And that linked him to Celine?'

He shrugged, nodded. 'It wasn't much, but I spun up a few what-ifs. What if all those years ago, Celine's lawyer was actually Ethan? Or what if he was more than just her lawyer? He'd faked his death once already, what if it wasn't the first time? What if Peter Rosen hadn't really drowned, and Ethan was actually her son?' His mouth twisted. 'I didn't really buy it, it was too . . .'

Jodie filled in the gap. 'Grotesque?'

He nodded, swallowed hard. 'But when you disappeared, I went crazy, I couldn't pick up your trail anywhere, no one had seen you. I was scrambling, I had to *do* something. So I followed my only lead, got a copy of Ethan's photo over to Celine's old neighbours in North Dakota.'

'The Blanes?'

'Took a while to find them, but they confirmed the likeness and I called the cops. When I got to Celine's house and I heard the shot, I thought . . .' He halted. Tried again. 'I thought I was too late.'

Jodie touched his fingers through the mesh. Eventually, she whispered,

'I left you for dead. I thought Caruso had found you, and I just left you for dead.'

Novak looked bewildered, and she tried to explain: the black jeep at the motel; the mess in his room that she'd interpreted as signs of a struggle; the pain and guilt she'd felt at abandoning him to Caruso. Novak's brow finally cleared. He reached a finger through the mesh, gently tilted up her chin.

'I get it, it's okay. If it was Toby, I'd have done the same thing.'

Jodie lost track of time.

For days or weeks, she wasn't sure which, she paced the cold, ten-by-ten cell: toilet to bench; wall to wall; cinderblock to cinderblock. To and fro; backwards and forwards; over and over.

Until one grey, shivery morning, an officer rattled at the wire mesh screen and held the door wide open.

41

Jodie closed her eyes, tilted her face skywards. The sun felt hot and glossy on her skin, pouring over her like a warm, soothing liquid.

The sounds of the island washed through her: waves shushing against the sand; voices lilting in Belizean Creole. She opened her eyes, shading them from the dazzle, then picked up her paintbrush and looked across at her daughter.

Abby had chosen to sit far apart from her mother, plonking her sturdy little frame on a towel several feet away. She sat there scowling out to sea, flinging fistfuls of sand into the air in front of her.

Jodie drank in the miraculous, wondrous sight of her. The years had melted away some of Abby's plumpness, but her cheeks were still round, her wrists still circumscribed by a chubby, rubber-band look. Abby's gaze flickered her way, resting briefly on the squeezy, poster-paint bottles that Jodie had left out for her. So far, she hadn't touched them.

Three years ago, Peter had told Abby that her mother had left her. That Jodie hadn't wanted her little girl any more. Who could blame Abby for keeping her distance now? She was waiting for the moment when her mother would leave her again.

Jodie loaded her brush with cadmium red, resisting the urge to hug Abby close, to rush the healing process. She risked another quick glance. Her daughter was peeking through her wild fringe of curls, sneaking looks at Jodie's canvas.

Novak had driven them to the airport. He was busy these days, getting his life back in order. He'd lost the scoop that had meant so much to him. Calling the cops had leaked his story, and others had beaten him to the punch. So in the end, he'd written a human interest piece. The story behind the story. A reconstruction of Peter's journey from abused young boy to tormented, twisted adult. It was a powerful account. Unflinching. The *Boston Globe* published it to wide critical acclaim, and Novak had a string of new assignments as a result.

The Caribbean breeze frisked around Jodie's shoulders. She glanced at Abby, who was standing up and scuffing at the sand with her feet. Novak had wanted to join them on the island, as soon as his custody case was over. His ex-wife had relented, and they were reaching a settlement, working out the best arrangement for their son. Putting their child first, like normal parents.

354

'I'll fly out in a few weeks,' Novak had said. But Jodie knew it was too soon. So much had to be mended first between herself and Abby.

They'd driven most of the way to the airport in silence, the tyres slushing through the melting ice and snow. When Abby had finally fallen asleep in the back, Novak said in a low voice,

'Would you have shot him? If Celine hadn't done it, would you have pulled the trigger?'

Jodie stared at him for a moment, then turned to look at her sleeping child. Her heart soared and danced at the sight of her. At the flushed, round cheeks, at the chubby fingers curled into fists. Suddenly, Jodie had felt again the weight of the gun, felt her own fingers flexing around the trigger. She'd turned and stared back out at the snow.

'Some things are worth killing for, wouldn't you say?'

Waves hissed against the sand, the briny air mixing with the sweet scent of fried food: conch fritters, fry jacks, spicy rice and beans. Abby kicked at the sand, sidled closer. Jodie's chest turned over, her arms aching with the need to scoop her up and hold her. Abby sneaked another look at Jodie's canvas. It was almost finished, though her attention was barely on it.

The foreground showed a dark, tunnel-like enclosure, forged by earthen walls and canopies of palms. It led out to an epicentre filled with light and colour. Not the fantasy colours of her old paintings, but the true festive hues of Ambergris Caye: cheery blues and yellows of beachfront huts; cobalt-blue sky, aquamarine ocean; carmine, purple

355

and magenta blossoms; bougainvillea, hibiscus, morning glory.

Abby moved closer, fetching up beside the easel. She picked up Jodie's palette, sniffed at the paint, her button nose wrinkling at the dense oiliness. Then her expression cleared. Turned thoughtful. As though the smell had conjured up buried memories. Abby blinked. She stared at Jodie. Seemed to reassess her.

Jodie gazed back at her sturdy, robust little girl. At the dark eyes and brows that were so like Peter's. She thought of Anna, Lily's daughter, weakened by faulty, inbred genes. But not her Abby. Thank God, not her Abby.

Samples A and C share insufficient genetic markers . . . excluded as the biological father . . . Sample D . . . Probability of Paternity greater than 99.999% . . .

She recalled the DNA samples she'd sent off three years ago to the lab. One for Ethan, one for herself, and one for little Abby. And a fourth for Lucas Olsen, the young Danish architect who'd been so enchanted by her paintings.

Their affair had been brief, a snatched respite from her oppressive marriage. It was over and Lucas back in Copenhagen before she'd even known she was pregnant. Her intimacies with Lucas and Ethan had overlapped and she'd spent the pregnancy plagued with worry. Then once Abby had been born, all doubt had vanished. Abby's likeness to Ethan was strong and unmistakable.

But the lab results had confirmed the truth. That Lucas

was Abby's father. And yet she looked so very like Ethan. But not because she was his daughter. She looked like him because she was his granddaughter.

Jodie gazed at her little girl, risked a smile. Abby stared back.

Jodie had already been in touch with Lucas. He was married now, but he and Abby had a right to get to know one another. As for Jodie, she'd had more than enough of family. She'd make sure Lily was looked after. But where Jodie came from, who she looked like, none of that mattered any more. She held Abby's frank gaze, saw her own past, her present and her future reflected back to her there.

Abby snuck a look at the squeezy bottles. She reached out a hand, fingered the caps. Jodie held her breath. Then Abby picked up a bottle of vibrant yellow, and with a mischievous glance at Jodie, upended it over a bowl, squeezing out glowing colour till it overflowed.

She flung Jodie another rascally look, then plunged both hands into the bowl, dunking them up to her wrists. She lifted them out, held them, dripping, stretched out in front of her.

Then with a wide smile that lit up her face, she clapped her hands together, over and over, spattering flicks of bright, light yellow into the air like sunshine.

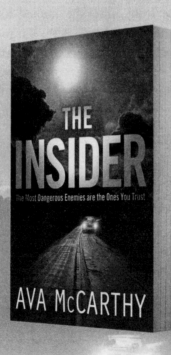

THE COURIER

CAN SHE PULL OFF HER MOST DARING HEIST EVER?

'A DELIGHT...THE TANG OF AUTHENTICITY COMES OFF EVERY PAGE'
DAILY MAIL

THE COURIER

A HARRY MARTINEZ THRILLER

AVA McCARTHY

Approached to crack a safe by the owner's suspicious wife, reformed hacker Henrietta 'Harry' Martinez can't resist the challenge. Now her client's absconded with a fortune in diamonds, leaving Harry sole witness to a brutal murder. And next in line for a ruthless assassin who doesn't like loose ends...

Hide Me

IN A GAME WITHOUT RULES, THE WINNER TAKES ALL.

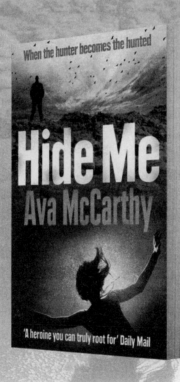

When the hunter becomes the hunted

Hide Me
Ava McCarthy

'A heroine you can truly root for' Daily Mail

Security expert Henrietta 'Harry' Martinez has been hired by casino boss Riva Mills to expose a ruthless scamming crew. When the crew's expert hacker is brutally murdered, Harry goes undercover as his replacement. Trapped in a deadly global underworld that encompasses international terrorism, organized crime and drug cartels, Harry soon finds that when you play this game, you play for your life...